Pops of Violet

PART 1

BUBBLY DUET

Y.V. LARSON

Printed in the United States of America

This book has been professionally edited and has been combed through many times. If you spot a typo, please email Y.V. Larson directly, or reach out via social media. Please do not report it to Amazon because this could lead to the book being removed.
Cover Design – Lune Aesthete
Editor – Scarlett Chase from Scarlett Pen Edits
Proof Reader - Erica C.
Alpha Readers – Angelica Heitbrink, Patricia Conway, Brandi Augustine,
Character Art - ART by ALEKSA

Formatted with Vellum

Trigger Warning

Please read the following list if you have any triggers. Note that these could be considered spoilers!

If you have any questions or believe I missed a trigger warning, you may reach out to me through social media, or via email: Author@yvlarson.com

- Nightmares
- Anxiety
- Panic Attacks
- Injuries
- Violence
- Mental health struggles
- Alcohol and drug use
- Mentions of childhood neglect
- Mentions of parental death
- Mentions of past violence and kidnapping (not of main characters)

This is a spicy MMMF why-choose romance, meaning everyone including the three men are also in a sexual/romantic/loving relationship. Part one ends on a cliffhanger.

Author's Note

The Wilted Duet world continues with Violet's story. This duet can be read as a standalone, but if you want to avoid spoilers, reading The Wilted Duet before The Bubbly Duet is recommended. You asked for more spice, and Violet is ready to deliver! Angst, heat, groveling, betrayal, trauma, high emotions, and revenge await. Dive between Violet's…pages… and fall in love and maybe a little hate.

There is a basic Wilted character cheat sheet in back if you need it!

Dedicated to

Those who need the reminder that not all thoughts are facts. Anxiety can be loud. So let's be louder for Violet, for those in the back, and for you.

YOU ARE LOVED

Prologue

VIOLET

There's something strange about trusting someone. You know without a shadow of a doubt that they love you endlessly. They'll do anything for you. But it's that anything that makes it...odd. Questionable.

Because love, loyalty, and devotion can alter truths.

A girl asks her mom if she's smart after making a mistake. Her mom tells her she's the smartest girl in the world. But the girl knows that isn't true because she literally just messed up in front of her mom.

Did her mom lie to spare her feelings? Or, did her mom tell her the truth?

See? Perception is everything.

I'd love to say, of course the little girl's mom truly believed that, and she may have, but the little girl might never believe those words because her mom loves her enough to lie. Fib. Withhold the truth. Sugarcoat.

What do the people who love us not *say?*

And how do I stop filling in the blanks?

This isn't a simple math problem or a bad choice I made with my hair. I love my hair. Long, blonde with purple streaks, it's awesome. I love it, even when I don't love myself.

My bad choices go far beyond the norm. The guilt of my decisions drags me down every day no matter how fast I've tried to run from them. I've found that there's no place far enough to hide either.

I've taken my love of traveling and adventure and morphed it into a way to escape my issues. But they've followed me. Or, more accurately, *I* am the issue.

No matter how many times my mom attempts to reassure me that my guilt is misplaced, I don't quite believe her. Because she loves me more than anything in the world.

She would never admit it was my fault that she was kidnapped and held captive for the better part of a week.

Seven years later, Blue Bennett, my adoptive mom and cousin by blood, has moved on. Why can't I? Why, when she tells me I did nothing wrong, do I narrow my eyes and try to read behind her lie?

Because it *is* a lie. It *was* my fault.

No matter how many times I reread the messages she sent me when she was in the hospital all those years ago, I can't quite accept them.

I remember it as if it were yesterday. Mom was slumped in the hospital bed missing four fingernails, unable to speak because she was almost strangled to death, and needing quiet because of her concussion.

Text after text of her trying to make me feel better

only made me feel worse and has added to my guilt every time I think about it. I should have been coddling *her*. Not the other way around.

As I reread our messages in an attempt to finally believe her words, I only feel worse. I don't think I'll ever fully trust my mom's words.

TEXT THREAD FROM 7 YEARS AGO

Mom 🩵: I'm okay, V. Please don't worry about me. The doctor says in the next few weeks everything should start feeling normal again.

Me: I'm so sorry. This is all my fault. I should have told you what was happening. That man...I didn't know he knew you. I swear. I'm so sorry.

Mom 🩵: Violet. In no way do I blame you. That man was sick and was searching for me. Nothing would have stopped him.

Me: Just because you don't blame me doesn't mean it's not my fault. I should have told you sooner. I was just...I don't know.

Mom 🩵: V...I love you so much. If you need to hear that I forgive you, then I absolutely forgive you. But please know that this was my past coming back to haunt me. You are not to blame.

Mom 🩵: Look at me.

Mom 🩵: This. Is. Not. Your. Fault.

The fact that she couldn't actually speak the words until days later broke my heart and solidified my thoughts on the matter.

I may question my mom's reassurances, but I definitely don't trust myself any longer.

One

VIOLET

Unpopular opinion: A sexy tattoo artist texting you at nine at night asking if you made it home safe is annoying.

Of course I respond. I'm not that cruel, even if it's a one-word answer. I haven't seen Jamie for two weeks because I was on another road trip for work. He shouldn't even be thinking about me. Booty calls don't ask these kinds of questions. As far as I'm concerned, Jamie shouldn't give a shit about me once we've both had our happy ending.

I don't give that man much to care about anyway. He doesn't know anything about me besides the best way to drive my body crazy. He lets me into his apartment, and I dive right for his mouth and belt. No talking. No feelings. No attachment.

When he messages me asking if he can come over and help me *relax,* I decline. He's too pushy tonight. Plus, he knows the score—I go to his house for a good time and leave before passing out.

"If you keep huffing like a feral cat, I'm liable to throw a damn pillow at your face."

Laughing, I throw my crappy phone down by my feet and banish Jamie from my mind. The tingles between my legs will just have to deal with waiting a few days. Plus, angry sex with Jamie is the best.

Cassidy takes a sip of her wine and narrows her green eyes at me. "Jamie bothering you again? Wait, let me rephrase that." She sits up straighter, and her messy red bun flops to the other side of her head. "Is the hot tattoo guy with gorgeous long hair who rocks a man bun and has muscles big enough to toss you around, trying to take your relationship further?"

"There is no relationship." I'm quick to shut that down. No way am I getting involved with someone. I'm a mess and, according to my therapist, I'm scared of making a mistake. Again.

My friend rolls her eyes and snuggles further beneath her blankets. "Are you willing to admit you like him at least? He's been your fuck buddy for five and a half years. You realize that says something right?"

"We've had like ten two-minute conversations, Cassidy. There's nothing for me to like beyond what we get from each other." She opens her mouth to argue with me, and not for the first time, but I stop her. "I have to unpack my gear and start organizing my images," I say, standing and intentionally leaving my phone behind.

I don't need it. There's nothing on it besides texts and phone calls. Also my location since one of my mom's husbands, Felix, demanded I have it on at all times.

Yes, I said *one of*. She has four, and no I don't call them versions of *dad*. They are Jared, Declan, Felix, and Roman to me. Role models, protectors...they're family.

See? I have plenty of people to ask me if I made it home safe. And all four of them did as well as Mom. They worry about me all the time. Which is understandable considering I do some risky hikes to get good images for my boss.

I'm a ghost content creator. I photograph the gorgeous landscape pictures that my boss takes credit for and posts on her socials. Keeping far away from social media is my objective, and I've done a pretty good job of it.

My personal life and my family are for my eyes only. Well, Mom gets a lot of my pictures and videos now. I recently upgraded from my grandpa's old flip phone even though I didn't want to.

Gosh, I miss Jared's dad. I'll call Grandpa Derrick in the morning.

My heart pangs as I connect my camera to my laptop. Moving through the motions of emptying my hiking bag and starting a load of laundry, I allow myself to miss my people. Maybe I should go home for a visit soon.

Sighing, I glance at my open doorway. Cassidy knows to leave me alone when I stomp out on her like I did. It's rare, but she knows not to push me on some things, and there's no way I'm letting Jamie into my heart. Hell, he's not even allowed in my bed.

Sometimes I wish Cassidy would come give me a hug when I'm like this, but a louder part of me tells me it's better this way. I'm afraid I'll say something I'll regret if she comes to me.

Tears fill my eyes as I look around my bedroom. I only spend two or three weeks here a month, but it looks like I don't even live here. This is my home base, and all I have is a bed, dresser, and a purple quilt I can't seem to part with.

Everything else a twenty-five-year-old woman might have isn't here. My makeup is hidden in the bathroom cupboard with my toothbrush and hygiene stuff.

All of my clothes are tucked away, and my shoes are hidden in my closet. There's nothing to be seen here. No photos on the wall or a random necklace on the windowsill.

No decorations. Those are all in boxes at my mom's house. *If she saw my room now...*

Shaking those thoughts away, I mechanically get ready for bed. If Cassidy hates how sad my room is, then it would for sure break Mom's heart.

My room at our old apartment in Chicago was an explosion of color and photos of me and my friends. It was a mess, and *obviously* lived in. But that just reminds me of my mistakes. I can't settle. Hell, I'm not even on Cassidy's lease. I just pay rent and use this room to crash for a few weeks between trips.

Cassidy and my odd jobs are all I have here, but it's enough to keep me coming back. Detroit fuels my inspiration with its artsy depth, so that's another reason I keep coming back.

That's all, though.

No part of me gets excited to come back after a long trip to see Jamie. He's pushy and far too possessive for my liking. My body may enjoy him, but that's all he'll get.

At least that's what I tell myself as I scoop my phone off the couch and read his unopened text. It's sweet and a little bossy. I don't eat dinner like he reminds me to do, and I don't sleep well like he hopes.

Jamie has no power over me. I'll scream that at the top of my lungs even as I imagine him between my thighs while I rub the pad of my middle finger over my clit.

I have to stay strong in my stance to stay alone even as I slip into a fitful sleep. I'll continue convincing myself it's better being single and detached as I struggle to stay warm at night.

The nightmares, the chill of January, and my burning eyes tell me *I'm* a liar. But I lie to myself because it's easy. Because I don't trust myself. Because most of the time I don't even love myself.

Two

VIOLET

"Motherf—" I quickly cut myself off when an older lady whips her head around to glare at me. To be fair, it looks like she's having a pastry with her grandchild. *Oops.*

Although I don't say anything because I've made that mistake before, and that woman was not happy with my insinuation that she was old enough to be a grandma. Even though, spoiler alert, she actually was a grandma.

I wiggle my fingers at the crabby lady and turn back to the scone that decided to ruin my day. Honestly, I was seconds away from taking the perfect shot when it just...crumbled.

It may, *may*, have been my fault for rearranging it for the ten thousandth time, but really? The shape was all wrong anyway. Maybe I can convince the barista to give me a stack of cookies to take a photo of instead.

I chose the scone because the blueberries peaking

through the carbs would really pop in the early morning sunlight.

Sometimes I have no idea why I do these random jobs. I love taking photos and have a knack for knowing what sells on social media, but the coffee shop and hair salon don't *excite* me.

The nightclub is fun. I'd just rather be on my hikes and take pictures when it feels right. This is forced even if it's artsy and offers me some income.

"Hey, Sweets."

"Really?" I grumble under my breath. When I woke up this morning I had a plan, and that plan did not include fumbling around with a scone. And it definitely didn't involve Jamie freaking Murphy helping himself to the seat across from me.

"That nickname can go right in the garbage with my prop," I sass, leaning back in my chair.

He looks even better in the daylight. His dark brown hair is pulled back from his face in a man bun. A few wavy wisps have escaped their entrapment and tickle his lightly scruffed cheeks. The black gauges in his ears shine in the sunlight, and I notice he's replaced his cartilage hoop with a silver one while I was gone.

I hate myself a little more when sadness rips through me at not being able to see his dragon tattoo that climbs up his neck. Jamie is a work of art, and it drives me crazy.

In his bedroom, that's great. Out in the real world where we aren't meant to see each other, it's infuriating.

"Come on now," he rumbles while eating said prop. "We can't waste free food."

"Who said it was free?" I snap even though it was free. Of course, he just raises an eyebrow and smirks at me.

My clit pulses. I really, truly, hate seeing Jamie around Detroit. It makes the boundaries I've set very hard to maintain, especially when he's feeling particularly pushy.

I'd rather continue talking about the half-eaten scone, but Jamie has other ideas. "What are you doing tonight?"

My body heats at the underlying question, but I have plans that don't involve his hands on my body. "Going to Club Surreal."

"Work or pleasure?"

It's a fair question considering I help take images for their socials too. I narrow my eyes even as my tummy swoops. While I answer his question, I'm trying to figure out how to get him to leave. "Girls' night."

He nods and reaches for my iced latte. Before his fingers can wrap around the cup, I bat his hand away. Only, Jamie has a bit of a dominant streak. Moving fast, he snatches my wrist in a firm grip that makes my breath catch.

"Sharing is caring, Violet," he scolds and grabs my drink with his other hand. He takes a sip, and that simple act of wrapping his lips around my straw heats my blood. Right up until he sucks a third of my fucking drink down.

"You asshole!" I snap and yank my hand free.

A scoff comes from beside us, and this time I don't

give the old woman a smile. My mood is effectively ruined, so everyone gets a glare today.

Jamie releases my straw, licks his plump lips, and slides the dewy cup back to me. "Feisty this morning," he murmurs.

I sigh and slump into my chair. Being called out for my crappy attitude always makes me feel worse. I never used to be like this—so quick to anger. Pushing Jamie away is for the best. How do I get him to see that?

"What do you want, Jamie? I'm trying to work." Even I can hear the defeat in my voice.

He frowns at me and leans forward. "I came in for a cold brew, saw your beautiful face, and remembered that my messages asking how your trip was went ignored. So, thought I'd ask face to face."

Why does he care? I keep that question to myself though because the last time I said something along those lines, Jamie went off on an angry rant. For some reason, he can't come to terms with the fact that we're nothing more than a good time.

"It was great," I respond, giving him only a smidgen of what he wants. "That all?"

"Jesus, Violet," he says, leaning away from the table with a hurt look. "That's all you have to say to me after being gone for two weeks?"

I'm honestly confused now. "What do you mean? I've been doing this traveling job for years, Jamie. Why are you so upset?"

He just stares at me. My heart thunders away in my chest as my discomfort skyrockets in response to his rising disappointment.

"Right," he grunts, shuttering his expression. Jamie stands and tells me to have a good day.

I watch him with my heart in my throat as he orders at the counter. My eyes follow his every move as he pays, receives his coffee, and leaves the cafe.

Swallowing multiple times, I try really freaking hard to shake off that encounter. I miss when Jamie would just flirt with me. His sexual innuendos are always off the charts spicy. Why does he have to push me like this?

Sure, I play the dense asshat to his face and whenever Cassidy questions what I'm doing. The truth is that I *do* have feelings, and most of them are really awful to deal with.

I'm not stupid, but I am a little confused.

Hurting Jamie isn't something I want to do, but we both agreed on what we are. I hate that he's changing our dynamic. Even if I decline and avoid, he's still ruining everything.

I'm afraid it's time for me to put a complete stop to what we're doing. Seeing him so upset and disappointed in me all the time is taking its toll. I don't have more to give him.

This is me. Detached, aloof, a little rude, and incredibly sad. He doesn't need this shit. I should end it with him.

So, if that's the best option for both of us, why does it hurt so much to even imagine?

Three

VIOLET

My third lemon drop shot goes down easier than the first two. I decided on the way here that it was going to be a four shot and water in between kind of night.

The torrent of emotions running through me after my unfortunate meeting with Jamie this morning left me feeling off-kilter. I know from experience that when I'm feeling this way, getting trashed is the last thing I should do.

Cassidy doesn't need to hold my hair back tonight or catch me from faceplanting the minute we step outside. I'm thankful her other friend joined us tonight so I'm not completely on the hook for hanging out with her.

The fact that I can't fully enjoy my night because of Jamie throwing me off twelve hours ago has me feeling a little bitter.

"You okay, sweetie?"

"Ugh," I groan, looking up at the cute bartender. "That nickname is off limits."

He laughs like I'm telling a joke. I'm not, and I don't get where everyone sees this "sweet" side. Maybe I look younger than I feel.

"Alright," the bartender says. He's nice to look at, but not my type. "You okay though? You're crying on my bar."

"Oh." Crap, I wipe my cheeks, mortified. *How long have I been crying?! How drunk am I?*

"Another?" the blond man offers, holding up a bottle of vodka. I nod, feeling incredibly numb. For real, how did I not realize I was crying? "Don't worry about it, sweet thing."

Before I can snap at him for calling me by another crappy nickname, a masculine voice I would know anywhere does it for me.

"Don't fucking call her that."

To top off Jamie's declaration, I throw my fourth shot back and relish the slight burn down my throat. The bartender raises a brow at me when Jamie slides him a large bill. I nod and wave my hand before taking a step away from the bar.

"Where are you off to, Violet?"

I mutter something and continue to weave my way through the crowds of people. My head is beginning to feel the effects of the four shots I've downed in the last hour. So when Jamie's warm hand wraps around my waist from behind, I melt willingly.

This, his body wrapped around me while I'm all

buzzy, is what I know best. I can do *this*. Hard conversations, emotional connections, no. The hard outline of his cock pressing against my lower back, yes.

Heat engulfs my earlobe, and Jamie's rumbly tone sends shivers down my spine. "Coming home with me?"

I'm nodding before I can really think about it. But that's the best part of Jamie and me, there's no need for me to think about anything. He may have been the one to put me in a mood today, but he's also the one who can help me forget and just *be.*

Cassidy has her friend, so I'll send her a text in Jamie's car. I need this. I need Jamie to chase the ickiness in my mind away. At least for a little while because...well...I deserve to feel like a piece of shit.

I grab his hand and step toward the door. "Let's go."

Bang!

Jamie's apartment door slams, indicating it's time to take my corset off. I removed my leather jacket in the elevator. Or, should I say, Jamie did right before he pressed me up against the cold wall of the moving box.

Stumbling slightly, I make my way to his kitchen island and toss my little black purse onto it.

Vaguely, I notice the warm hue of the dimmed lights around his industrial-style kitchen. His apartment is *meant* for sex. Brick accent walls, black furniture, and tall windows—it's sexy.

I fumble with the clasps of my lacy top, but my hands are soon replaced by larger, warmer ones. Humming with pleasure, I rest my palms on the island and allow Jamie full access to undress me.

Unfortunately for my needy nipples, Jamie trails his fingers away from the clasp, and brushes my hair over my left shoulder. My pout shifts into a delighted shiver as he kisses a trail from my bare shoulder to my ear.

"Violet," Jamie murmurs against my neck, sounding pained.

Taking matters into my own hands, or feet, I toe my black booties off and spread my legs apart. Bending so my ass presses against him, I rest my elbows on the chilly marble.

"Touch me," I moan, grinding on him. "Please," I add, because I don't need him demanding manners right now. *Damn dominant dick.*

A low groan vibrates the air between us as Jamie presses into me. His hands trail down my sides and land on my hips. "Violet—"

"Jamie!" I cry, drowning out his serious tone. My panties are soaked, I'm bent over his fucking counter, and he hasn't taken my top off.

Shifting my hand down, I unbutton my jeans myself. I push back so I'm standing on my own, and remove my pants. Dressed in nothing but a black lacy thong and a matching corset, I turn around and wait for Jamie to pounce on what I'm offering.

"Fuck."

Hair tussled and eyes hooded, Jamie takes in every inch of my body like he hasn't kissed them a thousand times before. I bite my lip and try to enjoy the way he's looking at me. But as soon as his eyes find mine and soften, I remove my top without a struggle.

Urgency and a dose of fear eliminate the awkward effects of alcohol.

"Violet, listen—"

I could collapse to my knees right now and give him the best blowjob ever, but that's not the way into Jamie's pants. Wild, right? Here's a man who would rather be kissed and caressed instead of sucked on like a tasty treat.

So, like I've done many times to this man, I prowl toward him and place my hands on his chest. He takes a shuddering breath as I run them up and over his shoulders then clasp them around his neck.

Stray strands of Jamie's hair tickle my temples as I pull him down until we're sharing a breath. I look him in the eye because that's the final move that will ensnare him.

You'd think after five and a half years of using this man for my pleasure, I'd be able to shut everything else off. Ignoring the extra twirl in my tummy and thump in my chest is almost impossible as our eyes meet.

I see too much in his crystal blue eyes, so I do what I do best; avoid. Smirking, I let out a breathy sigh and press my naked chest against him.

Then, like the horrible human I am, I use my final, most effective weapon in my arsenal. No, it's not my toned, tanned body, or my long blonde hair. It's my mouth, but not the way you'd think.

No. It's manipulative, and maybe a little cruel. After five and a half years, I know how to bend Jamie Murphy to my will. And what he needs are words.

"Touch me, Jamie. Please." And finally... "I need you."

Four

JAMIE

I can feel the heat of Violet's breasts through my T-shirt. Absentmindedly, I scold myself for removing my damn jacket. This woman is a temptress, and my lack of control around her pisses me off.

What also drives me to rage is how flawlessly she plays me. Violet knows how to get her way when it comes to me, and I allow it. I'm not blind to her tricks, but I also give in because it's easier. This way, I still have my slice of Violet. She doesn't give much beyond her body and screams of pleasure, but the extra bits I've seen are oh so sweet.

I'm aware of what caused this woman so much pain. What was shown on the news seven years ago is where I got my information, but there's so much more than articles and social media posts. Violet and her family went through something unspeakable, and the effects on V makes it hard for her to accept any form of kindness or care.

The guilt inside her is robbing us of our potential. I'm almost at my wit's end. Not with Violet. Never with Violet.

I'm just about done with watching her run from me. Even as she strutted her sexy ass toward me, she was still running. Always running from any kind of conversation.

Violet thinks she's a pro at keeping shit casual, but *casual* ended four and a half fucking years ago. Who knows what she thinks is going on here, but nobody has a fuck buddy for this long. At least none that I've heard of.

Unfortunately, she's deluded herself into thinking her hot pussy is all I'll ever get from her. I see it in her reluctance to leave my arms every time we spend a few hours together.

There's a lingering look of tenderness every time she looks back at me through the window as I walk her out. She's stopped trying to convince me she doesn't need me to walk her out—that's just another indicator that not all is as it seems.

Violet is not a fucking booty call.

She's everything. Even when I'm annoyed with her for not allowing me to speak and for tempting me with her words.

"Touch me, Jamie. Please. I need you."

Only Violet Bennett can bring me to my knees. Nobody, and I mean *nobody,* plays me the way she does. They aren't allowed to. I'm a dominant man, and I get what I want.

I want Violet's heart, and fucking hell I *know* I have

it. She may not know it yet, but she's mine. I haven't touched another woman in four and a half years, and I'm pretty damn certain I've been her only partner too.

As willing as Violet is with me, she doesn't sleep around. I know what she's up to. Keeping tabs on her and ensuring her safety is my number one priority.

I'm a fucking tattoo artist in downtown Detroit. I know *many* people. Sketchy and legit. Hell, I ink half the MC population around here. Violet has plenty of people looking out for her.

It just so happens that they're always willing to report their observations at my request.

"Please," Violet begs again, blinking up at me with her sparkling eyes that say more than I think she realizes.

A sound similar to a growl rumbles up my throat and propels me forward in a fierce, possessive kiss that makes my sweet girl gasp. Violet's used to me dominating her and fucking her senseless, but tonight shit's going to change.

By the time I'm done with her, she won't be able to take one goddamn step toward the door before dawn.

With the power of all the angst between us, I grab her thighs and pick her up. Her legs wrap around my hips, and she immediately moans when her hot cunt presses against my cock.

Both of my hands are on her bare ass as I stride for the island. The bedroom is too fucking far, and if Violet really has *zero* patience to listen to me talk, then I won't make her wait.

A chuckle slips from my lips when she squeals at the

chill of the marble on her cheeks. With the taste of lemon on my tongue, I pull away to look down at the woman panting beneath me.

I reach into my back pocket and snatch the condom I stashed there before I went to pick her up earlier. Crashing girls' night was always on my agenda.

"Take me out. Now," I demand, loving the way her eyes glaze over with desire at my no-nonsense approach. While she works to release my solid dick, I rip my shirt off because nothing feels better than Violet's hard nipples grazing my chest when I fuck her.

"Good," I groan as she encompasses my boner with her soft hand. Nibbling on her bottom lip, Violet eyes the weeping tip of my cock. "I'll fuck your bratty mouth later."

It's a promise and also a threat. I'm telling her there's no way we're just having sex before she leaves. She'll stay until I let her leave.

We've pulled all-nighters before, and it's usually after she tests my patience a little too much. Violet has tried to pull away from me in the past, and right now the signs are all there again.

Too bad I'm not letting her go.

"Enough." I grab her wrist and drape it over my shoulder as I use my other hand to slide her panties to the side. Her pussy lips are swollen and wet, just begging for me to take care of her tight hole. She needs me; it's as clear as the juices on her thighs.

As quickly as I can, I sheathe my cock in the unwanted protection.

Clawing at my neck and dragging me toward her

entrance with her feet, Violet wiggles and meets my gaze. "Jamie—"

I narrow my eyes and push forward, effectively cutting her off. "Sorry, Sweets. You decided we weren't talking tonight. Take my cock like you begged for it. Because you fucking did." I punctuate my rude comment by thrusting all the way inside her tight pussy.

"Yes!" she screams, sounding much louder as my ears begin to pound with the thundering of my heart.

Wet, warm, and rippling, Violet's body encompasses me. "Fuck. Yes."

She throws her head back, inviting me to nibble her throat. I hum in appreciation as I lick a droplet of sweat from her neck. Forcing myself to focus on her pleasure helps me ignore the sheer need to empty my load in her and make her mine. Permanently. Someday I'll bury myself in her goddamn womb and come over and over again until she has no choice but to admit we're each other's forever.

Her wet heat sucks me in and ripples around me like she's thinking the same thing. I make it my mission to drive into her with purposeful thrusts to see how high I can get her perky tits to bounce. Red, rosy nipples reach for me, begging for my tongue. And because this is Violet, I give her whatever she desires.

Gasping and mewling, she claws at the back of my head as I nip at her tits.

My balls draw up in desperation, but I battle it away. Violet needs me, and I'm going to fucking get her there.

"Jamie! More!"

Fucking hell. The chill of the counter touching the tops of my thighs every time I push forward grounds me and helps me hold back the urge to come. Her toned thighs jiggle around my hips, drawing my attention to their pretty bounce.

Violet's legs slip along my ass cheeks as she loses her grip on reality. *Not good enough.*

Snarling like a feral beast, my hair falls from my man bun and I yank out of her. I grab her ass, pull her from the counter, and twist her around until she's bent over the same spot I chopped a tomato earlier.

My fingertips dig into her hips as I yank her back. She pouts and begs me to help her reach the orgasm I feel rippling around me when I plunge back inside. *So good.* Reaching around because I can't deny her anything, I slip my fingers between her folds. She's fucking soaked for me. The sounds of my claiming are obscene, but it drives me higher and higher. Violet loves it filthy too.

"You like that, V? You're so fucking horny for my cock, your juices are dripping to your knees."

"Shit. Shit. *Shit!"* she moans, and it takes only two rubs on her clit for her to explode around me.

My eyes cross as the pressure building inside of me releases in a torrent of pleasure.

"Violet!" Roaring her name like it's our first time, I drag her to a standing position by a hand on her throat. Unable to help myself when I look down at her taut nipples, I graze them with my rough hands.

She shivers in my arms, and huffs when my softening cock slips out. Just as I feel her straightening, I scoop her into my arms bridal style and silence her protests with a kiss.

Small hands push at my chest until I pull back. "Jamie, what are you—"

"I'm taking you to my shower—"

"No."

Though she cut me off with another sassy denial, I know how to make her stay. "So I can lick your sweet pussy."

I can practically see the wheels turning in her eyes, so while she's thinking about my declaration, I rush us to my room.

Just as we're entering my attached bathroom, I hear her whisper, "Okay," and breathe a quiet sigh of relief.

She's still mine for a little longer.

Five

VIOLET

Early morning sunlight shines through the open curtains of Jamie's bedroom. The low lighting highlights the mistake I made last night. *At least the sun hasn't even lifted above the horizon yet.*

It doesn't matter though, because the damage has already been done. The amount of time I slept in Jamie's bed doesn't matter. What does matter and makes me feel sick to my stomach is that I closed my eyes to begin with.

I'd like to be mad at him for keeping me here and wringing as many orgasms from me as possible. Sure, I manipulated him first, but he then used my weaknesses against me too.

The push and pull is as exhausting as his stamina. And I don't mean his ability to get it up all night long because, let's be real, Jamie's almost thirty. I don't think it's possible for any man to have sex for seven hours straight.

I don't think I could handle that either. But what

Jamie does have is the ability to keep me on edge even after bringing me to orgasm three times.

I'm not one of those women who can come six times in an evening. It's unfortunate, yes, but the times I reach four are pretty exciting. Jamie has been the only person to get me to four.

And he did last night. I blame the spine-bending fourth orgasm for me passing out in Jamie's bed. It may have only been a two hour long sleep, but it shouldn't have happened.

I've only slept here after some particularly drunken nights, and even then, Cassidy came to get me at dawn without question.

Waking up sprawled across his bare chest has scared me shitless. I wasn't too drunk to go home last night, nor was I feeling clingy. I was just...comfortable.

That's why I'm currently standing in Jamie's bedroom doorway and chewing on the inside of my cheek. I've dressed and combed through my hair with my fingers, so there's nothing left for me to do once I grab my shoes in the kitchen.

So why am I still looking at Jamie's sharp jawline and thick eyelashes?

Flashes of last night assault my mind as I study his tattoo.

"You taste so sweet," Jamie mumbles between my legs. There's that word again.

Tingles race through my core with each stroke of his warm tongue against my pussy. He's so skilled that it makes me wonder who all he practices with.

My mind tries to haul me in a different direction by wondering how many women Jamie is sleeping with this month, but his fingers grip my thighs and spread them wider.

I huff, my neck flinging back at the burn in my muscles. Flexible sure, but Jamie's wide and he's forcing me to take his broad shoulders.

"Jamie!"

To shut me up, he slides a finger through my bottom cheeks and probes my other entrance. He likes to tease me with anal play, but he has yet to take me there. I'm not against it. Hell, I crave it. But when he says, "Someday I'll have all of you," the need shrivels up and dies.

Instead of acknowledging his reverent comment, I reach down and drag my hands through his hair roughly. He grunts when I pull on the long strands then shoves his naughty finger in my pussy instead.

"Yes!" I cry hoarsely and lean up on my elbows. I'm not going to reach my peak for a while longer since I've already had two orgasms, but I will enjoy the pleasure he's willing to give me.

Unable to help myself when Jamie rests his head on my thigh, I give in to the moment of intimacy and trail my fingers along the beauty of his dragon tattoo.

Slowly, with deliberate attention, Jamie pumps two fingers inside of me while nibbling on the crease between my leg and vagina.

My breathing turns ragged, and my tongue pushes to the roof of my mouth to keep me from saying something he might deem as sweet. *Realizing just how romantic the sexy moment became, I yank my hand away from the intricate lines of his ink and slump back on his bed.*

Similar to then, I pull my hand away from my chest. What am I doing watching him sleep, acting like that was a fond memory? Those are only meant for people in love and I—can't complete that thought, I realize.

Because someone in love wouldn't treat the other person the way I've treated Jamie. See? I don't love him.

I only feel bad.

Guilty. Like always.

I'm always feeling so fucking guilty.

Swallowing thickly, I try not to look around Jamie's apartment as I hunt for my shoes and purse. Except, the cozy plaid blanket on the back of the large couch in front of the fireplace makes each step even harder.

When I notice the purple mug by the coffeepot, I falter but continue. Spying my jacket hanging by the door along with my purse, I hustle toward them.

I can't get out of here fast enough. Yet I feel like I'm dragging my feet. Jamie's apartment has such a cozy vibe that's trying to suck me in. At least that's what I'm going to tell myself.

Quietly, I pull my jacket and shoes on. I've escaped

Jamie's home more times than I can count, yet it gets harder and harder each time. The door snicks shut behind me, and I rush for the elevator. Blinking rapidly once I'm in the small box, I try to keep the memories at bay.

Jamie with his cold hand under my shirt, but not grabbing my boob. He held my lower back with a gentleness that I can still feel.

I blink again and shake my head.

But then... *Jamie's lips are under my jaw as he bends his knees to reach my sensitive spots.*

No, I can't think about this right now. I'm leaving his darn apartment and going home.

Jamie pins me to the wall and lifts me up as he stands to his full height again. The only thing that stops us from ripping each other's clothes off right here and now is the ding of the elevator door opening.

Ding!

Jolting, I puff out a breath and rush for the main entrance. I already told Cassidy not to pick me up this morning, and with how distraught I am, I'm glad.

Snow falls from the sky, and I thank the chilly flakes for their ability to ground me. It's less than a twenty-minute walk home, but I feel like I might need much longer to clear my head of that man.

With each step away from his apartment building, the tension in my body increases. *This shouldn't feel this wrong.*

Six

VIOLET

I don't know what I'm doing anymore. All of my choices seem super messed up.

My night with Jamie has been playing on repeat in my mind. Over and over again, I recall how manipulative I was. This isn't who I want to be.

Sniffling, I press my forehead further into my bare knees. I'm huddled on my bathroom floor wondering if I can swing another road trip this week. Getting away sounds great, but I don't think I can make it work.

I can't stop wondering what Jamie wanted to say to me before I offered my body to him. Filling in the blanks hasn't been helping my mood. My phone has been taunting me for two days—*call him*.

But calling means talking, and we don't do that. I feel freaking sick to my stomach.

What I'm doing isn't working, but I have no idea what else to do. Every move I make adds to the anxiety that steals my happiness every day. Second-guessing has become my personality.

A cramp assaults my tummy, making me blow out a pained breath. My period is always worse when I'm home. Being on the road and focusing on my adventures is the perfect distraction. Or maybe it's the exercise. Or the fact that my stress is only related to the hike.

I'm a minimalist. One backpack, a fanny pack, and my camera are all I need on my trips. Home-cooked meals like the ones Cassidy likes to make are always missed, but a good apple and a protein-packed granola bar do the job when I'm away.

Life is much simpler outside of the city. Away from people.

Life is easier on the run from the things that make me feel.

Feelings fucking suck. I'm not like my mama with her potty mouth, but some statements definitely deserve the F word. Feelings, good or bad, result in anxiety for me these days.

Here's another example: My intellectual and emotional confidence is fucked.

"Violet!"

I shake my head even though Cassidy can't see me. The bathroom isn't locked, so she can come in if she wants, but no way am I getting up right now.

"Dinner is ready!"

Being brought to my butt by Mother Nature humbles me. I really need to be nicer to Cassidy. She's my best friend and always looks out for me. Hell, she tells me she loves me like a sister, and I've not once used the L word with her.

I'm stingy because the deeper the connection to

someone, the more it will hurt when I eventually mess everything up.

A soft tapping on the door pulls me from my thoughts. "You okay in there?" my friend asks.

She sounds worried, and that brings tears to my eyes. Swallowing, I try to shove my emotions down. "Fine! I'll be out in a bit," I reassure her, hoping she'll leave me in peace.

Who am I kidding? There is no peace when the cramps from hell are twisting your insides around like a freaking noodle on a fork.

Cassidy's silent, but I don't hear her walk away. It makes me feel worse that she's hesitant to talk to me. Admittedly, my attitude has gotten worse since the holidays.

Mom and her husbands were great, but they were also worried about me. Mom's girlfriends were there on New Year's Eve as well, and sometimes they ask too many questions. Many of those questions I chose not to answer which only fueled their concerns.

"Do you have water in there with you?" Cassidy's voice comes once again.

I frown, lift my head, and tuck my towel around me further. *Where did I put my water?* Remembering how I crawled out of bed this afternoon from my crappy nap, I pout. "Ugh, no. I think it's on my nightstand."

Now I hear her footsteps retreating from the other side of the door. Knowing Cassidy is most likely going to pamper me for the rest of the night, I stand and wrap myself in my purple robe. She doesn't need to see me naked right now. I'm bloated and feeling pale.

Am I getting sick on top of being on my damn period?

The messy French braid I refused to wash in the shower hangs down my back, and my eyes are half open. Looking in the mirror isn't an option, so I lean my butt against the counter and curl my arms around my tummy.

"This sucks," I murmur to myself as if I haven't struggled with horrible periods for over ten years.

"Knock knock! Coming in," Cassidy yells through the white wooden door and pokes her head in with a big smile. *I miss when I smiled so freely.*

"Hi," I whisper, throat thick. "Thank you." She hands over my favorite water bottle. State park stickers decorate the light purple sides. *So pretty.*

"That time again?" Cassidy asks, shifting around on her feet. She's nervous, and I feel the same. I know she wants to help me and comfort me, but she's holding back. I'm not very touchy these days. But, my goodness, I do want my friend to hug me.

Maybe...Maybe I can ask.

Just contemplating it makes a tear slip from my sleepy eyes. I nod in answer to her assumption. "My back hurts like I fell off a darn cliff and landed on a rock."

"I'll grab your heat pack from your room and bring it out to the living room. The casserole I made will help you feel all cozy and warm. Plus, I was planning on making the *fun* brownies tonight."

I narrow my eyes at the bubbly redhead. Absent-mindedly, I recognize I also used to talk a mile a minute like she just did, but there's no use in thinking about the past when my uterus is currently trying to flee my body.

"Did you know it would start today?"

Cassidy shifts on her feet. "Well, maybe? The signs were all there. You get a little stabby a few days beforehand."

I can't help it; I laugh and it feels so freaking good. Cassidy beams at me and rushes forward to give me a big hug that I didn't consent to but needed so much.

"Violet," she whispers with her head on my shoulder. "I know the holidays are hard for you, and you have some stuff going on. But I'm here for you."

My laugh turns into a choked sob. Thankfully, she doesn't comment on it. I hold on to her tighter to show my appreciation and love. Because I *do* love Cass. She's my best friend, and she's put up with all my bullshit for years now. How she isn't sick of me I'll never know.

"Thank you," I croak and pull away when she releases me.

As she exits my bathroom, she turns to say one last thing that I've never heard before. "The voices in your head aren't real. Nobody is saying the things you're listening to. Not all thoughts are facts."

I slump against the counter when she disappears around the corner. As Cassidy dishes up my dinner and takes care of me while I'm not feeling well, a new war rages in my mind.

My brain will never rest, not with the anxiety that rattles me daily. But...Cassidy might have given me the weapon I need to at least breathe.

Not all thoughts are facts.

Seven

VIOLET

"That one is pretty," Cassidy murmurs, looking over my shoulder at the colorful display.

I hum, studying my options and waiting for one to jump out at me. This is the third store I've drug Cassidy to with me this morning. To keep her happy, I bought her an iced latte and promised we'd get lunch on our way home.

She's been eyeing me since I woke up and demanded she come shopping for notebooks with me. Not much gets me out of the house during days one through three of my period, so I understand her confusion.

Then there's also the fact that I haven't told her why I need a new notebook. I have a stack of unused ones at home, but none of them feel right for my inspiration.

"So, V..." Cassidy sounds so gentle, making me smile. "Care to tell me why we're running around Detroit looking for a notebook? Is there a specific one I should be helping you look for?"

I shake my head. "I won't know until I see it."

"Oookay. Is this like a hormonal thing?"

At that, I giggle and roll my eyes. "How would this be a hormonal thing?"

The ice in her cup jostles as she throws a hand in the air in exasperation. "I don't know, Violet. What's with the notebook fixation at seven in the morning on a damn Sunday?"

"It's almost nine," I point out while walking toward the next display of notebooks. These are a little smaller which I like better than the full size. I need to be able to bring it around with me in my fanny pack.

"You woke me up at *seven*!"

Glancing over my shoulder at her, I smirk when I see the bewildered expression on her face. I also notice that she has a cute notebook with bows on it tucked under her arm. The coffee in her hands is almost gone too.

"I'll explain once I find it. Shh." I shoo her away with a hand and my debit card. "Go to the coffee shop and get me some donut holes and whatever you want. Please."

Cassidy snatches my card and skips away to the checkout counter to buy her new find. I stare longingly after her and wonder when the last time I bounced happily through a store was.

I miss how bubbly I used to be. That was the word everyone used to describe me. *Bubbly*.

After slipping out of Jamie's bed the other night and walking home in the super early morning sunlight, I've come to realize just how much I dislike who I am without those bubbles.

Holding on to my annoyance at how everyone else misses the happiness I used to radiate is a defense mechanism. My therapist told me so. I haven't spoken to her in about eight months, but I think she would approve of this idea I have.

Every time I feel the bubbles rising to the surface, I pop them with a sharp comment or a wicked taunt. I would like to be happy again. Drowning the anxious, mean thoughts that try to contend with my desired positivity, I take a deep breath and turn back to my mission.

I deserve to be happy.

It's with that thought, that *factual* thought, that I find what I've been looking for. Purple and white, the small notebook stands out like a beacon of hope. I had hoped to find one with bubbles on it; instead, this one has flowers.

It reminds me of Mama. The woman who has become the brightness I need in these dark years like I was for her.

Now I just need Cassidy to come back with my money. Then, I'll be on my way to vanquish these nasty anxious thoughts that have been trying to ruin my life for seven years.

No more. *Hopefully.*

Explaining my plans to Cassidy makes me feel a bit odd. Of course she just nods along and smiles like my idea isn't weird, but I'm uncomfortable.

"Hey, Violet?" she calls to me, snapping me out of my weird feelings. When I look at her, she grabs my hand. "Thank you for sharing. I'm really glad my random word vomit last night sparked some motivation."

"Oh," I hum, looking down at the pretty notebook on my lap. "Yeah. Thank you."

She laughs quietly and continues. "Are you alright?"

I sigh. "I'm feeling, I don't know, off."

Nodding, Cassidy seems to agree with my guess. "Yeah. Well, I've known you for like five years, and this is the most I've seen you reflect on yourself. This is a *good* thing. Personal growth is hard, though, because it's all up to you."

Ugh, she sounds like my therapist. Even though I'm internally rolling my eyes, I do agree with her. If I plan to change, to grow, and be a better person, then I must figure it out myself.

"Yeah," I repeat as I slowly lose myself in my thoughts. "It feels corny, and like someone would make fun of me if they knew I was journaling."

Cassidy frowns. "Wait, what the hell do you do with

your stack of notebooks in your room if you haven't been journaling?"

Confused, I look up at her. "What?"

"I thought you were already doing stuff like this." She gestures to my new possession. "Considering this is like your millionth notebook you've come home with in the past year."

Blinking at her, I try to wrap my head around what she's saying. To be clear, her statement isn't confusing; I'm just having a hard time concentrating. There are a lot of thoughts that need to be unloaded on these pages, *and* my cramps are wrapping around my uterus as well as my lower back.

Glancing behind Cassidy and toward my bedroom, I can see one of my small stacks of adorable notebooks on my nightstand. "I just think they're pretty."

My explanation of my collection makes her laugh. "Well, I hope you find a use for them in the future. Maybe they'll become journals." She stands from the couch with a small smile and tells me she's going to go get some groceries.

Curling tighter around my favorite blanket and heating pad, I run my fingers across the printed flowers. A tap on my shoulder reveals Cassidy with her jacket on and a pen in her hand.

"Love you," she murmurs, and before I can gather the courage to say it back, she's gone.

With her encouragement and affection, I settle in and prepare to release my demons in the pretty binds of a notebook that reminds me of my mama.

I can do this.

Journal Entry

Fact or lie? The game I played today.

Nobody wants me around because I'm annoying. LIE - I think.

Cassidy doesn't actually like me. She just wants to keep me around to pay rent. LIE.

I don't know who I am anymore. Fact.

My collection of notebooks is dumb. Uncertain.

I'm rude. Fact.

I'm abrasive. Fact.

I hurt people's feelings. Fact.

Cassidy walks on eggshells around me. Fact.

I manipulate. Fact.

I'm an unfeeling bitch. Lie.

I feel too much. Guilt being the number one emotion. Fact. FACT. FACT!

^ I deserve it. Fact?

Eight

JAMIE

I respect women; I really, really fucking do. But when women don't respect me and are toeing the line of sexual harassment, my manners start to slip.

"Get your fuckin' tits off my shoulder."

I'm putting some blame on all the gruff biker guys I tattoo. Those men are assholes, and it might be rubbing off on me, but damn are they good to have on hand.

"What do you mean?" I wish the buzzing sound of my gun was loud enough to cover the cringy ass whine coming from the brunette in my chair.

Leaning back removes her unwanted touch, and focusing on patching up her fresh ink helps me ignore the batting of her fake ass eyelashes. I taught myself a long time ago not to judge what other people get tattooed on their bodies, but when young chicks with no sense of self respect waltz in and demand a tattoo I've done a million times for women who look just like her...yeah, holding my judgment back is hard.

"You may remove the bandage in two hours. Keep it clean, wash with gentle soaps, and Aquaphor is good to keep it from drying out. Any questions you have will most likely be answered in the packet Jake at the front desk will give you when you pay."

The brunette gapes at me like she's shocked I'm not sucking on her pushup bra or some shit.

"Any other questions, you can call the front desk," I continue while I open the door and head out into the lobby.

I know she's following me because I can hear her huffing like a petulant child. Jake makes eye contact with me and smirks. He's young, and I hired him as a favor for the local MC. He's a prospect in need of some real-world work before he starts doing the illegal shit. I have no clue really, but the kid is fucking hilarious and can read people pretty damn well.

Rapping my knuckles on the counter of the desk, I turn to the pouting woman and am about to tell her to have a nice day when a streak of purple and blonde zips by the large windows.

I'm running out and make it onto the sidewalk before I even realize what I'm doing. "Violet?" I yell, rushing to catch up to my girl.

Thankfully, she stops and turns, giving me the time of day. I'm surprised if I'm being painfully honest. I expected to chase her down and demand that she actually speak to me.

I haven't heard from her in a few days, which isn't uncommon, but I miss her damn it.

"Hi, Jamie," she says with, I shit you not, a soft smile on her perfect face.

Is my jaw on the ground? Where's her scowl or sultry look?

"Hi, Sweets," I reply and watch her lips twist a little. This time it's not in annoyance, at least I don't think it is, because she starts shifting on her feet and red rises on her cheeks. "What are you up to today?"

"Um."

Fascinated, I watch Violet struggle to communicate with me. Her hair is down in its usual waves, but she has half of it pulled back in two pigtails that are so damn adorable I can't help but smile. I'd prefer she had a hat on in this cold weather, but I'll just be glad she has her big winter coat and boots on instead. Her jeans are on the baggy side today, and I really, *really* want to know what shirt she's wearing. Not in a sexy way, but because I rarely get to see my girl in normal fucking street clothes.

Like many times I see her around the city, her camera is around her neck. The photos she can take with such a simple device are incredible. I can't imagine her with a ton of material like lenses and tripods—Violet is a minimalist who doesn't like to be dragged down by *stuff*.

She lifts the camera I was just admiring, and wiggles it at me. "I had an inquiry about dark, more gothic images for their business."

When she shrugs like that's all she's going to say, I lift a brow. "I'm not freezing my ass off out here for minimal answers, Violet. Finish the story."

Frowning down at my thin long sleeve, she takes a step forward as if she's going to warm me up, but of *course,* we're interrupted. And the touch that grabs my bicep is from the woman I left at the front desk with Jake.

Violet stiffens at the same time I do. "What are you doing?" I growl low while glaring down at the woman who needs a serious come to Jesus moment.

"I wanted to thank you," she purrs, and fucking hell, her jacket plunges to show her cleavage. "You have a lot of skill, Jamie."

My muscles bunch to yank away from the bitch who has no fucking right to touch me. Instead, she pulls away first and struts her ass right by the woman of my dreams with a pleased grin.

"What the fuck?" I rumble, shivering in disgust. I'll need to tell Jake that she is no longer allowed to book with me. Maybe she can be seen by one of the other artists, but with the way she just disrespected Violet, *no fucking way.*

"Well." Violet snaps me out of my mental note taking with her shaky voice. When I look at her again, I see the slight sheen in her eyes. "I should be going."

"Wait." I rush forward to grab her and ensure she doesn't cry, but *fucking Jake* yells my name from our door. "Violet—"

The smile my girl gives me is so fucking sad my stomach twists with concern. I've seen her emotional only a handful of times, and that's when she won't let me fuck her because of her period...*oh!*

"You should go." Her tone is quiet and almost defeated.

"Jamie! Get your ass in here. We have a situation!"

Code for some idiot passed out, I bet.

"Hold your fucking horses!" I shout at Jake, but when I turn around Violet is turning too. "Violet, please."

Wiping a tear, she breaks my damn heart. *What made her fucking cry!?* "See you later, Jamie."

"JAMIE!"

Whirling around to glare at the prospect who is just fucking asking for a punch in the face, I bellow, "JAKE! I'm going to fire your fucking ass!"

His face pales. Fucker knows if I fire him, he won't get patched in. He's proving himself and apparently needs a fucking lesson in patience.

"V—" When I turn back to my girl, she's gone.

Sagging, I sigh when I realize I missed another chance at taking our relationship to the next level. It will be okay, because I have a plan.

First, I have to set a young asshole straight. Clearly he hasn't heard of Violet, but he will have no doubt now about interrupting me when he sees the blonde with purple streaks in her hair ever again.

His prez knows, so he fucking should too.

Nobody comes between me and Violet Bennett.

Showing up at Violet's apartment isn't my best idea. She's a very private person, so this could be a super big mistake. I've only done this a few times, and it was at the beginning of our *thing*.

That was when I didn't know she had a job traveling and was gone far more than I had realized. Her roommate looked confused to see me, which hurt a bit because even years ago I thought Violet and I had something special.

Only reason I knew her address is because she demanded to see if I could be a gentleman before slipping between my sheets. V has always been addicting with her sass and toxic power she holds over me. But that's not to say I'm not demanding and addictive to her either.

Shit, if we ever do become an official couple, we're seriously going to need to work on communication.

Violet's my forever woman. Forever can't last if we're toxic toward each other.

I know V's sass and rude mouth could be a lot of fun if we paired it with my patience and smiles. We could be fucking awesome together if she would just stop fighting me.

Which is why I'm patiently waiting for someone to answer the damn door because the tub of ice cream I brought is not going to last all night out in their hallway.

Finally, the lock disengages, and the door handle turns. I hold my breath, hoping like hell it's Violet who's home tonight. Maybe she'll be alone. Maybe she'll let me in for the first time.

I just want to see her space and catch a few more glimpses into who Violet is. My woman is a fucking tease, leaving me with scraps while I pant after her as she leaves me in the dust. *She has to want me as much as I want her*.

"Ah, Jamie."

Fuck. Seeing Cassidy brings a wave of disappointment over me, making my smile drop.

"Jeez. Nobody ever looks that upset to see me," she teases while rolling her eyes.

Cassidy is a beautiful woman, even in her baggy sweatpants and sweatshirt. Her bright red hair gives her an edge, but what I appreciate about her is the loyalty she shows to Violet.

Cassidy is my woman's roommate and best friend. I'm not into her, but I need her to like me. Cassidy would be the best ally I could get.

"Good evening," I greet, trying to look over her shoulder. "Is Violet around?"

Cassidy narrows her eyes at me as if she's trying to read my mind. "You don't come here. So why are you here now?"

She sounds annoyed which surprises me. I've run into her and V when they're out, but I haven't been on their doorstep in a long ass time.

"I want to give Violet some ice cream. She didn't look so good earlier today," I explain, trying to placate the questioning redhead.

Crossing her arms, Cassidy cocks a hip. *Christ, I forgot how sassy she can be*. She and Violet together, especially after a few drinks, are a force to be reckoned with at the club.

"'Kay, but like, why?"

I can't tell if she's testing me or genuinely confused about my being here. The chill of the ice cream makes my fingertips burn, but I'm not that much of a pussy that I set it down. Instead, I tuck it under my arm, thankful for my leather jacket.

"Is Violet here or not?" I snap as gently as I can. "I'd like to see her. To make sure she's okay."

Her chin lifts, and I know I'm not getting past her. "She's in the shower. I'll take your offering and let her know you stopped by."

Shit. Fuck. I know a dismissal when I hear one.

"Alright." My attempt at keeping my grumble out of my voice doesn't work, making Cassidy smirk and hold out a hand. *Damn her*. "Thanks," I say and hand over the ice cream. Parting with it fucking sucks because that was my way in.

She doesn't move to close the door, and I'm still rooted to the spot in hopes of seeing Violet. I barely notice Cassidy's face soften while I'm trying to plan the best way to get myself invited in someday.

"Jamie. If you want her, you're going to have to keep pushing. She may gift you a centimeter here or there, but if you want *more,* you'll need to challenge her."

I nod, already working on some ideas. "Great, then you get it. I'll need your help with her birthday present."

"We'll see," she says cryptically, and closes the door

in my face. I don't have Cassidy's number, and I don't need it. I'll be back and get it then.

I'll keep coming back for as long as it takes to get a glimpse of Violet.

Nine

VIOLET

I'm losing my mind. Actually, *Jamie* has lost *his* mind.

Who does he think he is texting me shit like this?

Jamie: Hi Sweets. I want you to know a secret that's super important for you to think about okay?

Jamie: I haven't been with anyone else in years. Just you.

I'm angry. No, I'm livid.

He can't be telling the truth. I saw the way that woman was all over him yesterday outside of his tattoo shop. He may not have had sex with her, but he probably got a blowjob as a tip.

The hurt I felt at seeing her fawning all over Jamie yesterday was uncalled for. I can't be jealous of a fuck buddy for having others to warm his bed.

Jamie's hot. Hotter than hot. No way he's just settled

for me all these years. Heck, I'm gone half the time. I figured he has someone in his bed every night I'm not there. Surely, his stamina and needs require more than I've been giving him.

"You look like you either need to punch something or have a stiff drink? You alright, girly?"

Groaning, I hang my head and rub my eyes. They burn, and I can’t tell if it's from the lack of sleep, staring at Jamie's messages, or unshed tears.

"I'm fine," I grumble. Maybe it's all three of those things, because I'm becoming more and more overwhelmed by the minute.

It's only been two days since Cassidy enlightened me about the requirements of personal growth. What I once thought was a good idea to think about has completely opened the floodgates.

My journal has pages and pages filled with so much back and forth it hurts to look at. The anxiety must be radiating from me because everyone I've come into contact with frowns and asks if I'm okay.

No. I'm not okay!

Seven years later, and I've accidentally ripped most of my walls down. Turns out, I'm more messed up in the head than I thought.

Tasha tugs on my hair and spins me around in the chair. She's the salon manager and likes to hang out with me while I take my pictures for their social media.

Her pixie haircut is on point today, reminding me of my mom's friend Janine. She's always checking on me too, but I've always told her what she wants to hear.

Tasha is the same way. A dog sniffing out a bone.

Raising a perfect brow at me, Tasha waits for me to spill my guts. I don't though, which, like the dramatic person she is, sets Tasha off.

"Oh my god! Is it a man? Tell me someone has finally been able to get you to settle down! Yay! This is amazing."

"Tasha..." Reece, a hairdresser I would kind of consider a friend, frowns at his boss.

Tasha doesn't hear him, or she might just ignore him because her hands keep waving around in my face talking about makeup and a hairdo to sweep this mystery man off his feet.

"My goodness," she gushes, "this is the best news! I wasn't sure we'd ever see this day. How did he knock the scowl off your beautiful face? Did you let him hug you?"

My throat thickens with pent-up emotion. Most of it feels like hurt, but another part is frustration. Who does Tasha think she is talking to me like this? We're not besties. Hell, she employs me, and we only see each other for an hour a month.

"Tasha!" Reece snaps, turning from the older woman in his chair. The stranger looks at me with pity, which does nothing for my feelings.

Can I feel offended even if what Tasha said is true?

"What?!" Tasha throws her hands in the air then slams them on her hips. With her crappy attitude aimed at Reece, I slip from the chair while clutching my camera to my chest like it's my only lifeline.

Reece looks so angry with Tasha, yet when he glances at me as I make my escape, I don't see pity. If he were into women, I might give him a chance after his show of support and kindness. *Yeah, right,* I scoff in my mind. *Maybe if Jamie didn't exist.*

I nod at Reece in thanks, and rush from the salon. The bell above the door dings, and I know Tasha will be running after me, so I rush into my car before locking the doors. I'm stomping on the gas and peeling away from the curb without a backward glance.

I would say I have a lot to think about, but my mind already has that under control. With every passing second, a new thought enters my mind.

How could Tasha say those things? She was right though.

Do I really come off so cold and horrible? Maybe not horrible but probably cold.

I never used to be a cold person. That's not who I am.

Maybe I never should have donned a mask like my mama did. But Mom didn't shield her entire self and personality from the world. Just the things she thought would hurt those she loved.

But that's what I did, right? Because my personality proved to be gullible and senseless. Bubbly and happy don't mean smart. I thought the person harassing me online was only annoying. Until he created more accounts and started demanding my location. Only when I started feeling scared, I told Mama.

I thought it was all part of being famous on social media...My videos and content of Blue and me received so much love I thought it was normal to have a few creeps in my DMs.

My naïveté almost got my mama killed.

So, I chose to mask it all. Violet with the smiles and

skipping legs who befriended everyone has become a husk filled with pain and longing for the life she used to have.

I miss who I used to be. But why does it have to be so painful to come to that realization? Confronting the toxic traits I've acquired to keep people away from me is so damn hard I don't think I'll ever be able to do it again.

This is a one-time thing. I'll only deal with my crappy trajectory once because at my core I have a soft heart and a bubbly soul. I'm not cut out for another rewrite. Plus, how many chances will I get?

Not remembering the drive to the underground garage at my apartment is a bit sketchy, but at least I got myself here. A little processing didn't kill me this time.

Slumping against my seat, I turn the car off and squeeze my eyes shut.

I don't want to be the person people look at with shock if they think I have a boyfriend. Being humiliated today was the final straw. This camel's back is broken.

Which is probably why, when I turn my phone on and see Jamie's new message, I burst into tears.

> Jamie: Let me know when you're ready to admit I'm the only partner you've had too. I'll be here. I'm a patient man, Violet. 💜

Ten

JAMIE

I pride myself on keeping my cool. Always. Even faced with fucking MC men who like to swing their guns around, I'm pretty damn chill.

Violet undoes me. I've been worried for days.

As frustrating as it is for her to disappear on me for extended periods of time, I've always managed just fine. V hasn't been ready for commitment for a long time, except I'm starting to question how she feels lately.

She's always made her stance on our relationship very clear, which is *fine. Christ, now I sound like a woman.*

"It's not fucking fine," I growl, throwing my fork in my kitchen sink. "Where the fuck is she?"

Deep breaths stopped helping yesterday. Rational thought hasn't existed for a while. I have no clue what I was thinking sending her those messages.

I'm a patient man. I swear I am.

So why the hell did I text that shit? I wanted to push and get us moving in the right direction, but I'm afraid I've pushed her *away*.

Yeah, I'm *afraid*.

Violet is fragile. She tries to be tough, but, *my god* her eyes bleed with pain. Even in the throes of passion, I see the internal battle she fights. I feel the way her body softens against me right before she stiffens and pulls away. I'm not the only one afraid—Violet's scared.

She's scared that we're real. *I'm not crazy*. There's no question in my mind that what we have is real. No matter how many times she tries to distract me with her body, her heart, mind, and soul have my attention too.

Hanging my head, I try to wrangle my thoughts into something helpful. *I could go to her apartment, but what if she just needs some space? When is a good time to demand that she talk to me?*

Like I've done a thousand times, I glance at my cellphone in hopes it lights up. Then I tap the screen, praying I missed a message or call. *Nothing*.

My chest tightens, and I feel my throat working as a frustrated shout builds. Unraveling isn't an option, but it seems like I'm coming apart at the seams without my woman.

Knock, knock!

My childish explosion settles and dissipates as I rush to the entryway. I skip the peephole and rip the door open, but I never expected my excitement to turn into heartbreak.

"Sweets..." I whisper, shuffling forward. Her eyes are bloodshot and she's in pajamas. "Are you—"

"Don't ask me if I'm okay," she snaps, but it's weak.

I've never seen her so openly vulnerable or struggling. I feel my knees wobble, wanting to crash to the ground in front of her and beg her to tell me how I can help.

"Because you're not..." I venture a guess, already knowing I'm right. I'd bet my last penny that she doesn't have any lingerie on tonight, which is saying a lot. Violet came to me dressed like she wants to cuddle and watch a movie which has never happened before. Each visit she's ready to seduce—not tonight.

If I thought I was unraveling, what has Violet been going through? I should have gone to her sooner, but maybe this is a good thing? She's showing emotion, *and* she came to me.

Shifting on her feet, I jolt into action and usher her inside my apartment. *What a fucking idiot,* I scold myself, annoyed I left her in the hallway for so long.

"Where's your coat?"

Internally, I breathe a sigh of relief when she rolls her eyes at me. I let it slide since she's taking her shoes off and looks like she's going to stay. *Stay forever, please.*

Violet proceeds to remove her sweatshirt, leaving her in a white crop top that makes my dick perk up. Then she turns around, and I see her red eyes again.

I'm about to beg her to tell me what's wrong when her lips part and she does what I want without me asking. "You've caused a lot of problems for me, Jamie Murphy."

My heart stutters, and my gut roils in retaliation against me because I should *never* be the one causing problems for my woman. I should say something, but my tongue is stuck to the roof of my mouth.

I watch slightly terrified as Violet slumps onto one

of my barstools. "There's so much going on in my head..." she whispers, no longer making eye contact. "There are too many feelings..."

My feet start closing the distance. Her pain is calling to me, and I'm incapable of ignoring the sheer emotion pouring off of her in waves.

Then, fucking hell, she looks up at me, and every muscle in my body coils tight. "I'm sorry I ghosted you, Jamie."

Holy fuck.

My jaw is about to hit the floor, but a tear slips free from her beautiful gray/green eyes, and my trajectory shifts from shock right into kissing that tear away.

Control gone, I snatch Violet from the stool and crush her to my chest. "Violet," I croak, petting her head and breathing in the strawberry shampoo she uses. "Stop crying please. Fuck."

Her shoulders are trembling, and my shirt is damp where her face is buried. I swear my heart swells with the way she clings to me, but also breaks because she's not okay.

It's hard, but I push Violet back so I can look at her face. As soon as our eyes clash, a sob rips from her chest, and I *snap*.

My right hand grabs her jaw and catches her tears as I slam my lips down on hers. It's not out of passionate need, but sheer desperation to make her stop hurting.

For once, I *don't* want to talk to her. I'm terrified that if I asked more questions, the more Violet would cry. It physically fucking hurts me to see her cry. It's avoidant as fuck, but I want to make my sweet girl feel better.

With Violet's tears on my cheek and my left hand gripping her ass, I caress her tongue with mine.

I hate that I can't tell if her whimpers are because she's sad or because she's horny. Maybe both? Only one way to find out.

With a soft snarl, I back her into my living room and force her down onto the couch. My knees finally give out like they wanted to do as soon as I saw the anguish in her features.

"Jamie." She's trembling still, but her tears have stopped. "I—"

With my eyes locked on her from my kneeling position, I peel her sweatpants off and trail my fingers back up her legs. Absentmindedly, I notice the prickliness of her legs, and pride blooms in my chest. An odd reaction to leg hair, but I'm fucking thrilled she came to me *not* dolled up and perfect for once. She's still perfect, maybe more, because this version is *real*.

"Fuck." Her thong is pink cotton with little martini glasses printed on the fabric.

Violet's hands move to cover her panties, but I bat them away and glare at her. She shakes her head, and the red of her cheeks makes me grin. "They aren't—"

"Shush. I fucking *love* you like this."

Violet chokes, and I panic a little on the inside. *Did I just say that?*

"Ja—"

Laying a stinging slap on the inside of her thigh, I scold her. "Enough. Let me make you feel good."

It's a demand, and one Violet allows. Just to prove my point about her cute underwear, I leave them on and pull them to the side while I begin our night of total pleasure.

No talking. Not tonight. My heart can't take her tears. Unless they are caused by me finding her G-spot, orgasms, and edging.

I'll help her forget, then I'll hold her after. I'm not taking no for an answer tonight. She's staying.

Eleven

VIOLET

I've never wished for a tube of mascara so much in my life. Lacy thongs are uncomfortable as hell, but a pair sounds amazing right now. My cotton panties and sweatpants on the bathroom counter mock me. *What was I thinking coming here like this?*

I'm not my mom. Blue Bennett loves her clothes and makeup, but for me those things are just armor. Masks I can hide behind. I am not Mom. Not strong, not fearless, or epic.

How could I come here and show Jamie just how depressing I really am?

"Martini undies..." I sigh, and hang my head to splash some water on my face. My oldest, most comfy thong should not be anywhere near Jamie's apartment.

Yet, I let him eat me out with them *on*. Insert face palm.

God, I could cry. I feel so embarrassed and even more strange than when I decided to come here.

For some reason I really needed Jamie tonight. I've

been struggling to understand the torrent of emotions and overwhelming thoughts in my mind since Jamie texted me the other day.

We need to talk, and that was the main reason I came over here. To say what, I'm not even sure? But ignoring him, *ghosting* him made me sick to my stomach.

I've seen the damage miscommunication can cause.

My goal is never to hurt anyone, let alone someone who I know cares about me. *Love,* Jamie had said. He can't possibly love me when he doesn't know anything about me.

Except that I wear grungy panties and baggy clothes when not seducing him...

Grumbling to myself as I dry my face and put my clothes back on, I try to think through the best way to get out of here. I know I came here to talk, but I should at least have jeans on and a bra with a wire.

With one final glance in the mirror, I try not to cringe at my messy hair. Patting it down with water didn't seem to do much I guess. Slowly, I open the bathroom door and tiptoe down the hallway. I had left Jamie in the living room so I could get myself under control.

The closer I get to the main area, the louder his deep voice becomes. *Who is he talking to?*

"I intend to do just that. Promise." His voice echoes down the hall. His shoulders and head come into view where he's sitting on the couch, and I see him nod. "Yeah. She's amazing."

The pinch of my brows is starting to give me a headache. *Is he talking about me?*

Keeping my steps light, I try to gain a little information about Jamie through his phone call. If he's not talking about me, then I'll know his text was a lie, and I can leave without having a heart to heart.

I see his lips twist as I get closer. "I understand, Mrs. Bennett."

As if he punched me in the chest, I gasp on my next breath and rush into the living room. Jamie whips around, startled, and that's when I see *my fucking phone* held up to his ear.

"What the hell are you doing?!" Shock and betrayal rip the words from my mouth in shrill distress. "Are you talking to my mom?!"

Jamie's crystal blue eyes are wide, but they hold a sense of calm that confuses me. He opens his mouth, and when I expect him to make *me* feel better, he talks into the phone. "Don't worry, Blue. I'll fix this. Have a good night."

He hangs up, and I launch myself forward to snatch it from his strong hand. I grapple for my device and fling myself off of him as if his touch burns me.

"How dare you?!"

He stands after I back away a few steps. With his hands in the air like he's trying to tame a wild animal, Jamie coos, "Violet, please listen."

"No!" *Childish response, but I'm not taking it back.* I'm pissed off and taken by surprise in the worst way right now.

Jamie doesn't back down. "Your phone was ringing, and I saw your mom's name on the screen. I wasn't going to answer, I swear—"

"You swear, but *you did!*"

My breaths are coming fast, but what Jamie just did crossed a line. I wasn't ready to tell my mom about him. I don't even know what I would freaking label him as.

She's going to have so many questions. Oh hell, what did they talk about while I was in the bathroom? How long was I in there?

"I wasn't," he assures me. "Then I got it in my head that there might be an emergency when Blue called a second time. So I answered. I swear I didn't say anything bad. She just wanted to make sure you're okay and—"

"WELL I'M NOT OKAY!" The truth explodes from my heart like it's been waiting an eternity to be brought to light. "Now, not only am I super fucking confused and sad, Jamie, I'm angry too!"

"Violet—"

"NO!" Rushing for the door, I shove my phone in my sweatshirt pocket. "You crossed a line!"

Before I can reach the small table with my keys on it, Jamie's there blocking my way with a look of anger and desperation. "All you fucking have are *lines*!"

My breath stutters and my hands go numb in response to his booming voice. Jamie has never sworn at me or raised his voice, so the anxiety that rushes through my veins is born of uncertainty and maybe a little fear.

He's not done, though.

"I told your mom you were fine and that I would make sure you stayed that way. I can't fucking do that if you block me at every turn with all your damn boundaries and walls!"

"They're there for a reason," I say, my voice dropping into hurt territory.

Jamie throws his hands in the air like he's done with my bullshit. Maybe he is, hell knows I would be at this point.

When he turns his back to me, more of my pain slips free with my tears. "I've made some really horrible mistakes in my life. You don't know—"

He whirls around, eyes wild, and fists his hands, forcing my heart into my throat. "Of course I know what happened! That was national news *seven years ago,* Violet!"

I can't breathe. All I can feel are my toes twitching, begging me to run. *Of course he knew. How dumb can one person be? I'm such an idiot.*

"Seven fucking years. It's time to move the fuck on."

I'm done. Done with this conversation, done with Jamie thinking he knows what I've been through. There is no moving on from the trauma my family endured.

Pushing past him, I bolt for the door and snatch my keys from the small table in the entryway.

"Violet, wait!"

Jamie's voice is far away and completely disappears as the blood rushes through my eardrums. He did what he had to do when faced with someone who's ruined lives.

Jamie has officially pushed me away.

Twelve

JAMIE

I have never felt like such a fuck up in my entire life. There has never been anything so profound, so important for me *to* mess up. Which is why when my dad calls me right after Violet leaves, I'm tongue-tied.

"Jamie? What's wrong?" my dad asks, sounding gruff. Mom's voice is muffled in the background, but I can tell she's concerned.

Groaning, I flop my head back on my couch. "I fucked up, Dad."

"What did you do? Is Violet okay?"

My parents have known about Violet for years and are constantly asking about her. Not in a pressuring way, but with a need to check in and make sure she's doing well.

Violet doesn't know how invested my parents are in me winning her heart, and it's going to stay that way until I get her to meet them. Mom will wrap her in a hug and give away all my secrets, I just know it.

"I—" My throat clogs with emotion.

"Is she with you?" Mom asks and tells my dad to put me on speakerphone. "Let me talk to her."

At that, I smile. Lucy Murphy is the kindest woman in existence. Who I know for a fact is going to ream my ass when she hears about what I said to Violet. My mother already considers Violet her own in a way.

My smile fades as I sigh. "She left. I said some shit I shouldn't have and—"

"What did you say?" Mom cuts me off, her tone as harsh as it can get. Last time I heard it, she was scolding one of the MC brothers for his vulgar language at the tattoo shop when ladies were present.

What a day that was...

"Jamie!" Dad snaps, and I'm suddenly grateful we aren't on a video call.

Fuck. "I told her she needs to get over what happened to her mom."

Exactly as I predicted, my parents demand to know the full story. I offer them part of it and explain my feelings on the matter. They provide ideas of what she must have been thinking, which makes me feel so much fucking worse.

By the end of the call, I'm on the verge of tears and an anxiety attack. Calling a cab to take me to a bar with the best liquor is the best plan I can come up with at this point in the night.

An unknown amount of alcohol later, something touches my arm. No, *someone.* Which I'm only able to distinguish by the voice coming from near my shoulder since I refuse to lift my head and face the world.

"Alright," a manly voice begins. "I couldn't come up with a pick up line, so I'm hoping my honesty at *least* earns me a glance beyond your jawline."

Shocked enough to look up at the man, I'm a little stunned by how someone masculine can be so...so...pretty. His short brown hair is a mess of waves, and he keeps his scruff close to his striking face. Brown eyes gleam at me, but that's not what really catches my attention. The man behind him eyeing me like a snack with an arm wrapped around the guy touching me does.

"Excuse me?" I murmur, a bit weirded out by these two men.

"Love the man bun," the other guy says with a lift of his chin. In the low lighting of the bar, I notice he too has a man bun; but his hair is much lighter than mine, and the beard he's rocking sets us apart. Well, that and his incredibly wide chest and muscles. *Is this a real-life lumberjack?*

A snort from the leaner man startles me. "No, Nate is not a lumberjack. He does work with wood, though. And he's *really* good at it," he adds, winking at me.

My dick jolts, enjoying the way his voice deepens with his dumb innuendo. I've been with plenty of men before, but I've always preferred women. Or at least I have since I met Violet.

"Aw, no frowning." The short-haired guy introduces himself. "I'm Ellis."

"Jamie," I respond politely, still uncertain what the couple wants from me. It's obvious they're together in some capacity.

Ellis watches me glance down at the buff arm around his waist. "I'll cut to the chase since it's clear my partner can't keep his hands off of me. We're looking for a third tonight and maybe onward too. Let us buy you a drink, show you a good time, and see what happens?"

Nate leans in to Ellis and whispers something, then Ellis adds in, "Please."

I cannot get a read on these two for the life of me. What I do know is my dick is hard from the attention and how taboo what's happening right now is. And my heart hurts a little less under their intense gaze.

"Actually," I say, twisting on my stool to face them. Ellis licks his lips as he looks me up and down. I'm guessing the bigger guy could match my dominance, and I'm feeling the urge to test Ellis a little. "Why don't we move to a booth and *you* show me just how interested you are, Ellis?"

His eyes flare with surprise and lust. Glancing at Nate, they seem to share a silent conversation before Ellis nods.

My stomach flips with a bit of nausea, but I battle it back. I'm not in a committed relationship. I've fucked up so bad I'm not sure I'll ever be forgiven, and these two would just be an escape. *Just how Violet was using me.*

As my heart clenches, I stand and realize Ellis and I are the exact same height. Nate seems to be a few inches taller which will be interesting. *No it won't because they are just a distraction.*

Nodding to the back corner, I lead the way with my drink in my hand. I'm not so drunk I can't walk straight or think properly. Just drunk enough that I'm making questionable choices and falling into a pattern I told myself I was done with.

Once I've settled myself in the center of the round booth, I rest my arms above the back cushion and relax. "Sit," I command Ellis, using the power I have in this situation to my advantage.

He moves so he's between me and Nate, so I'm betting he's the one that wants to do the touching. As I suspected, Ellis licks his lips and slides in until he's inches from me. Nate sticks to Ellis' side and watches us with a keen eye.

"Voyeur?" I ask, not willing to shoot the shit right now. Maybe in the morning I'll realize I'm being a dick, but Nate doesn't even bat an eye when he nods.

Smirking at the big man, I wait for him to stop his man when Ellis reaches for me. Lean fingers open the buttons of my shirt without hesitation. *They've done this before.*

Quickly I down the last of my beverage and sink into Ellis' sensual touch. Honestly, he is too soft.

Nothing like Violet's desperate need to feel my skin on hers.

"Underneath the table," I bite out, trying to keep myself calm but am getting more agitated the longer this stranger is taking to suck my dick.

"No," Ellis replies, not even looking me in the eye. He just watches my chest heave with exertion as he drags his blunt nails across my abs. "You can wait. I want to see if I like what we picked out first."

What the fuck? Maybe my assumptions about him were wrong. He's not completely submissive. When I catch his eye, there's something hard there that confuses me. But I don't care about the interesting complexity of this couple. Not one bit.

"I'm not merchandise." My argument is weak, especially when he pinches my nipple.

"No?" Ellis hums. "Pretty sure I'm trying you on for size before we exchange numbers."

"Relax," Nate rumbles to both of us when Ellis and I continue to glare at one another. "Enjoy. Both of you."

"Fuck off," I snap at the big guy. My annoyance dissipates when Ellis slips beneath the table when I look away. "Fuck."

"Ellis likes to push buttons," Nate murmurs, eyeing me like he's making sure I don't kill his partner.

"I—Fuck," I groan. Ellis wastes no time pulling my dick from my jeans. His hand is hot and firm as he grips my solid length.

Nate nods, eyes flicking beneath the table and back up to me rapidly.

Where Violet teases me and drives me wild with need, Ellis swallows me whole immediately. I fight to keep my arms on the backrest of the booth. The darkness of the bar and thumping music hide our activities, but in no way do they steal from the complete sexiness of this moment.

A man *in a fucking relationship* is sucking my cock in a public space, while his partner watches with so much intensity the pressure in my balls is already building.

"Ellis," I grunt as his tongue swirls around the head of my cock. Then he's swallowing around me, making me feel every contraction of his tight fucking throat.

"That's good. He likes it when you moan his name," Nate says like he can read his partner's mind.

I barely register his words though because the added rumble from Nate rises me higher and higher until I'm barely hanging on. Then, *fucking hell,* Ellis gags and digs his fingers into my legs like he needs to hold on for dear life.

He does. Copper fills my mouth as I bite down on the inside of my cheek to keep from shouting as I spill my cum inside Ellis' hot fucking mouth. I don't even care if he swallows—all I know is these two stole my worries and gave me pleasure for five minutes.

They might be the drug I'm looking for.

Thirteen

VIOLET

It's been two days since I stormed out of Jamie's apartment. The sun is setting like it had that night when I showed up at his place, and all I can think about is him and his words.

How do I get over the worst mistake of my life? He made it sound so easy. As if I'm *choosing* to drown myself in sex and misery.

But aren't you? a mean voice whispers in the back of my mind.

Hours pass as my mind tries to wrap itself around the mess of feelings and thoughts. I feel like this is all I am these days—a storm of uncertainty and questionable points of view.

There have been a few times as I drove to my mom's house in Chicago where I thought this might be a bad idea, especially in the dark, but I couldn't stand being in Detroit any longer. Memories of Jamie and reminders of the sad life I've created for myself assaulted me at every turn.

After Mom texted me that her husband, Roman, was making my favorite banana bread tonight, I thought long and hard about what I needed. My conclusion sits right in front of me.

Blinking back tears as I stare up at my family's beautiful home on the outskirts of Chicago, I notice that Mama left the porch light on for me. That's nothing new though. She reminds me of the house code frequently and lets me know the light is always on if I ever need to come home.

My eyes burn as I kill the ignition and peel myself from the driver’s seat. Without thinking, I grab my backpack and tiptoe up the porch steps.

It wasn't long ago that I was waving goodbye after our holiday celebrations. I didn't think I'd be back so soon and definitely didn't think I'd be returning a changed woman.

Because there's no denying I won't ever be able to go back to my cold, detached ways. I'm alive again for the first time in years, which is why I'm hurting so damn much.

Life holds beauty. Life carries pain.

Letting myself inside, I inhale the scent of fresh bread and appreciate the calm silence of the late night. Everyone's in bed, which is perfect because I'm not ready to talk just yet.

They'll have so many questions. I've never come home unannounced, so they'll know something's up. Denying their assumptions will be futile because Mom's partners can read me like they raised me. They didn't. They just inserted themselves into Mom's life and learned everything they could about us so they could win her heart.

Mom and I are a package deal, so they needed to win my heart too. Felix's protectiveness, Roman's warmth, Declan's ability to lighten my mood, and Jared's understanding were everything I could have hoped for in new additions to our support system.

With a slice of bread in my hand and my water bottle, I curl up on the couch. I'm too tired to go upstairs to my room, and to be honest, I'm afraid I'll hear something that will make my ears bleed if I do.

It's best to stay down here just in case.

My mind turns sluggish as the heat from Mom's blanket surrounds me. With a full belly, I drift off to sleep, finally feeling like I made the right choice in coming home.

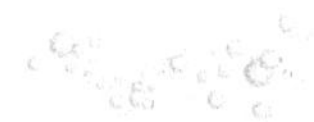

"I'm so glad she's here," a deep voice rumbles. *Roman*.

Something tickles the top of my head, and I decide to open my eyes. The living room is dim, so the sun must not be fully up yet.

"Do you think we need to kill someone?" With that response, I realize it's Jared playing with my hair.

I huff a laugh, feeling happier than I have in *way too long*. "No killing," I deny and shimmy until I'm sitting up to look at my mom's men.

Roman's wearing his usual black sweatpants and

sweatshirt. His short black hair is wild, but it fits his ear piercing and neck tattoos pretty perfectly.

Jared's darker skin contrasts the tight white T-shirt he's wearing. But I don't notice much else about him beyond his frown. Jared never frowns.

"Kiddo..." Roman murmurs, sitting beside me and drawing my attention.

Sighing, I bring my legs up to sit cross-legged. "I just needed to come home."

Tears are already blurring my vision, so I look down at my lap. Tugging the blanket tighter around me, I try really freaking hard to find the strength to open up to them.

"Violet."

"Shit," I curse beneath my breath, not realizing Felix was sitting on the other side of the living room. "Good morning, Felix."

With an eyebrow raised, he silently scolds me for cursing. Which is wild because Mom curses like a sailor.

"Is that fucking Violet I hear?!"

See?

Leaping from the couch, I rush right into Mama's embrace as she too runs to me. The sob I've been holding back since I got in the car last night finally breaks free.

Muffled beyond my cries, I hear Felix telling Mom that he was just waiting for me to explain what's going on. I cling harder to her, not wanting to do this in front of all four of her men.

I just want my mom.

Thankfully, Mama understands me the way I knew she would.

"Can Violet and I each get a cup of coffee, a few slices of banana bread, and some fruit? We will be in the library."

Thank goodness. The library is her reading room with beanbag chairs, twinkly lights, stacks upon shelves of books. It's her escape and is the perfect place for me to open up once and for all.

I just hope all this time away from home hasn't diminished her motherly advice because I really need Blue Bennett to step up and untangle the knot in my brain.

Fourteen

BLUE

No mother who loves their kid as much as I do *ever* wants to hear how they've been struggling for so long. Of course I knew Violet had changed since my kidnapping, but learning how she's held back from her friends and potential love interests hurts me in a way I didn't know I could hurt.

For the past hour, V has been slowly but confidently explaining what's been going on. Wrestling my own inner turmoil has been hard, but staying present for Violet matters far more than my worries.

I'll cry on Roman's shoulder later while listening to Felix tell me it's not my fault. Jared will agree and explain how every young adult needs to go through some shit in order to grow. Then Declan will make a joke about his *growth* because the four of them hate to see me cry.

"What's his name?"

"What?" she asks, frowning and looking at me like I've grown another head.

Leaning back in my chair, I wipe my fingers free of butter and prepare myself to dive into Violet's tortured psyche. *That's dramatic.*

"Violet," I start getting serious so she knows shit's about to get real. "I've been listening to you for a while now. You've told me that you've been keeping people at a distance. How even when they push you, your response is aggressive or standoffish. That is not who you are, V, which is why I'm going to be giving Cassidy a big birthday gift this year. What I want to know is who *else* you've been denying your beautiful heart?"

She's pale and shifty. Her body language tells me my hunch is right. That this is more than just a profound realization that her way of living isn't working. There's more going on that she's hesitant to voice.

I understand; I really do. Saying things out loud makes them very real.

Internally I laugh, realizing I'm going to have to push her to talk about Jamie. "Have you forgotten a man answered your phone a few days ago? Violet, I'm trying to get you to admit all on your own that this guy is important."

"Jamie is not important. He's just a fuck buddy. The only one I have, but still. We don't even talk. I make sure of it."

Oof. Poor guy has his work cut out for him.

Without any hesitation, I scold her. "Don't bullshit me. You've never come home unannounced. Tell me what happened after I talked to Jamie."

I'm done letting her brush shit under the rug. I've been supportive and loving, but maybe I should have been a little harder on my kid. The early twenties are so important, though. *Fuck. Parenting never gets easier.*

Shoving away from the coffee table on the floor, Violet stands and begins pacing around the room. My heart aches and pounds in my chest, but I don't let her see the worry raging through my bones.

I've watched her bubbles pop while chewing on my nails, hoping like hell she'll figure herself out with time. Truth is, I miss my bubbly girl so fucking much. I miss the way her hair would flip and bounce as she'd skip through our apartment. Even at eighteen years old, Violet had a childlike happiness that was infectious.

She was always dancing and creating videos for her social media, but that was the beginning of our downfall. Violet was being harassed by someone who ended up being a man from her biological mom's past. Not ten minutes after Violet opened up about the creepy accounts messaging her, Clarence kidnapped me and held me captive for the better part of a week.

Violet has yet to forgive herself for the choices she made. Yes, she should have told me sooner. No, she is *not* the reason Clarence came after me. He was a monster who set his sights on me when I was a teenager. It's a good ass thing he's deep in the fucking ground.

Right along with Violet's abusive biological mother who died three years ago. Drugs. Rest in peace, bitch. I still can't believe I survived growing up with Linda. Violet was my bright light that kept me in her orbit just as I was preparing to flee Linda's life when I was eighteen. I stayed for Violet and I wouldn't change a thing.

Shielding her from Linda and her long line of men was my greatest accomplishment.

Violet's quietly muttering to herself as she stomps around. I let her work through her feelings since it seems like she's overwhelmed.

I'm not the greatest person for her to talk to about her feelings, but I can help her work through them. What comes out of her mouth forces me to take a deep fucking breath.

"He told me to get over what happened." Violet throws her hands in the air. "Who says that?! He said I'm hanging onto it, and all my boundaries are getting in the way of my happiness, or something."

Well...

"It's not like I don't know that! I hate it. I hate the person I've become, but it's better this way. Right?"

Shit. She turns to me when she asks that.

I've spent my fair share talking to therapists, so I *think* I know what to say. "Do you think it's better this way?"

Violet doesn't skip a beat, and I'm honestly surprised by the sheer epiphanies occurring before my eyes. "NO! It's not fucking better this way. I'm lonely and always questioning myself. I have a notebook at home where I write down all the lies my anxiety tells me every day, and half the time I'm not even sure if they are lies."

I feel the tears building and my chest tightening, but I hold them back and nod along with V even though she's not looking at me anymore. Witnessing her breakdown, or maybe it's a break*through,* is epic and so damn heartbreaking.

"How can you tell which are the lies?" I ask, genuinely curious and wanting to get her thinking about it from a different perspective.

She stops pacing and stares down at her feet. Nibbling on her lip, Violet thinks through my question which I'm proud of her for. It's easy to snap out an *I don't know,* but it's clear Violet wants to work through this rut she's found herself in.

"I-It's embarrassing, but I ask myself if Cassidy or Jamie would agree with the statement. You and the guys are too biased to be pinned up against my mean thoughts."

I hum, thinking about my next question. "It sounds like you're doing a lot of hard work to find yourself again. I'm wondering if sifting through all your thoughts and feelings would be easier if you asked yourself questions."

She frowns and says, "Like what?"

"Like, what makes you happy? *Not* what should or used to, but what makes you happy today. And *why* do you keep going back to Jamie? Why is he the only guy you've been seeing? If you were to talk to him, what are the things you would want to know before deciding to spend more time with him? The only way you'll learn to trust yourself again is by asking questions and talking to other people."

Violet sucks in a breath and turns to me with wide eyes. I'm not sure what I said that stunned her, but I lean forward and take her hand in mine. "I love you so much, Violet. A long time ago, someone special told me that having confidence in the ones we love is enough and oftentimes the only way we can really help them."

Staring down at me, my kid cries silently, but she's listening intently. *God, I love her so much*. This position reminds me of all the times I crouched down while she sobbed about her skinned knee or sad feelings.

A tear slips free from my eye now as I look right into her soul. "If there is *anyone* in the world that I believe can handle this shift with heart and realness, it's you, V."

We're both crying openly now, and I swear the love that I have for her quadruples for the millionth time since I met her when she was seven. Violet may be my cousin by blood, but she is my daughter through hardship, experience, and love.

"I have all the confidence in you, Violet Bennett."

Fifteen

JAMIE

I'm no stranger to Violet's silence, but this time everything is wrong. Promises were never made between us, yet I feel as if I broke something. Not only did I hurt her with my words, I've let another touch me.

It feels wrong. I feel wrong.

The longer I stare at my unopened texts to my sweet woman, the angrier I get with her. It's not fair, but when feelings are involved sometimes all rationality flies right out the damn window.

I shouldn't have told her to get over the shit that happened with her mom. I know that. Hell, everyone should know that.

Allowing my frustrations to get the best of me after she got mad wasn't right. Talking to Blue Bennett on the phone that night gave me hope. Violet's mom was kind and a little suspicious.

Promising to look after Violet was easy. I dove right into wanting Blue and her men to accept me in Violet's life. So much so that when Violet yanked the dream away from me, I lashed out.

I'll never lash out at her again. I'm prepared to swear on it if only she would text me the fuck back.

My stomach has been in knots since I came down that stranger's throat. Another thing I shouldn't have done. Violet will need to know if we ever make us official. *What will she think of me?*

I'm not worried about how she will feel about my being bisexual. I'm talking about the fact that after an argument with her, I went and fucked around almost immediately.

We aren't together. I haven't promised loyalty. There's just no way my heart, body, and soul will accept that because I pledged myself to Violet a long time ago. Silent or not, I came to the conclusion that I was hers.

Now I've given myself to another. And I fucking *enjoyed* it.

Anxious nausea swims at the base of my throat. The sensation only builds the longer I stare at my goddamn phone. Then a notification comes in, and I have to swallow the bile that rises rapidly.

Ellis and Nate want to meet up for appetizers. I'm not an idiot; I know our night wouldn't end there.

My anger builds when I realize there's a giddy feeling buzzing in my veins at the idea of seeing them again. Exchanging numbers felt good in the moment, but I've regretted it since. Except right now, hanging out with two sexy men who *want* to be near me, I don't regret a damn thing.

I send off two messages. The first goes to Violet as a

final attempt for the evening. Deciding to give it four minutes, I wait for her to respond. She doesn't. *It's Friday night. Where is she?*

Because of her silence, I send out the next text to Ellis. I agree on a place and time to meet up. I plan it so I have to leave in a few minutes and not give myself any extra time to realize this is a shit idea.

I know wholeheartedly that I'm going to feel sick after my evening, but I can't bring myself to stop it from happening. Ellis and Nate draw me in and seem to know just the right time to pull me into their orbit.

They're intoxicating.

Just like Violet, which is probably why I decide to make a quick stop on the way.

The last time Cassidy opened her apartment door for me, I was in much higher spirits. Sure my girl wasn't doing well, but she was still a bit mine then.

This time, only negative feelings drive my voice and my actions. "What do you mean she's not home?"

Cassidy shifts around on her feet, looking nervous as hell to be talking to me. "Violet left a few nights ago. She's safe, just not here."

"Then fucking *where*?" I snap, my voice rising in exasperation. "She's not due for another trip that I know of."

Cassidy frowns and glances down at the ground. "Jamie, I'm not going to tell you where she is."

"Why the hell not?!"

"HEY!" an older man down the hall bellows. "Watch your mouth around the young lady or I'll be forced to mess up your face."

The man is hardly more than skin and bones who probably couldn't walk to me without his cane, but I admire his protectiveness. "You're right. My apologies to you and Cassidy," I attempt to amend.

"Thank you, sir." Cassidy smiles at the old man then turns to me, her eyes hard. "Violet cried for a long time after she left your place, Jamie. Leave her alone or I'll send our guardian neighbor to your doorstep the next time you hurt her."

My deep breath doesn't do anything to calm my raging emotions. "I know I fu—I know I hurt her, Cassidy. Why do you think I'm here? Please just tell me where she is."

"No."

My neck heats as my jaw clenches. "Who is she with?"

"None of your business."

A low rumble starts in my chest as my mind comes up with scenarios. Each is worse than the last, and they all have a common denominator. "Is she with another man?"

Cassidy's lips twitch, and for the life of me I *cannot* read her damn expression. "Probably. Four. Maybe six depending on how inconsolable she is."

"What the fuck?!" I roar, turning away from the door

with my hands ripping my hair out only to come face to face with the old man.

"Leave. Now." His voice is menacing, sending chills down my spine. His story must be a good one.

My inhale is noisy, but it does its job and forces me to calm down. I take another because just the thought of Violet being near another man makes me murderous.

Suddenly, a flash of Violet between Ellis and me with Nate hovering nearby assaults my mind. Squeezing my eyes shut, I bat the idea away and force myself to address the situation at hand.

"I'm sorry, Cassidy." That's all I've got right now. I should leave. I need someone to take my mind off my woman.

My reaction is unfair. I'm running to two men to help me feel better. Why can't Violet do the same?

Because I want her to run to me, but she doesn't want me running to her.

My phone buzzes as I'm stomping out of the building. The slam of freezing air on my heated cheeks shocks my system and makes me yearn for the positive attention of the two people waiting for me.

Why does it have to be like this?

Sixteen

VIOLET

Exhausted, I lock the door behind me as I enter my apartment. I may have only been gone for two days, but stepping into the depressing space of my bedroom makes it feel like it's been months.

There's something about visiting my mom and family that alters me. Many times I feel sadder and weighed down after seeing them because they remind me of my mistakes and what I've lost.

This visit was healing. My mom had some very blunt wisdom to share, and it was exactly what I needed.

Coddling is nice, but I needed someone to look me in the eye, see me, and tell me how it is.

The fact of the matter is, I'm not going to really grow or learn if I don't face this head-on. I've been battling a war in my mind, but I was still hiding behind pointy objects and loud drums. All the questions and feelings that have been trapped inside need to come out.

Mom seems to think talking to Jamie is a good idea.

The glare she leveled at me every time I ignored Jamie's texts would have told me that if she weren't so darn vocal.

Felix, Mom's alphahole man, was actually the one that stuck up for me. *Let him sit in the shitstorm he created, sweetheart,* he told her. The other three guys agreed and began devising ideas that would be good for Jamie to try when it comes time to grovel.

The truth is that I haven't been punishing Jamie by ignoring him. I needed space. It sounds toxic, and not responding wasn't the best choice I made, but I don't owe him anything.

He hurt me. He also sparked a tsunami of feelings that sent me running home to process what the hell was going on with me.

Now home and faced with my bare bedroom, I feel different. Like I really need to get some pictures set up on my nightstands and put some artwork on the walls.

This room is me. Bare. Minimalistic. And dull.

Everything I never used to be.

And exactly what I don't want to be.

This room is me. We both have potential, and we're crying out for life and color.

With that thought in mind, I pull my phone out of my hoodie pocket and slump onto my bed. "Alright, Jamie. What do you have to say to me?" I murmur at the dark screen.

Turning it on, I send a quick message to Mom and Roman that I made it home safely, then I'm ready to face my fears.

Jamie Murphy has *a lot* to say.

His messages start incredibly frantic and apologetic. Exasperation bleeds into his words as we get closer to today's date. He wants to know if I'm safe and begs for me to allow him the chance to apologize in person.

I can feel the anger through the screen as I read the messages from this evening. Again he's asking me where I am, and if I'm coming home soon. That's all he asks, but I can tell there's more he wanted to text me.

"Cassidy!" I call out as I stand.

Skipping into my doorway wearing nothing but a towel, Cassidy smiles at me. "Hey, I rushed through my shower to come see you!"

She looks so happy to see me that I can't help but smile. "Missed you. Did Jamie come here? I got a text asking when I would come home, so he must know I wasn't here."

Her face twists into a scowl. "Yeah, he was here like an hour ago demanding I tell him where you were."

"Did you tell him I went home for a few days?" I should have known Jamie would have come to find me if I ignored him. He's always so pushy. No way would he take my silence as acceptable after our fight.

A sly smirk tugs on her freckles around her face, so I brace myself for what she's about to say. "No. I didn't tell him where you were or who you were with."

"*But?*" No way that's all she said. She looks way too proud of herself for that to be all.

Cassidy turns around and heads to her bedroom. I'm hot on her heels waiting with bated breath for her to tell me what happened. My heart is pounding, and I'm not quite sure why.

My friend disappears into her closet, but I wait, knowing she's getting dressed. I'm not surprised when she comes out in a short tight dress considering it's Friday.

Bypassing me, she sits in front of her floor-length mirror and starts applying her makeup. "He asked if you were with a guy. The vein in his forehead almost burst when I told him you were actually with *four* men. Maybe six, since there was a possibility your mama's male friends were visiting too."

"Jesus," I breathe, scrubbing my hands down my face. "Please tell me you told him they were family and didn't make me sound like a hussy."

Frowning into the mirror, Cassidy looks at me in the reflection. "I left it open for interpretation because I thought it didn't matter."

My breath explodes out of me as I throw my hands in the air. "Of course it matters, Cass! Why would you do that?!"

"Why does it matter?" Her voice is so damn calm it makes my annoyance rise, which, if I were using my brain, I would realize is her intent.

"Because now Jamie will think I slept with a ton of other men after our fight!"

"So?"

My chest inflates as I prepare to bellow that I don't want Jamie to think that about me because it matters. Because *he* matters.

Instead of falling for her sneaky trap to get me to admit my feelings, I shift our conversation as the need to see Jamie grows. "I'll DD for you tonight."

Cassidy smirks. "You going to see him, huh?"

Flipping her off over my shoulder, I walk out of her room to freshen up. I'm not sure what I plan on saying to Jamie tonight. I just know I have to see him. To hear his voice. I need him to wrap me in his acceptance and encourage me to open up.

I don't bother texting him, but it's not a conscious choice. Many times I show up at his place looking for a good time.

This will be a tough time, but it's the only next step.

No more running.

For mid-January, the night air isn't as biting as it usually is. So when I find out the club Cassidy is meeting her friends at is a few blocks away from Jamie's apartment, I decide a walk will help clear my head.

I was ready to drive myself to his place, but Cassidy kept asking me questions. Many of them were intrusive and made it obvious she had had a few shots before we left the apartment.

I did my best to tune her out during the drive, but even seven minutes in the car with her in that state was too much.

Now here I am, bundled in my winter coat and not feeling all that bad for Cassidy as she stands in line in her teeny dress. A man she walks up to wraps his arms around her, making my jealousy flare.

I already told her goodbye, so I quickly turn my back and start my stroll to Jamie's place. The next two blocks are thumping with nightlife, forcing me to weave through stumbling groups and women complaining about the winter freezing their cleavage off.

By the third block, things calm down a little. Stuffing my hands in my pockets, I groan when I realize I left my wallet in the car. Whatever, I can use Tap to Pay if I have an emergency.

Glancing around, I take in the buildings and squint to find Jamie's down the road. With an intentional deep breath, I sift through my thoughts.

I'm ready to talk to Jamie about how I've closed myself off from connection. Honestly, if he's willing to wait while I work through some of my issues, I might want to try something serious with him. *I think*. Questions and getting to know him will come first.

Mama's advice wraps around my anxiety and gives me guidance until every sense of sanity is ripped away from me with a shrill scream that burns my vocal cords.

A thick arm coils around my throat as the stench of stale beer assaults my nose. "Give me your purse."

"I don't—" I croak, clawing at the man's arm. Unable to find purchase on his slippery puffy jacket, I continue to struggle as he digs through my jacket.

My phone is in my bra along with my car key. Relief floods me when I register that he won't have anything to steal from me.

"You fucking bitch! Give me something!" He turns frantic, releasing my neck, but I don't have the chance to suck in oxygen before he's shoving me to the ground.

A foot to my right hip makes me cry out and sends me spiraling into a full-fledged panic attack. Losing sight of the man as my jacket is tugged and ripped has me freaking out.

Blackness makes my vision tunnel, and suddenly all I can think about is everything that happened to my mama. Will this man hurt me like my mom was hurt? *Oh my god.* Can I survive this? I'm not as strong as Blue.

I'm not strong...I think to myself as I lose sight of the world around me. Weightlessness steals my senses, and I'm gone.

Not. Strong.

Seventeen

JAMIE

Admitting that I actually enjoy spending time with Ellis and Nate is hard, but it's true. Just sitting here listening to Ellis express how much he loves working as a nurse makes me happy. He left his previous job so they could be closer to Nate's mom in Ferndale.

The couple live only about fifteen minutes out of Detroit, near Nate's mom. They also shared that their property is a huge upgrade because Nate's woodworking and crafting business has gotten big enough that he needed a garage space to work in.

Their previous home was more like a bachelor pad, but now they have a detached garage near the back of their property. Nate even showed me some pictures of his custom furniture and wood carvings—I was impressed and a little mesmerized.

The way Ellis has gushed with pride regarding Nate's work brought me sadness. I want to hear Violet express enthusiasm about the tattoos I create. Having her show me off and being genuinely happy to flaunt me around would be a dream come true.

Nate's hand has been on my thigh throughout most of dinner. We kept it light and ordered a ton of appetizers while sipping our drinks.

The unspoken trajectory of our evening made my skin buzz and tingle as we talked. Sharing my story with them was easy after they gave me pieces of their lives.

I told them about my amazing mom and slightly gruff father. They live in Chicago, and when I told them that, there was a slight twitch of their posture that confused me. But they quickly shifted to asking about siblings, and I informed them I didn't have any.

Conversation was easy and connected us with every word we shared. It was nice not being cut off before my pants came off.

With that thought comes a lot of guilt, but I've reminded myself multiple times that Violet's gone. According to Cassidy, she's with multiple men. She's ignored me, and doesn't seem to care about me much anyway.

I know it's the hurt, defensiveness, and alcohol talking, but fucking hell I don't want to feel bad for finding a connection with someone else, *two someones* actually, when the woman I love is trying to convince both of us we won't ever happen.

Nate startles me as he leans in and whispers, "Hey, you okay?" His hand on my thigh tightens.

"Not sure," I admit and push my plate away from me. "I'm not sure about this." Gesturing to the three of us, I test to see if they can have a real conversation about *us.* Because goddamn it, I think there's potential for there to be something here.

"Tell us what you're thinking," Nate encourages me with a small nod. *He wants to hear my thoughts.*

Studying his manly features, I try really hard to be honest. "I'm torn between thinking this is just super hot and that the only thing we have is a sexy spark..."

"But?" Ellis prompts me. He leans forward, and I shit you not, the soft look in his eyes confuses me. Why does it seem like he actually cares?

"But this." I now gesture to the table and our comfortable setting. "It's not just that I want to bend Ellis over the table and show him my dominant side while you, Nate, stuff his bratty mouth."

Ellis groans and takes a sip of his beer to cool off. Nate laughs, making me smile and realize how easy this feels.

"It's not just the attraction. Talking to you both, hanging out, being in your presence is...nice."

"Hear that, babe? We're nice," Ellis mocks, smirking at Nate who rolls his eyes.

"Fuck off," I huff and nudge him with my foot beneath the table.

"Careful," Ellis teases. "You know I'll crawl down there and make sure you don't kick me."

Before I can come up with a retort, Nate steers us back in the right direction. "We feel the same way, Jamie. We've been looking for our third for a long time, and you've come as a surprise to us as well. So what's holding you back?"

"Or who?" Ellis chimes in, with his eyebrows raised. "We're not blind. I can see the hurt every time you smile and the guilt every time a dirty thought crosses your mind. Does someone already have your heart? And would we like them?"

I frown as the image of all four of us together flashes through my mind and sends blood rushing to my cock. "I don't know. I can't even get her to commit to me."

"Well, I'd like to meet her," Ellis states seriously just as my phone begins to vibrate in the pocket beside Nate's firm grip.

My stomach swoops when Nate doesn't release me as I dig my cell phone out. They watch, making me feel warm.

Nate is so damn intense it's easy to get sucked into his unreadable gaze. "You gonna answer that?" he rumbles, nodding at my hand.

I jolt and answer the call without looking at the screen. "Hello?" Jesus, my voice is so deep and rumbly you'd think I was about to get my dick sucked again.

"Jamie, where the fuck are you? Open the door right now."

Immediately my palms begin to sweat, and my back straightens. "Bash?"

"Who the fuck else?! Open the door. NOW!"

Bash is an MC brother who's on rotation keeping an eye on Violet when she's in town. The club never contacts me, and they aren't supposed to unless there's a concern about V.

As fast and loud as the crack of a whip, I'm out of my chair and rushing for the restaurant door. Nate's shouting behind me, and Ellis accompanies him. I have no time or fucking ability to give them my attention when I have Bash demanding things of me sounding scared.

"I'll be there in five. What's going on?" My chest is tight, but my voice is calm. How? I have no idea because on the inside I'm freaking the fuck out.

Bash curses, and there's some shuffling. "Violet's hurt."

Throwing myself into my car, I'm peeling out of the parking lot with Nate and Ellis on my ass. With Bash on speakerphone as I speed through Detroit, I beg for more information. "What happened?! SHE'S HURT?!"

Bash grunts. "Unconscious. Breathing's a bit rough, but otherwise she seems fine."

"FINE?!" I shout, narrowly missing a fire hydrant.

The shuffling coming from Bash's side of the phone call pisses me off. I should be there. I should know what's happening. Violet shouldn't *maybe* be fine. *FUCK!*

"She has a big jacket on. It's ripped a bit, but I can't tell if there's any damage beyond the fact that she was passed out when I chased the guy off."

"Chased who off?! What happened?"

Bash loses his patience with me and snaps, "Just fucking get here!"

He hangs up on me when I'm about a minute away from the apartment. As if on autopilot, I call Nate. He picks up almost immediately, and his steely tone booms through my speaker. "What's going on?"

"Vi—Someone I care about is hurt outside of my

apartment. She needs help. I have to help her. I should have—"

Nate cuts me off, maybe sensing my impending rise of guilt. "We are right behind you. We'll help in any way we can. It's not your fault, Jamie."

I shake my head even though he can't see me. It's absolutely my fault. Being available for her if she needs me is all I ever want to be. Yet I was at dinner with two men, fantasizing about how good they must be in bed, when she was...what? Attacked? Assaulted? Mugged?

Swallowing, I slam on the brakes in the parking garage. "Follow me," I say, finishing the phone call.

Aches and sharp pains pierce the heels of my feet as they slam against the ground in a frantic need to get to my woman. My sweet Violet.

Ellis and Nate fall into step behind me, each running just as fast. They don't know what's going on or who Violet is, yet here they are, determined to help me and an unknown woman.

I watch, pissed off, as the elevator closes and rises. Stairs it is. The burn in my thighs is well deserved and the least of what I should be punished with right now.

After what feels like an eternity, I'm bursting through the stairwell door and sprinting down the hallway. Then I see her in the arms of Bash. Her blonde and purple hair tumbles over his arm making my lip curl up in a possessiveness I didn't realize I contained until now.

"Violet!" I gasp, already reaching for her and punching the code into my door. Bash gives her to me willingly, but he's no longer my concern once I hold her small frame against my heaving chest.

"Sweets," I cry, my throat thick with horror. She's so pale and still.

After depositing her on my couch, I start piling blankets on her because I have no clue what else I can do. *Shit, what do I do?!*

"Jamie," Bash rumbles from his spot against my kitchen island. His face is serious and beckoning me forward.

Nate and Ellis look worried and like they bit into a lemon, but I can't blame them. I probably look like someone just killed my fucking dog and threatened my mom at the same time.

"Please sit with her?" I croak out. "I need to talk to Bash."

"Of course," Nate agrees thickly, glancing at me for just a second before his eyes go back to Violet.

"I'll check her pulse," Ellis whispers, moving closer.

Good, he'll watch over her for the few minutes I need to figure out just what the actual *fuck* happened to the love of my life.

VIOLET

The first thing I notice is the scent of Jamie's aftershave. Next comes the total warmth of what can only be from a fire and a whole pile of blankets.

"Sweets?"

I hum in response to Jamie's gentle tone. *How did I get here? And why is my head pounding?*

"A friend of mine brought you here when he found you unconscious down the block."

I must have said my thoughts out loud. *Wait*. Gasping, my eyes fly open, and I force my heavy frame into a sitting position.

"Woah, hey," Jamie coos, reaching for me. "You're okay. You're safe."

Looking down in panic, I realize the weight on top of me literally was a pile of blankets. Jamie must feel the heat radiating off of me, because he starts removing the top layers.

"You were cold," he murmurs, explaining the mountain I woke up under.

"Wh—" I cough, feeling all out of sorts. "What happened?"

Jamie looks me in the eyes, and seems so serious. "Bash, my friend, said you were mugged. Or as much as you could be without having anything valuable on you."

"But I passed out? He didn't do anything to me, did he? The mugger?" *Oh my God. What happened to me?*

Jamie shushes me and places a hand on my chest above my boobs. "Breathe, Violet. In and out. Shit."

Lightheaded with chapped lips, I feel myself starting to slip away again. *Why is everything so fucking hard?*

"Damn it, Violet!" Jamie curses and scoops me into his arms. My tummy swoops and my head lists back a little with the force of his lift. "Breathe, my love."

My chest feels tight and so heavy as he settles me in the crook of his arm on the ground. Time slows as I study the black wavy pieces of hair that broke free from his hair tie.

Confused, I realize his face is blurring and looking more nervous as time passes. "V! Take a fucking breath!"

"Jamie? Is she okay?" a voice says just as a second new voice swears.

"Hold on, guys," Jamie demands and doesn't take his eyes off of me. "Violet, I—Fuck it."

The pressure beneath my breast bones becomes

almost unbearable, and I swear Jamie's face gets closer to mine. *Am I passing out again?*

Warmth encompasses my lips at the same time my eyes flutter closed. My mouth is opened by something firm and demanding, forcing a gasp to expand my lungs.

Jamie rips himself back from me and moves me to straddle his lap instead of being comfortable lying in his arms. "Yes. Yes, Violet. Keep going. Another one."

Eyes locked, Jamie encourages me to take gulps of air with him. Each inhale becomes longer and deeper, helping to bat away the buzzing in my mind.

"Jesus, Violet..." Jamie whispers once I catch my breath and slump against his chest. "You scared me."

"Sorry," I mumble into his chest. "I haven't had a panic attack in a long time."

Jamie's chest vibrates with a rumble. "I didn't know that. This is what Bash said made you pass out when you were attacked."

Attacked. Just like Mama.

"I was coming to see you..." My voice trails off and my eyes begin to burn. What already felt like it was going to be a difficult night was made so much worse. "I needed you..."

"Violet, I'm so sorry I wasn't there. Fuck, Sweets. I'm sorr—"

I grip his shirt and tug without lifting my head. "No, I mean I needed you in general. Not when that guy mugged me. I did some soul-searching and wanted to ask you something."

His arms tighten around me, and I feel like he's trying to force me under his skin. *Never close enough.*

"Anything," he promises, "you can ask me anything."

Steeling myself for the door I'm about to open, I lean back and search his gaze. He looks so scared and fierce. A contradiction, but one that makes asking my question much easier.

"What's your favorite color?"

Jamie beams so darn bright it surprises me, but what makes me jump is the choked noise from behind me. Twisting, I ignore the flare of pain in my right hip as I move.

Nothing matters beyond the conflicted gaze of two men I never thought I'd meet in person. My past sits on Jamie's couch, watching me with so much scrutiny and uncertainty that my breath has no choice but to stutter and stall.

"Ellis?" I rasp. "N-Nate?" Tears officially fall from my eyes as guilt and sorrow begin to push at the barriers of my body. "How—"

I can't finish my question out loud, but Jamie picks up at a decent spot. "You know them?" he asks me, sounding shocked, which answers my question of whether he knew.

Ellis' eyes bore into mine, and I swear I see something cruel flicker in his brown eyes, but it's gone quickly with a shutter that blocks me from reading him. Nate seems conflicted, and I don't blame him because this is a surprise for all of us it seems.

"Yes. We know Violet." Straight and to the point, Nate admits our unfortunate connection.

"How?" Jamie snaps, holding me tighter. "Did you know I was with her?"

With me? Fuck, I should get out of here.

Peeking behind me, I ask Jamie, "How do you know them? Are you with—"

Jamie's face turns red, and when I glance back at the other two, Ellis smirks. "Seems we have the same taste, *Bubbles*."

A knife to my heart would have hurt less than the reminder of everything I threw away. That nickname distracts me a little from what happened tonight.

"Ellis, I'm sorry—"

Ellis waves a hand to cut me off which makes Jamie stiffen, but Ellis doesn't seem to mind ripping my feelings apart. I don't blame him. I've seen firsthand the damage of ghosting someone, but I did it anyway.

"I'm sure you are, Violet. But it's been seven years. No need to lie now."

"What?!" I gasp. "No. I'm not lying. I'm so sorry! I never should have blocked—"

Ellis' eyes turn cold and steely, making me recoil. "We don't fucking care, Violet. We're here because the man we're pursuing had an emergency. Unfortunate that it was *you*."

"Wait a fucking second," Jamie interrupts this heartbreaking moment with so much rage it makes me cry harder. He stands and sets me on my feet, making me flinch in pain. "You don't *ever* talk to Violet that way. What the fuck?"

"You don't—"

Jamie cuts Ellis off. "I don't know how you know my woman, but you won't speak to her ever again if you can't be fucking polite and kind. She's been through enough without your verbal lashings because you got your feelings hurt almost a decade ago."

Jamie steps so he's standing in front of me. Reaching out, I grab his forearm. "Jamie. I hurt them. I ghosted them, blocked them, and changed my number. We were in a serious part of building an actual relationship, and I-I ruined it."

Full on sobbing, I try to defend the men on Jamie's couch. They have every right to hate me and tear me down. What I did was cowardly.

"Absolutely fucking *not*!" Jamie snaps, wrapping an arm around my hip and dragging me to his side. "Nobody talks to you that way."

Copper fills my mouth because the only way to keep from hissing in pain is to bite the inside of my cheek. I vaguely remember the mugger kicking my hip as I fell to the ground.

Jamie levels Nate and Ellis with a glare so hellish, I shut up. "And no way in *hell* are you allowed to think you're *pursuing* me when you're clearly a fucking asshole with no emotional intelligence to comprehend the woman you clearly loved back then was exposed to something so traumatic it altered her life."

Ellis sits up straight at Jamie's words, but the man holding me isn't done. "Violet has worked *hard* to understand her choices and decisions. She deserves patience and care. You may be owed an apology and an explanation, but in no way are you owed the opportunity to hurt her further. Now get the fuck out of my apartment. I hope that if I ever see you again, you'll rethink your stance on Violet because she's mine even if she hasn't accepted it yet. We're a package deal. Get out."

Stunned into silence, I watch as Ellis and Nate slowly uncoil from the couch. Ellis stays in his place with his shoulders tight and his face unreadable. Nate, on the other hand, walks toward me slowly.

Each step he takes makes me stiffen further. Jamie watches every move Nate takes, and the closer he gets to our two-person huddle, the more I notice about him. Seven years made this man more rugged and wide. He's intense.

Jamie clutches me tighter once Nate is within touching distance, and there's no way I can mask the wince this time. Nate zeros in on Jamie's hand and reaches for me.

"Don't fucking touch her, Nate," Jamie growls, and it strikes me just how intimate Nate's name sounds coming from his lips.

Nate pays him no mind as his thick fingers reach for the hem of my sweatshirt. I suck in a breath at his closeness, but pout a little on the inside when Nate is so careful not to touch my bare skin. *No, Violet. No. This man hates you,* I scold myself.

"I don't hate you," Nate whispers, glancing into my soul quickly before his eyes narrow on my hip. "Ice this. And try to keep weight off your leg for a few days."

"What?!" Jamie gasps, releasing me and moving. His

new position shoves Nate out of the way and blocks my two regrets from my line of sight.

While Jamie fusses over the nasty bruise, Nate and Ellis slip out without another word. For some reason, that hurts more than all the insults and accusations Ellis could throw at me.

Nineteen

JAMIE

What the fuck just happened?

"Jamie—"

Violet's tone sounds pained as I walk away from her, so I stop and grab her hand. Pulling her along with me, she stays silent as I rummage through my freezer.

With an ice pack tucked under my arm and Violet's hand in mine, I dampen a rag with warm water. The silence is thick with so many things we need to talk about, but first making sure she is okay is more important.

Settling her back on the couch, I avoid eye contact, wrap her in a blanket, and ensure the cold compress is in the right spot for her to ice her hip comfortably.

Then, I sit beside her and begin wiping her face with the warm towel. Blotchy and damp, her cheeks tell the story of her pain. So much happened tonight, I don't even know where to start.

Especially not when I could literally throw the fuck

up. I let Ellis give me a blowjob. He's from Violet's past, and now they're my present...or past. Ellis' treatment of Violet tonight was sickening.

How could anyone treat this sweet woman with such disdain?

"We had plans," Violet whispers so brokenly I have no choice but to listen. "I—We loved each other."

Finally, I look into her eyes and see they're aimed over my shoulder and unfocused. Like she's remembering them.

"I never met them in person. We made plans to meet before Thanksgiving, but Mom was kidnapped on Halloween. Everything changed."

Barely breathing, I continue to run the towel over her pale skin. Slowly I move to her hands and soak in every word she graces me with.

"The police confiscated my phone. Grandpa gave me his old flip phone with a new number. No social media. No contact with friends. I unintentionally ghosted them."

I've known Violet avoids and refuses to interact with any kind of social media. What happened to her mom being tied to Violet's social accounts, I can understand why she cut it from her life.

Her fingers twitch when I drag the cloth between them. Ticklish maybe? My smile is soft as I do it again and watch her wiggle. I'm learning so many things about my woman.

"Mom was rescued." Violet takes a shuddering breath. "And I was in the clear to go about my life like normal again once everything came to a close. But..."

She couldn't.

"I couldn't." Tears trickle down her cheeks once again, so I shift and wipe them away. Breaking my heart, Violet continues. "The flip phone became my best friend. It kept me within the boundaries I needed to feel safe and like I wouldn't make the same mistakes again."

Fuck, it hurts just listening to her vague explanation of what she felt and still feels. Thinking about how deep her well of pain actually goes makes me a little murderous and a lot clingy. The desire to drag her onto my lap is strong, but I hold back for now. Once she's done talking, I'll snuggle the shit out of her. Right now I'm afraid that if I so much as twitch, she'll stop talking.

She sniffs, and her eyes dull even more. "I never spoke to them again. We were building something *real,* and I ran from them."

"Because you were scared and traumatized," I interrupt, unable to stand the self-loathing I hear in her voice.

Violet blinks but doesn't look at me. "I loved them. Why didn't I lean on them when I needed them the most?"

"The same reason it's taken you five and a half years to open up to me, Sweets. Am I right?"

At that, she finally looks me in the eye and absolutely *breaks*. "I'm so sorry!" she sobs and drops her face into her hands as her body shakes with anguish.

"Shit," I hiss and pull her to me. "V, shh. I don't fault you for anything. Please, just breathe."

I'm going to lose my mind if she drops into another

panic attack. Who knows how her body can deal with all the stress that's clearly wreaking havoc on her body.

"I'm sorry," she croaks into my chest. It's barely audible between sniffles and sobs.

With her cradled in my arms again, I run my hands along her legs and arms in an attempt to ground her. I continue to coo sweet things, *true* things, as she cries. It takes a while, but she eventually settles.

"My love," I whisper, feeling choked up. "Everything is going to be okay."

She sniffles and looks up at me. "You-You aren't mad? I-I'm messed up. I pu-push the people I care about away. Who-Who does that?"

Kissing her forehead, I bask in the fact that she admitted she cares about me. My heart swells even though each thump hurts a little with the beatings it's received this evening.

After years of falling in love with this woman, I'd like to think I've learned enough about her that I can answer her tearful question. "Someone who loves with their entire being would sacrifice their own happiness to keep the ones they care about safe. You've been in self-preservation mode for so long, Violet. That extended to your circle of loved ones because you care *so fucking much*."

"I just don't want to get anyone else hurt, but it seems like all I've done is hurt everyone with those choices too! B-But everyone's better off without me."

"Well," I huff and squeeze her tighter, "that is the biggest lie I've ever fucking heard."

She sucks in a breath and seems to look past my

eyes and into my soul. She needs to see that I'm telling the truth.

"You've been living under the assumption everyone is better off without you, but I'm fucking *miserable* every time you're on a trip. Hell, you leave my apartment and I *ache*, Violet."

Her mouth pops open in surprise. She'll have to get used to it though because I'm done holding back. Violet's trying to change, so it's time I start encouraging her growth.

Violet frowns and tries to push away, but I don't allow any movement. "You're staying right here, Sweets. Get used to it."

Her brows furrow even further, then she bites her plump lip. "But what about Ellis and Nate? They said—"

My throat rumbles in response to the reminder of *what they fucking said.* "What about them, V? They treated you like shit, so they are nothing."

"Ellis said they're pursuing you."

I shake my head. "Fuck that. Fuck them."

"Did you? Fuck them, I mean," she asks softly. *Is she afraid of my answer? Will she leave?*

A ball of stress forms in my throat as I come face to face with the reason for most of my fucking guilt. "No, we didn't fuck. Ellis and Nate approached me at the bar the night we fought. They offered to fool around and hang out."

Eyes wide, Violet hangs on to every word I'm forcing out of my mouth. She prompts me to continue with a strange tone. "And then?"

Blowing out a breath, I lay it all out there. "Ellis gave me a blowjob under the table while Nate watched." Violet gasps, and my gut coils tight with dread, but I have to keep going. "I went to dinner with them tonight."

"Like a date?" She again tries to sit up, looking pale and horrified, but I hold her tight. If she asks me to let her go, I will, but not yet. Not until I'm done explaining.

"I-I'm not sure. Nothing else happened because I got the call that Bash was outside my door with my unconscious woman."

At that, she looks away from me. I give her a second, then pull her face back to mine because what I'm about to say is really fucking important for her to hear.

"Listen, Violet. I didn't know about your connection to them, I swear. It's fucked that the one time I mess around with someone else in *years* that it was your past loves."

Her bottom lip wobbles, and I swear I break out in a cold sweat. *Have I broken her heart? Ruined everything? She was coming to me tonight to talk and figure things out...Have I destroyed our chances?*

What she says surprises me, though. "Do you like them?"

"I—" *What?* "No."

"You hesitated."

I feel my face twist into a scowl. "Had you asked me this before Ellis treated you like a fucking prick, my answer may have been different."

"So you're conflicted because of me. Without my connection to them and their negative feelings about me, you like them? Saw something with them?" I open my mouth immediately, but she begs me not to lie.

Fuck. Now *I* want to push her away so I can pace and work off these feelings building inside of me. "Yes," I grit out, studying her facial expressions like a hawk.

"And me?" Violet whispers, sounding sad and hesitant, but she needn't feel that way.

"You? Violet, you're *everything*. There is nothing with them without *you*. Package deal, remember?"

Everything I'm saying is the complete and honest fucking truth. I don't know if Violet can believe me, but she knows I care about her. I've never hidden my feelings and always pushed her for more. *She knows*. And if she second-guesses me, I'll prove my love again and again until the day I die.

"Jamie..." Violet chews on her lip.

Unable to help myself, I press a quick kiss to her plump lips. "Yes?"

"I want to see them again. I need to make things right. Maybe be friends. There's this guilt inside of me that will fester and eat me alive because I hurt them with my silence. No more silence."

"Anything you want," I agree, already planning to be there every time so I can protect her from their anger. "I'll be there."

"And...and it's okay if you want to continue seeing them, Jamie."

"No fucking way. Not without you, and quite frankly, they have some attitude adjustments that would need to happen if I hang out with them again." I'm reeling. She should be demanding I never see them again, right? There's so much confusion and strange connections that it's making it hard for me to understand where she's coming from.

"Jamie," she coos, placing a warm hand on my cheek. "I've taken enough from them. I won't take you away too. I'll still be here. What I'm saying is that I'll be okay if you end up doing stuff with them. Honestly, it's the least I can do."

"What the fuck? No. That's messed up, V."

Shaking her head, Violet snuggles into me as drowsiness begins to weigh her down. "I'm just saying you have my blessing. They were amazing to me, and I hurt them, Jamie. I'll try to fix things with them so this isn't weird. Just don't write them off, okay?"

Fuck. What the hell? I'm saved from having to respond when her left boob starts vibrating between us.

Violet wiggles and snorts a little. "Forgot that was in there." Then her hand is beneath her shirt and pulling her phone out. "Shoot. I have to drive Cassidy home."

Absolutely fucking not. "No. I'll drive you both home."

"But my car."

"Fine. I'll drive you and Cassidy home in your car, then crash on your couch so you can drive me back here in the morning. Or, I'll drive you and Cass home in my car and pick you up in the morning to get your car. *Or*, you go curl up in my bed, I'll pick Cassidy up and bring her home, then I'll snuggle you all night long."

I know which option I'd like her to choose, and by the way her eyelids are drooping, I think I'll get my wish.

"Promise you'll come right back?"

Nuzzling the top of her head, I stand with her in my arms and bring her to my bedroom. Two panic attacks, a mugging, a big revelation, and truth bombs drag her into dreamland as I promise, "Nothing could keep me away."

Twenty

NATE

We knew we would see Violet again someday. Imagined it even.

None of the scenarios we pictured came anywhere close to what happened tonight. We figured we'd see her, tell her that her actions caused a lot of hurt, and really make her understand the consequences of how she treated us.

Ellis' emotions on the subject have always been a bit more volatile than mine. Over the years, my anger has diminished as I've grown. I'm thirty-one years old. I'm capable of empathy and understanding that what happened to Violet's mom changed her life.

While the rage has diminished, it's really fucking hard to tamp down feeling like the woman we loved betrayed us. She ghosted us. Left us without a word. Just disappeared.

Socials were taken down, her number changed, Violet left us to pick up the pieces of the life we planned which she shattered.

Ellis has always wanted to give her a piece of his mind, and I admit I've wanted to educate her on the impact she has on others, but the way tonight unfolded has left a bad taste in my mouth.

Because Ellis and I are partners in every sense of the word, I carry half the blame for how wrong our meeting went. "I don't feel good about this, El."

He mutters curses under his breath. Not lifting his head to look at me, Ellis continues to drag his hands through his hair. His posture is that of a defeated man with the weight of bad choices weighing him down.

With his head hung low as he sits on our couch, Ellis shakes his head. "Me neither."

Damn it. Had he said anything else, it would have made me feel better. Like what we did was warranted. Had he said something toxic like Violet deserves it, I might have been able to brush my feelings aside and just nod along.

"Fuck, Ellis. Jamie's pissed, and Violet isn't acting like herself."

At that, Ellis scoffs and looks at me. "Of course she wasn't acting like herself. She just got mugged, then saw our angry faces. She feels guilty as she should!"

I'm sure she does feel guilty, which is what we wanted. Ellis and I were planning a *life* with that woman. And she ripped our hearts out. She should feel fucking bad.

But how Ellis is reacting sets me on edge. This might be one of those times I take a more dominant approach with him. He needs some guidance and for me to narrow his path a bit because I'm not comfortable doing more of *this*.

Silence wraps around us. Our living room hasn't felt this cold since we moved in a few months ago.

There's another part of this situation that's weighing on us. I need to get him thinking about more than his anger and need to defend our actions. "What about Jamie? He's loyal to her. And we...we what? Do you want to continue this thing with him?"

"Do you?" Ellis asks me, eyes boring into mine. Challenging and making me sit up straighter.

If he wants to push, so will I. "You like him, and so do I, but this is so complicated, Ellis. What we did—"

Ellis shakes his head, cutting me off. "They can't know."

"They?" I raise a brow knowing he means Violet and Jamie. He's already protecting her feelings and doesn't even realize it. "Seeing Violet stirred up old feelings for me too."

"Damn it!" Ellis explodes and leaps from the couch to pace. "I'm so fucking angry with her, though! She abandoned our future, Nate!"

"I know, El." Watching him closely, I note the tension in his shoulders and give him the space he needs to vent. Better at me than at her.

"Threw us away like we were nothing! Violet was our everything. We clearly didn't matter much to her if she could just turn her back on us without a word!"

Our drive home was silent, so I was expecting a big blowup from my partner. His emotions run so deep in every aspect of his life. Which is one reason he's hesitating to reenter the medical field.

Ellis cares with every atom in his body, so this reaction he's having is a result of his own trauma of losing the woman he loved. I'm the calmer, dominant one of the two of us, which allows him the space to express his heightened emotions when they push against his sanity. I won't allow him to lose himself to his trauma though.

"We shouldn't feel bad for getting back at her! And we were never supposed to actually like Jamie. Fuck. FUCK!"

Ellis' wild eyes tell me he's had enough. "Enough," I interject as I stand. "We fucked up. But the repercussions might be good. It could all be fine. If we want to make up with Violet, we can. If we want to actually try for something with Jamie, we can."

"They would never forgive us," Ellis says brokenly. "We have to keep it a secret."

Bile burns my throat, but I fight the reaction down. "Ellis, I don't know. Wouldn't it be better to tell them?"

Ellis rolls his eyes and steps away from me in agitation. "Sure, let me think. Hey Violet. We saw you at a coffee shop a few weeks ago with Jamie. Then when we saw him at a bar, we drunkenly decided it would be fun to get some payback by luring the hot guy you're clearly with into our bed."

I grind my teeth while Ellis mock laughs as if this is funny. He continues his tirade. "We didn't think he'd actually go for it, but he did, and damn revenge tasted *good*."

"Son of a bitch, Ellis, stop. This isn't productive."

"But it's the truth!" he bellows at me, and my palm itches to spank his ass. "And one we must take to the grave if we want to be in any kind of relationship with them."

"But—"

Ellis swings a hand through the air as if physically cutting my words off. "We. Can. Not. Right now we have the upper hand, as we should. Violet needs to apologize and make up for all the hurt she's caused. If she finds out about our reasoning for entering Jamie's life, we lose our position."

"This isn't a fucking war, Ellis!" Anger simmers below the surface the longer he continues talking. Ellis is ready to fight his corner, and I don't think I'll be able to convince him my ideas are better.

"Yes it is! She hurt us way more than us fucking around with Jamie. It wasn't as bad. Right? It couldn't have been. And it doesn't matter because we actually care about him now. *Please,*" he begs, eyes wild and watery. "She *left* us. We can keep this one secret. We're owed a mistake."

My throat closes over as emotion strangles me. Fuck, I must be strong, but this is so much to deal with. Not to mention my protective side is screaming at me to go back over there and make sure she's okay. Violet was hurt tonight by a goddamn stranger, and here we are saying she deserves the hurt *we've* caused too? This is so fucked up. I just want to hold her and ice her hip.

I squeeze my eyes shut and shake my head. "What if they find out and we've built something amazing with them?"

"They won't because if something actually comes from us spending time with them, then they will see how real our feelings are. We won't fake shit. Hell, we couldn't fake it with Jamie when we met him."

The desperation pouring off of him tells me there's no way I'll win this battle tonight. Maybe he will change his mind soon, and I kind of hope he does. I have no idea how long I can hold on to this.

We aren't malicious men. We're hurt, and we did something for reasons we shouldn't have.

It doesn't matter that our motivation with Jamie quickly changed when we met him and were sucked into his bright blue eyes. We lied by omission. We used him to hurt her.

I might be taller and wider than Ellis, but my heart is vulnerable beneath all the muscle. Hurting them is not an option, so they'll never know. Doesn't mean I feel good about it.

Like a coward, I shift the conversation and wrap my arms around his waist. "So we won't let them go easily because *A* we deserve an apology and explanation from V, and *B* Jamie is under our skin and we want him?"

Ellis sighs and thumps his forehead onto my shoulder. "Sums it up."

I want to tell him I don't know if I can pull this off, but I let it go for now. Who knows, maybe Jamie will block us from his life, and Violet will run screaming the next time she sees us.

One thing is for sure though; we *will* be seeing them again.

Journal Entry

Fact or lie? The hard version.

It's my fault that Ellis and Nate are angry. Fact.

I broke their hearts. Fact.

They hate me. I think so.

They want Jamie. Most likely a fact.

I'm standing between them and happiness (Jamie) again. Fact.

I have the power to give them what I took. Fact.

I'm holding Jamie back from something that could be really wonderful for him. A fact that's been true for a looooong time.

I should step away from all three. Fact.

I can step away. I don't think I can.

I want to be happy too. Fact.

Jamie makes me happy. ....Fact.

Admitting that is hard. Fact.

I can handle sharing Jamie. We will have to see.

Twenty-One

VIOLET

My life has turned into something completely unrecognizable. Just a few weeks ago, I was *fine*.

Mom and everyone back in Chicago wouldn't agree, and I'm sure Cassidy would cry if I told her I was fine before. Honestly, they would all probably prefer I have a breakdown because they would have hope. Hope that once I crash and burn I will get better. I'd show my feelings and work toward a better future.

What's the saying? There's always a rainbow on the other side of a storm or something?

It's hard to believe that there will be something beautiful after this. Doubting there will be an *after* is where I'm at. A different metaphor might fit this better. I can actually imagine the scene that's making me tremble and chew my nails to the nub.

I'm drowning. The sun is shining, highlighting all the crystal currents around me. So beautiful, yet they drag me deeper.

The longer I'm underwater, the more air escapes my lungs. Bubbles sparkle and warp as they slip from my lips. They rise and rise until I lose sight of my life source.

I can't hold my breath any longer. Can't hold on to these small bubbles of air. I'm losing my grasp on life, and the fight is leaking out of me.

My final exhale burns my chest and climbs up my throat as the water becomes darker, murkier.

Then, it escapes and rushes for the surface. My bubbles literally flee my dying body to save themselves.

The longer I struggle, the faster I lose myself.

The more I think about it, that scene has lasted seven fucking years. I've been struggling for a long time, but I've made the suffocating pain easy to ignore by allowing the ache to burn inside of me. I've deserved it.

Now, to top it off, I'm faced with another horrible mistake.

I feel so, *so* awful for what I did to Nate and Ellis. Pushing them from my thoughts for so long didn't diminish the guilt. If anything, ignoring it made it so much worse.

Seeing them again and hearing the anger in their voices hit the boundaries I've put up. They're from a time in my life when I thought everything was going to be okay. When I was happy and hopeful.

Nate and Ellis had all my positive energy.

It makes sense that they were drawn to Jamie. Jamie is such an outgoing guy who demands smiles and conversation. They found a guy who can match their energy and laugh during the tough times. Jamie works with them.

He's everything I used to be.

Jamie's bubbly. A dominant kind of bubbly who has a lot of tattoos and can be a bit dangerous, but he's still excitable and loving.

Bubbly.

Bubbles.

My heart aches every time I recall how Ellis used his old nickname for me. It hurt more than anything he could have thrown at me. Ellis flayed me without even knowing it just by using one darn word.

If he knew how dull and sad I've gotten, he would never call me that again. Everything Nate and Ellis loved about me evaporated with every pop of the bubbles that made me, me.

I evaporated. I disappeared and didn't tell them why. Wrapped up in my own issues, I broke up with them using silence. The same way Mom's guys did when they were young.

Suddenly all the ways Roman, Felix, Declan, and

Jared groveled comes to the forefront of my mind. *I should grovel.*

Gosh, I'm so embarrassed and feel so bad I could throw up.

"Violet, are you listening to me?"

Blinking, I realize Cassidy's talking to me. She's sitting on the other side of the couch, staring at me with concern. "What? No, sorry."

"I'm not even going to ask if you're okay, because I can tell you're not. You were mugged just days ago," she reminds me unnecessarily. I don't correct her that that isn't what's bothering me.

Jamie explained that I was hurt when he drove her home from the club last weekend. He didn't tell her anything else. When he brought me home the next day, I didn't offer Cassidy any more information than he gave her. She knows I was mugged, and that's enough for now while I figure out how I'm going to fix my messes.

I have two men from my past pursuing the man of my present. The conversation about Jamie's and my future that I wanted to have has been put on pause because who knows what the heck will happen.

I've had way too much time to fester in my thoughts. For the past few days, I've listened to Jamie and continued to ice my hip and rest. It's nasty yellow right now, but it barely hurts anymore. Not like my brain.

There's a lot of pain in this situation, and I don't know where to start.

"Violet, helllooooo?"

Wincing, I focus on Cass. "Quick, tell me what you want to say because I'm super spacey."

"I need you to meet me at the address I sent to you on your birthday. I would drive you, but I have to pick something up on the way which is your birthday surprise. Sound good?"

"Sounds good," I agree, half listening because my phone vibrated while she was talking, and it's Jamie. We've been texting a lot, keeping things light, but I haven't seen him since he delivered my car to me yesterday.

"What did he say?" Cassidy smirks, eyeing my phone like there could be a nude on it.

Rolling my eyes, I pull my phone closer to my chest. "His favorite food is tacos."

Cassidy groans. "Lame reply, V. But so meant to be. You can always fuck with a taco."

Nodding, my mouth salivates a little. Taking a leap, I invite Jamie out for lunch, and of course, he accepts and declares I be ready in fifteen minutes.

I'm ready in ten.

Twenty-Two

JAMIE

The awkward silence in the car can't diminish the sheer giddiness zipping through my muscles. Veins too, but my muscles are all kinds of twitchy with the urge to reach out and hold her leg.

My jaw hit the fucking ground when she ran out of her apartment and smacked right into my chest. I hate how shocked she was that I would be at her door when I texted her I was here. She should know I'm a fucking gentleman.

Violet squeaked out an apology and quickly shut the door behind her. I couldn't help but laugh at Cassidy's joke to have her friend home before the sun sets.

Violet basically rushed out to my car, but a firm swat on her ass made her take a step back from opening her car door. *That's my job,* I reminded her and held her hand as she shimmied onto the seat. Plus, she should not be moving like that while she's healing.

I've been following her lead, knowing she has a lot

going on in her head, so I've allowed her to ignore the fact that she was mugged less than a week ago. The only time she brought it up was to ask what happened to her attacker. Telling her Bash was handling the report was enough for her to let it go.

I'm a little worried that we aren't talking about it, but I guess it's a good thing considering Bash isn't making a police report. The mugger is currently in "questioning" with the MC. I'd rather not explain to her what Bash and my friends are doing to the fucker that hurt her.

I'm just going to ride the high of her shyness for now. Her blush is the highlight of my day. It hasn't left since she ran into me. Even now with her body slightly angled away from me, her cheeks are pink.

I'm so damn pleased that she's wearing light-wash jeans with a multitude of rips in them. The peek I got between her jacket showed a simple black shirt. I hope it's long sleeve because it's cold as fuck, and I don't trust the restaurant to have good enough heating for my woman.

Parking the car a block away from my favorite place to get tacos, I turn to her already smirking. "Violet, you can avoid looking at me all you want, but I promise I know every single thing you're thinking without seeing your face."

As I hoped, Violet twists to face me with a scowl. "You can*not*."

Her scoff is fucking adorable, and if I have to provoke her to make her feel more comfortable about our first date, then you bet your ass I will. "No? So you're not thinking about how amazing I smell and how you can't escape my intoxicating scent when you're in my car?"

Holy shit. Her blush blooms so bright I can't help but call her out on it. "Your blush just rose ten degrees. Were you thinking about the cologne I put on for you today?"

Groaning, Violet drops her face into her hands. "Stop. Let's just go eat."

"Wait," I grab her seatbelt buckle to keep V from escaping. "First, tell me...were you wondering if I smell this good *everywhere*?"

"Jamie!" she gasps, her forehead pink with embarrassment.

My smirk turns into a full-blown smile. "Jesus, Sweets. I was just messing with you. I didn't think you were actually sniffing me like you're obsessed with me."

"Take me home," she demands with the most adorable frown on her face.

Reaching for her, I tickle her rosy cheeks. "I'm glad you wore your hair up today. You won't be able to hide behind those gorgeous locks."

My voice is unintentionally deep and reverent, which matches just how deep my feelings are for Violet. Her frown softens when I kiss her cheek and release her buckle.

"Alright. Let me feed you." *That* earns me a smile. "Wait there, Sweets. I'll come around."

My smile grows with each act of trust she gives me in the next five minutes. Violet lets me escort her out of the car, down the sidewalk, and into the restaurant. She even allows me to remove her coat and pull out her chair.

Violet Bennett is gifting me more of herself, and I'd be a fool to waste the opportunity to shower her with love and care.

Fuck knows she needs it.

Our meal was similar to the car ride here, but there was a key difference. Violet glanced at me every time she blushed.

I love how nervous she is with me, especially since I know everything about her physically. I'm absolutely willing to take the mental and emotional parts of our relationship slow.

Maybe.

"Would you like dessert, my love?"

Violet studies my face and cocks her head like she's thinking. "Why do you call me that?"

Internally I wince because I just told myself I could be patient, but that one slipped out. On the outside, I play up my cockiness and confidence. Violet doesn't need to know I'm nervous. She needs one of us to take the lead here, and I'm thrilled to be that for her.

"Because that's what you are, Violet. You're my love even if you aren't ready to accept it. I'll try to back off and—"

"No! No, it's okay," she rushes out, grabbing my

hand across the table. Chewing on her lip, Violet battles with what to say. "It feels nice."

Her tone is soft when she admits her feelings. Instead of lingering on the deep stuff, I kiss her knuckles and ask her if she wants dessert. Only Violet isn't the one to answer my question.

"Violet likes ice cream and chocolate-covered almonds like her mom." Ellis sidles up to the edge of our table with Nate on his heels. "Isn't that right, Violet? Or has that changed? I wouldn't know, since you know..."

My temper flares so fucking fast my mouth opens without planning to. "You fuck—"

"It's still true," Violet blurts, squeezing my hand pretty damn hard for a woman who is now white as a ghost.

"Ellis," Nate sighs, tugging his partner back. "Knock it off. Violet, I hope your hip is doing better. I'm sure it's been hard after the mugging."

Violet mumbles an unsure thank you all the while looking like she's about to cry. These two idiots are ruining our fucking date and her mood. My one goddamn goal was to keep her happy.

Ellis seems to shrug off his attitude and glances at Violet's hand in mine before he apologies. "Shit. Sorry Violet."

"It was good to see you both," Nate adds and tries to pull Ellis away. *Good riddance.*

"Wait!" Violet scrambles to stand and glances at me for permission. For what I have no fucking clue, but I don't like the desperation I see in her face to keep them here. "Stay. Have a drink with us."

"What the f—"

"Please?" Violet cuts me off with a sharper tone that actually makes me shut up.

Ellis grins, and I don't like that either. *What the hell is happening right now?*

"Sure," Ellis agrees, and walks around behind me while trailing his hand across my shoulders. It makes me shiver, but I play my reaction off by twisting my features into disgust.

Unfortunately, Violet was watching me the whole time. When I meet her gaze, she nods at me softly, like she's giving *me* permission. Again, *for what?*

What? I mouth at her while the other two settle into their seats and order a drink with our waitress.

Violet just lifts her chin at Ellis and widens her eyes at me. I don't know what the hell she mouths because I'm immediately snapped out of our intense stare down when Ellis opens his fucking mouth.

"This is cozy."

Fucking prick.

Twenty-Three

ELLIS

My plan? I have no fucking plan.

All I want to do is get under Violet's skin. Unfortunately, I'm finding it harder to hold on to my anger the longer I've been sitting beside her. It's been a minute and a half, but my negative feelings have been cut down by a third.

Jamie's cologne wraps around me since I shifted my chair to sit closer to him, but Violet's big eyes suck me right in. She's tanner than I would expect for the middle of the winter in freezing Michigan, which only adds to all of my questions.

"So where have you been fucking off to, Violet?" Internally I cringe because that was a horrible way to start this conversation. I force my face to stay neutral and a little bored, but, fuck, I feel sick.

"You can fuck right off out of this restaurant, you son of a—"

"Jamie!" Violet hisses, sending daggers with her eyes. Not a lick of makeup coats her eyelashes, endearing me to this new woman even more. "He can ask me questions."

"Not like that," Jamie snaps back, and I gotta say his protectiveness of her is a turn-on. It pisses me off though. Not because I want Jamie to protect me, but because Violet doesn't need him stepping between us.

"I'm not here to hurt the girl," I drawl and lean my elbows on the table.

Jamie shoves one of my arms off the wood and looks at me like he's about to punch me in the jaw. "Judging by the tears she shed over you, I'd say—"

"Jamie enough," Violet cuts him off, looking furious and like she might cry. "I hurt them first. Just stop and let Ellis ask his darn questions."

Nate's lips twitch. We make eye contact, and for once it's kind of hard to read my partner's mind. Frowning at him, I hope he will tell me what he's thinking, because I'm no longer certain he was biting back laughter.

Violet's deep breath is audible, drawing my attention back to her. "I'm assuming you know what happened to my mom?"

"Blue upgraded to Mom, huh?" Nate murmurs, sounding thoughtful.

Violet just nods and waits for us to answer her question. While I'm wondering how much to share because I'm not feeling very forthcoming with the woman who broke our hearts, Nate gives her all my fucking secrets.

"We do. Ellis was actually Blue's nurse right when she got to the hospital and woke up. Met the four guys attached to your mama too."

"Nate." My voice is growly and full of so much warning I'm sure the table next to us can feel the threat.

"What?!" Violet's shocked, and her already big eyes are wide as saucers now. "Wait, but I never saw you there."

Ignoring the wobble in her tone, I level her with a cool glare. "Nate and I had a trip planned. The dates were already taken off, so we went on a self-care trip. You know, to heal our broken hearts. Oh, wait. You already knew that."

Tears fill Violet's eyes as she recalls the plans we finally made to meet the woman we loved in person. We were going to start our life together when she ghosted us and made it very clear she didn't want to be involved with us when we were blocked and removed from her life.

"Ellis," Violet chokes, and Jamie's hand fists on the table like he's holding himself back. He would probably equally like to punch me and scoop Violet up in a hug.

"Yes? What do you have to say?" I'm an asshole, but I do want to know if she can defend herself in any way. We were going to meet her somewhere in Chicago. Maybe we were fools not to demand her address so we could show up, but she always teased that once she met us in person she would give us her address.

We knew she was nervous about sharing it, so we respected her wishes. I never expected to fucking hate myself for never forcing the issue though. If we had known, we could have found her.

"I–" she stutters and swipes the tears from her cheeks. Her trembling fingers make me frown. *Why is she shaking so much?* But she must read my expression wrong and flinches away from me a bit.

"I'm sorry. I—I ran."

I snort. "Well, that was pretty fucking obvious."

"Ellis," Jamie starts, voice tight, wrapping his big hand around the back of my neck and squeezing. "Don't get your wires fucking twisted. I'm *allowing* this conversation. You swear at her one more goddamn time and I'll drag you out of here with more than just a bruised ego, and you won't *ever* be allowed to see either of us ever again. You fucking understand me?"

Nate pushes his chair back, looking pissed at the sexy man's threatening hand on me. I implore my partner to stay in his seat with a small shake of my head.

Chills run down my spine, making me squirm as Jamie squeezes me a little harder. Quickly, so he doesn't get the wrong idea about my head shake, I nod and agree, "Yes. I understand."

I almost don't want to say it because I'm intrigued by the idea of Jamie manhandling me. The only thing that stops me from testing him are Violet's sniffles and the sheer despair drooping her dainty shoulders.

Surprisingly, I barely notice Jamie removing his hand from my skin. I'm stuck watching Violet try to gain control of her emotions.

With a deep breath and a moment of silence, I pull on all the empathy I honed from my career and try for the millionth time to see Violet as the victim she absolutely is, rather than the woman who abandoned me.

What I see breaks my heart. I feel my face slacken

from my usual frown as I take in her hunched posture and the way she's angled away from the table as if she's ready to flee at any moment.

Not *once* in the few times I've seen her, even when we first found her at the coffee shop, has she smiled. The Violet I knew *always* smiled. There could be many explanations for why her pink bow-shaped lips haven't lifted with happiness, but what about the odd detachment I've noticed?

I'm foolish enough to admit that I expected her to run into our arms if she ever saw us again. Of course I would have pushed her away, but I always knew her as affectionate and free with her love.

Her feelings radiated from her, even over text. Seeing her on a video call felt like a warm fucking hug. Even through a long distance relationship, Violet made Nate and me feel so loved and cherished.

What happened? Could she have really changed so much that I don't recognize this version of her?

Blue was the one kidnapped. Not Violet. Sure, V was traumatized by losing her mama and the chaos of everything, but what the hell altered her fundamentally?

I'm confused. This isn't what I expected.

Fuck. I figured when we found her again, she would be living her best life. Maybe started fresh because Chicago reminded her of what happened to Blue. But this? This version of Violet I'm just now actually *seeing* confuses me.

Anger is easy. Whatever the hell I'm feeling right now is fucking *not*.

Swallowing thickly, I lean toward her and say the only word that comes to mind. "Bubbles?"

To my horror, a sob bursts from her. I rear back with my heart in my throat as Jamie bursts from his chair. Nate grabs Jamie immediately and forces him to listen to his quiet words. I lose interest in their heated argument because Violet continues crying into her napkin.

She's not gone yet. I can still fix this fucked up situation.

Right? Fuck.

Twenty-Four

VIOLET

The only thing that could make me stop crying happens. Jamie steps away. He literally takes a step back.

I have no idea what Nate said to him, but I want to slap all three of them. Unfortunately my emotions are in depression territory. What I wouldn't give to have an easy anger switch like my mama.

Anger is easy...

"Hey Violet," Nate coos, now sitting beside me and looking like I'm going to burst into an explosion of kittens or something. "Jamie's going to the bathroom. I think while we have time alone, we need to clear the air."

I don't realize how stiff I've gotten until Nate tells me Jamie's *leaving*. Panic seizes my vocal cords as I look back to where Jamie just was.

To my relief, he's leaning against the wall a few tables away, staring at me. As our eyes lock, Jamie places a hand on his chest and nods at me. *He's not going anywhere. He will watch over me as I face my mistakes.*

At least that's what I think he's promising.

"V..." Nate touches my elbow, making me flinch and snap my gaze back to him. He doesn't seem to have noticed that Jamie isn't actually *gone,* or if he does, he simply doesn't mind my hero hovering.

Is that what Jamie is? My hero?

Mom would tell me Jamie isn't the hero in my story; I am. Especially when I feel like I can't get any lower because there's no telling when another person might leave. *I am forever. My loyalty to myself makes me my own hero.*

"Violet?"

Blinking, I realize I zoned out on Nate's face. "You grew out your beard," I murmur like an idiot.

Heat warms my cheeks, but I don't retract my statement because it's true. Nate didn't have a full beard when I knew him. It's not wild by any means. He keeps it cut nicely, but it's...*different.*

Just like I am.

Like Ellis is. I never knew Ellis to be cruel, but there's an edge to him now that scares me a little.

"He did. Many things have changed," Ellis confirms.

I cringe a little even though I'm not certain he meant that to sound as harsh as my heart felt it to be.

"What are you thinking about right now?" Nate surprises me with his question and gentle touch on my jaw.

Shifting back, I watch as his hand drops between us.

"Currently I'm wondering why you would want to touch me."

Nate cocks his head and scans my face. Who knows what he sees beyond my watery eyes and blotchy face. I am *not* a pretty crier.

"I—" Nate can't even get his thought out. I shouldn't be offended that he can't explain why he felt the urge to touch me. Hell, they're only here for an apology or to get in Jamie's pants, so it's time to get this show on the road.

I nod. "Can you just ask me your questions? Please."

Ellis and Nate make eye contact. I try not to let it bother me, but once upon a time I would have been able to read them like they do each other.

"Where did you go? After Blue was safe." Nate takes the lead, which is probably for the best considering Ellis hates my guts and can't say a single sentence without making his feelings for me known.

My back starts to itch as I break out in a nervous sweat. Don't get me wrong, I've been sweating since they sat down, but now I have their full attention. The weight resting on my upcoming words is suffocating.

"Everywhere. I took my car and made it my mission to stay lost for as long as I could."

I can tell by Ellis' scowl that my answer wasn't satisfactory before he even opens his mouth. "What does that even mean?"

I shrug and twist my hands in my lap. "Just driving. I stopped at state parks, camped out in my car, and visited new places."

Ellis is practically fuming next to me, so Nate asks

the next question. "Why didn't you come to us, V? We would have done anything for you."

Would have, past tense. I have no right to be so heart-broken by that distinction, yet I bleed anyway.

"I—" Swallowing, I attempt to will the ball of stress in my throat away. "I—"

"Really?" Ellis hisses, turning toward me completely. "You *have* to have an answer, Violet. We were planning on fucking marrying you. You're telling me you left us in the dust for a fucking road trip?"

"That's not—I didn't—" Stumbling over my words is the last thing I need right now. I'm still sitting here with them so I can provide them with the closure they need. Yet I can't get anything to come out of my damn mouth.

Ellis' voice is sad when he asks, "Was there someone else?"

"Ellis," Nate hisses, fists clenching on the table.

Shaking my head furiously. "No. Never!" I declare while telling myself he has the right to accuse me of anything. What I did was horrible. *Everything* I've done is fucking horrible.

My God. Just look at Jamie. This amazing man has been hooked on me for years, then the first time he seeks happiness elsewhere it's with my past. The three of them can't have a future together unless I get my act together and fix this.

"You can't blame me for asking, Violet." Ellis is *so* mad I start shaking.

"I d-don't blame y-you. It was all m-my fault."

My muscles wind tighter and tighter as my vision ping pongs between them. Absentmindedly, I recognize another panic attack is hovering just beneath the surface, but I can't let it consume me. They need to understand how sorry I am.

"So sorry," I force out, pleading with them to piece together the shattered pieces of the girl they once knew.

I can't tell what Nate is thinking, but his eyes widen and his shoulders look wider when I glance at him.

"Please," I whimper. "I'm sorry."

"Violet," Ellis calls out to me, so I turn to him and bring my hands beneath my chin to beg.

Please see me. See, I'm not malicious. I'm not bad or horrible. I'm LOST. I'm trying*! PLEASE HELP ME.*

"I was scared. So scared. I messed up, and Mama got hurt. I couldn't bear the thought of hurting you too. S-so I ran. I caused so much p-pain because of my choices. I couldn't—I couldn't—"

Warmth trickles down my cheeks as Ellis blurs. Now I'll never know what he thinks of my shame...and I don't think I would like to.

Just as a chair scrapes along the ground and deep voices get closer, I explode out of my chair and plead with whoever can help me. "I want to go home!"

Twenty-Five

JAMIE

"Jamie, I want to go to *my* home." In the passenger seat of my car, Violet sniffles while scowling at the side of my face.

I ignore her, my emotions way too fired up to have a normal conversation. Fearing I'll scare her keeps me quiet as I drive through the streets of downtown Detroit. I should bring her home, but I can't make myself do it. My white knuckled grip on the steering wheel won't budge on this.

Ellis and Nate fucked up *again*. How many chances can I give them before I write them off as a pair of fucking assholes who can't see what's right in front of them?

But that's not quite true now, is it?

I saw the confusion and shock on Ellis' face when he really looked at Violet. It was like he was trying to actually figure her out. When he did, I had to force my heart to stay steady instead of breaking for both Nate and Ellis.

Their worry was palpable when Violet started shaking. It took every ounce of strength I had to stay away, and fucking hell, it was one of the hardest things I've had to do.

As soon as she launched out of her chair, I was across the room and pulling her into my arms. Her plea to go home just about snapped my control.

The desperation and honest sadness etched into Ellis' features dulled some of the rage I felt for him. He pushed her too far, and he knew it. He'd better fucking learn from it.

Nate looked ready to take her from me and wrap her in bubble wrap. Unfortunately, I think they may have lost their right to comfort my woman.

Maybe if they hadn't made her cry and panic each time she's seen them, it would be different. I wish it could be different. Instead I'm driving her to my place alone, and I'm not letting her leave until she's feeling better.

"Jamie..."

I've always wanted Violet to show me more emotion and vulnerability. Now that I have it, I'm freaking the fuck out. I hate seeing her cry. Her usually confident posture has drooped, and the seductive lilt of her voice that I've become accustomed to over the years has faded into uncertainty.

Violet has been disarmed by Nate and Ellis. I don't know whether to kiss them or rip their spines through their throats.

"Jamie!"

"What?! Shit," I curse, looking over at her wide eyes. "Fuck. I'm sorry. V, I can't bring you home."

"And why the hell not?" She crosses her arms.

Thank fuck for small bratty mercies.

Whipping into my parking spot, I once again ignore her words. She stays in the car as I come around to her side, but she doesn't move an inch when I open the door.

"Violet. Come here, please," I say, voice tight, but I'm trying to be gentle. She shakes her head while looking out the windshield. "Now."

"Fuck off, Jamie."

Something tangible in my brain snaps. Reaching inside, I unbuckle her seatbelt and grab her calves. Violet gasps and starts to wiggle away from me, but her feet are already on the concrete and I'm pulling her out by her clammy hands.

"Goddamn it! Jamie, stop. I want to go home and sleep in my bed for a year," she exclaims as if that would get me to let her go.

"That is *exactly* why you're staying with me for a bit." Slamming the car door behind Violet, I tuck her hand into the crook of my elbow and start our march into the building.

"But—"

My feet take a turn, putting me in front of her with her dainty little nose millimeters away from my collarbone. "Violet," I warn, allowing her to see how I too am struggling. "You're coming inside. At least for a while until I know you'll be okay on your own."

Blue sparkly eyes bounce back and forth between

mine. Her chest rises and falls with a deep breath as her bottom lip wobbles. "Fine," she relents.

Grunting like a fucking caveman, I press a kiss to the corner of her mouth and lead her inside where it's warm. Thankfully she doesn't fight me the rest of the way to my apartment, but she's awfully quiet.

It's probably for the best though because I don't think I'm capable of being gentle right now. She's cried so much today. Getting some water in her is first on my agenda.

Some of the tension releases as we step into my apartment. I may be imagining it, but Violet seems to relax a little as well. She kicks her shoes off and hangs her jacket like it's the most natural thing for her to do. I love how comfortable my sweet woman is in my space.

"I'll get you some water," I mutter. Grazing her lower back with my hand as I walk past her, I strut into the kitchen with purpose.

As I'm filling the glass, my mind conjures up what they could have talked about. How cruel was Ellis? Did Nate demand too much from her?

"It's full," Violet tells me, shocking me out of my head. Cool water flows over my hand and onto the floor. Quickly I move to the sink and dump some before tossing a rag on the floor to mop up the mess I made.

My heart pounds in my chest as I slide the glass across the island to where Violet sits. On top of the counter with her legs crisscrossed, V looks like she belongs here.

"Here you go, Sweets."

She offers me a small smile which settles me a bit. "Thanks."

I watch like a damn weirdo as she takes a sip. "More," I urge, needing my woman hydrated again.

Eyes narrowed on me, Violet does as she's told, and before I know it, half the glass is gone. With that out of the way, it's time I figure out what the hell made her panic the way she did.

"I know you have questions," Violet says, sighing. She plucks at the strings coming from the holes in her jeans, a sure sign that she's anxious. "They wanted to know where I ran off to. I told them I went on a road trip to escape the reminders of what happened to my mom because of me."

I bite the inside of my cheek so fucking hard I draw blood. There will be plenty of time for me to tell her she's wrong, but right now I need to know the situation at hand.

"My answer wasn't good enough," she whispers, and I can't help but feel like she means *she* isn't good enough. "So Ellis asked me if there was someone else."

"He what?!" I snarl, my hands slamming down on the counter. That's a fucked up accusation.

Violet's lips twist as she sniffles. "I told him no and that I didn't blame him for asking me that. Then I—then I lost it a little. I apologized, but I don't think they believed me. So I kept telling them how sorry I was for leaving them the way I did."

Jesus fucking Christ. "What did they say?"

She shrugs, and my heart clenches at the sight. Reaching forward, I wrap my hands around her thighs.

"I don't know what they said, I guess. Or if they said *anything*. It felt like I couldn't breathe, and my ears sounded like they were under water. I was panicking. I needed them to believe me, but it felt like I was pleading with a brick wall."

I remember this part. This is when I started moving and heard the worry in Ellis and Nate's voices. Part of me doesn't want to tell her how scared they were so I can just keep her all to myself, but she has a right to know how her words affected them.

"Ellis kept saying your name," I begin slowly, forcing the words out. "Nate was trying to get your attention so you could match his breathing or something."

"Really?" Violet's frown is equally cute as it is heart-breaking. It should not be shocking that people care about her.

Nodding, I rub my thumbs along her thighs. "Really. When Nate stood up and Ellis started panicking right along with you, you launched yourself out of your chair."

Violet nods. "Then you were there."

"Then I was there," I confirm, smiling even though it hurts. "Do you remember anything between then and demanding I turn the car around?"

I lose her eyes, but I allow her to hide from me for a moment. She needs to know she's safe with me, even when I demand answers. All I want is to help her.

"You put my jacket on me and walked me out of the restaurant. I don't know what else. It's all kind of a blur because I was trying to control my breathing. I don't love panic attacks, you know," she teases, glancing up at me.

Chuckling, I grab her ass and scoot her closer to me so her crossed legs touch my hips. "Does anyone enjoy panic attacks?"

Violet nods. "Yeah. Readers love when the main character has a breakdown."

"What?" My eyebrows shoot up, a little surprised at this turn of conversation.

She nods with a little more life in her eyes. "Yeah. In books. The leading lady panics, and the guy or guys is supposed to swoop in and bring her back down to earth."

"We'll come back to that odd desire, but first, did you say guys? As in plural. Is that something you want? To have multiple men loving you and doting on you?"

Fuck. Violet goes pale and I know I've pushed the wrong button at the wrong time. Of course my sweet woman wanted multiple men in the past, Ellis and Nate.

"I'm sorry," I rush to apologize, and the light begins to fade from her eyes. "Sweets, stop. Come back. I'm sorry for pushing. I wouldn't judge you. Hell, I kinda like the idea of surrounding you with a few other guys. More protection, more eyes and soothing hands to keep you from putting those walls back up."

To my horror, a tear slips free from her right eye, and her lip begins to wobble again. "Fuck. Violet, why are you crying?"

She doesn't answer me. Instead, she tugs her knees up to her chest, dislodging my hold, and spins on the counter. With her back to me, she jumps down on the other side. "I'm gonna go wash my face," she mutters as she walks away.

Groaning once she's out of sight, I hang my head. A few more curses slip out of my mouth. Why must I always push her away? When will I figure out where the fucking line is with her?

I must figure it out quickly because I can't stand my sweet girl crying.

Twenty-Six

VIOLET

The woman staring back at me in the mirror looks like a lost little girl. When did my eyes start sinking into my skull and my eyebrows go unplucked? Maybe when I started spending all waking hours with tears in my eyes and my mind dragging me through the guilty pits of hell.

"I'm a mess," I whisper. The faucet can't drown out the exhaustion in my voice. I don't mean physically. I mean I am completely and utterly tired of trying to figure things out.

I feel like I should be able to pinpoint the exact moment everything took a turn. Was it when Jamie answered my phone and spoke to my mom?

Honestly, I think it was before that. My walls had begun to crumble with each interaction I had with him. Cassidy also chipped away at the boundaries around my heart with her hard truths.

I could be angry with all the shit being thrown at me, but all I feel is overwhelmed. Not to mention the mugging. I'm worried it might be causing me to slip into panic more easily. Like it triggered my nervous system and made me vulnerable. There's been no time or space in my mind to figure it out though.

Wishing I would have begun to change a long time ago doesn't help. But maybe if I had the chance to find the new me, I would be stable enough to deal with Ellis and Nate coming back into my life.

Scoffing at myself, I cup the cool water in my hands and splash my face. What a stupid thought. Ellis and Nate aren't here for me. They aren't part of *my* life. The only reason they're even talking to me is because they like Jamie. And I can't blame them.

A knock sounds behind me, and Jamie's voice rings out. "My love?"

Immediately, more fucking tears fill my eyes. Why is he so nice, so *loving*? I know he thinks Nate and Ellis are the reason for my emotional torment, but they aren't even half of it. It's Jamie and all the changes. I want him so badly, and I've fought it for so long that now I'm trying to embrace him while fighting against my past. It's too much.

The ball of emotion that halts my voice suddenly bursts in a growl of frustration. Whipping around, I yank the bathroom door open and glower at the handsome man who thinks he can steal my heart.

I'm not ready to admit he owns my heart, body, mind, and soul.

"Stop calling me that," I snap.

My chest is heaving and my breasts feel a little heavy. There. Yes. This is what I want. A fight. A sexy fight. Jamie raises a perfectly sculpted eyebrow which just pisses me off more.

Why am I standing here in a pair of jeans and a lame top when I should be in my favorite black lacy lingerie? Why am I self-conscious about my eyebrows?!

"Stop calling you what?" Jamie says, but his voice is too soft. Too understanding and gentle.

"My love. I'm not your love." Although, the ache in my heart when I deny his claim tells me otherwise.

His eyes flare, but he hesitates, eyeing me like he can see right through my anger. "I think you like it. Just as you like it when I call you Sweets."

Don't stomp your foot. Don't stomp your foot, I tell myself, though the urge to throw a tantrum builds as the gleam in his eyes brightens.

"Right, Violet?" Jamie prompts me to talk, but I'm sick of talking.

All the warmth that surrounded my heart when he called me *my love* minutes ago travels south. My foot lifts; instead of responding by stomping away from him, my feet carry me into his arms.

"V?" Jamie grunts out as I collide with his chest.

Needing him to shut up, I stand up on my tingling tippy toes and kiss him. As if in muscle memory, my arms rise and wrap around his neck, not allowing him to pull back. I need this. I need him.

He responds with so much passion I have to force my feelings down even harder. *Just sex,* I remind myself while the angel on my shoulder rolls her eyes.

Jamie's hands are heavy on my hips as he yanks my center right into his growing erection. Delighted, I grind against him and moan a high-pitched noise that *begs* for more.

I may have been crying moments ago, but now I'm ready to weep for a whole new reason. Except it's not new. Jamie does this to me frequently. He plays with my heart just as often as he plays with my pussy.

Lust drives my actions, leading me toward my next mistake. I release his neck to grab the hem of his shirt. My body immediately misses the warmth of his hands as they snatch my wrists.

"Violet, no."

Annoyance comes roaring back to the surface, and in its wake is a fresh dumping of tears that I can barely hold at bay. "Why?" I grit out.

Jamie looks pained as he peers down at me. He's trying to read my mind or at least pick up on where my change in behavior came from, but this is new territory for him. Heck, it's new for both of us. All I know is I need him to take my thoughts away and burn them in a—

"Because we need to talk, Sweets," Jamie says, trying to slam the door on my libido.

Shaking my head rapidly, I deny his claim. "No. Jamie, I can't talk anymore. I'm tired of talking. I'm tired of all the thoughts inside my head. Please just make me feel something *good*."

His posture melts ever so slightly, but still he hesitates to give in to me. I'm very aware that I could play this man like a fiddle to get what I want—his cock—but I'm trying to change. I want to be better.

"But are you okay?"

Holding in my laughter is hard, and my lips twitch anyway. What a dude thing to ask. "No, you sweet, sweet man. I am not okay. Which is whyyyy," I drawl, pressing my pelvis into his again, "I need you to make me feel better."

Okay, maybe I manipulated the conversation with my body like I usually do, but damn it I want him to press me into his bed and have his way with me.

Taking a chance on something I rarely do, I drag my nails across his scalp and tug his hair tie free. Curly brown locks tumble around his jaw, and as I shimmy forward, his long hair helps to block out the world.

Jamie shudders and dips his head so his nose tickles mine. "As soon as my cock is inside of you, Violet, you aren't leaving."

"Fine," I agree immediately. I've already broken my rule about spending the night here, might as well get over the fact that Jamie has my heart firmly in his gentle grip.

He pulls back an inch and looks me in the eye. "That had more than one meaning, but we'll go with just sleeping over for now. Let me know if you lift the talking ban," he teases, then seizes my lips in a kiss that steals any response I might have had.

My tummy swoops and flutters as he drags me into his bedroom. Stumbling around his sure feet, I laugh with surprise and happiness as he manhandles me. Fingers graze the underside of my tits, making my nipples tingle and beg for him. His teeth nip at my lips like he just can't help himself from taking a bite of me.

He's passionate, and judging by the hard outline of

his dick, he's excited. But of course, Jamie focuses on me. On swirling his tongue around mine the way I love and tickling the side of my neck one moment, then grabbing my ass the next. He's riling me up, chasing my pain away.

Jamie always gives me what I need.

My jeans are shoved down my hips, and as soon as the cool air breezes through the gap between my thighs, I shiver. He drops to his knees, already mesmerized by the wetness he aches to taste, but I need more than his tongue right now. I need his cock deep inside me, punishing and thick. I need him to stretch me wide and demand I remember him for all eternity.

I *really* need him. So while he's busy undressing and putting a condom on, I rush away with my pussy pulsing. I launch myself onto his bed face first, ass up, ready for him to fuck me into oblivion.

"No!" Jamie growls just as a slap rings out. Soon after, a stinging sensation lights up my ass cheek. "Naughty."

With more force than I was ready for, Jamie flips me onto my back and slaps my bare pussy. "AH!" Fire encompasses my clit, forcing the ache to burn brighter and steal my vision.

Fingers engulf my throat, making my eyes fly open in surprise. When my eyesight clears, I lock eyes with Jamie's intense ones. "This first time tonight may be hard and fast because you clearly need me to fuck the feelings out of you, but don't get it twisted, my love. You'll feel me in every single part of you. For that, I need your eyes and your luscious lips."

He grins all kinds of naughty and proud of himself. "Both sets."

"Idiot," I snort, but I'm quickly cut off with his thumb being forced into my mouth and him demanding I suck while he releases his heavy cock.

"Fucking hell, Sweets," he groans, swiping the head of his dick through my folds. My eyes roll into the back of my head at the simple contact only for his thumb to dive deeper and gag me in warning. I love when he stuffs my holes full and commands my body with his desire.

With my eyes solely on Jamie's face, I pay attention to the euphoria that alters his features into a look so tense yet relieved. I barely register the burn of his cock stretching me open—my body is accustomed to his at this point.

"Touch your clit before I lose my fucking mind, Violet."

Gasping around his thumb when Jamie presses his free hand on my stomach so I feel every inch of him, I do as he says. Giving me three hard and fast thrusts helps my nipples scrape against my bra. Then he slows to a pace that most definitely tortures him, but he knows it's what I need to orgasm.

Too much stimulation just distracts me from my task. I like to feel every drag of his cock inside of me as my walls begin to ripple and tug on him like he can't ever get close enough.

His hips swivel and his abs ripple. I don't know where to look, but the longer I eye fuck his body, the faster my fingers rub my clit.

Needing more, I reach a touch further so the pads of my fingers thrust between my lips and warm my clit. The drag of my touch gives me the perfect friction while Jamie pulls my bra down with one free hand and plucks one needy nipple.

"Fuck, I'm gonna suck on these later. I'll mark them and maybe fuck them. Look at them," he growls, and I have no choice but to follow his instruction. Looking down, I watch my tits bounce. It's sexy watching my body as I flick my clit and hold Jamie in my pussy.

"Fucking look. Your nipples are practically aching for my tongue and these?" He pulls his thumb from my mouth to grab both of my boobs. Pushing them together, he groans. "These are begging for me to slip my slippery cock between them and fuck 'em like I do your tight cunt."

Oh wow. I'm a panting mess, the slick sounds of his cock dragging through my wetness a hot soundtrack to his imagination. Biting my lip, I can picture it. The way he would glide between my boobs and reach for my mouth.

Jamie's hips snap forward like he can't control himself. It pulls my focus, but it feels incredible. "And these," he hisses, plucking my lip from between my teeth, "would love for me to splash my cum all over them because they're slutty enough to take anything they'll get."

Gasping, I arch my back, but he quiets me by stuffing his thumb back in my mouth. Like it always is with Jamie, my orgasm climbs so fucking high I feel like my muscles won't ever relax again.

This time is like no other. Well, that's not true. Because this time, we lock eyes as my pussy convulses around his hard length after a few minutes of his patience and my intent to reach my highest peak.

"Mhmmm," he rumbles, then pulls his thumb from my mouth. "Now fucking scream, my love."

I do him one better. I scream his fucking name like he deserves. "JAMIE!"

Twenty-Seven

NATE

My skin feels tight, and no matter how I move or stretch, I can't get the feeling to go away. The loud hum of my miter saw doesn't help drown out my thoughts. I abandoned my whittling set a while ago once I realized I definitely did not need downtime to process all the shit that's happened the past few weeks.

Fucking hell, it's only been like two and a half weeks since we met Jamie. So much has thrown me for a loop I'm surprised I can still man my power tools without losing a damn finger.

I'm not being smart in allowing muscle memory to guide me as I cut materials, but I just can't seem to give work all of my focus. Scratch *smart;* it's fucking dangerous.

Pissed with myself for being so irresponsible with my tools, I power down the saw and step away from my workbench. Unable to control myself, my feet take me to my phone.

Tapping the screen, disappointment fills me when I see Jamie hasn't responded to my messages. Plural. It's been two days since the disaster at the restaurant, and still he won't fucking answer me.

I'll never be able to wipe the complete despair on Violet's face from my mind. She was lost in so much sadness when she slipped into her fight-or-flight mode that I froze for a moment too long.

Maybe if I had reached for her hand or stood to hold her sooner, she wouldn't have slipped so far into her panic.

The fact that Ellis and I caused her to feel so horrible doesn't sit right with me. Fuck that. I feel like our actions are dragging me to hell, giving me constant heartburn with how much the organ stutters in sadness.

My fingernails dig into my palms as I replay our interactions with Violet. It's unfair to blame Ellis for all of it, but he does need to take accountability for his fucking behavior.

Speak of the devil. The heavy door opens and slams closed behind me, echoing through the garage.

"Hey, are you coming in for dinner?" Ellis asks, sounding a little confused. I saw his text telling me that the pork chops were ready, but I chose to ignore him.

"In a bit," I grunt out, not looking at him. I'm afraid if I do, I'll snap. He doesn't deserve my anger if he feels bad for what he said to Violet. What if he doesn't feel bad though?

"Nate?" Ellis sounds closer. "You alright?"

I don't have a second to breathe before his words hit me right in the gut, forcing me to spew out all of my frustrations. Whipping around, I pierce him with a glare and my words. "Are *you*?! Because I sure as hell am not after witnessing you trigger an innocent woman over and over again!"

Rearing back, Ellis looks like he might be sick. His brown eyes look hurt, almost sucking me in, but I stand firm because I'm furious.

Like a fucking asshole, he stands his ground too. Except his tone is much softer, sadder and genuinely sounds a little lost. "Violet isn't innocent..."

Growling like a beast, I force myself to stay in place. I will not punch the man I love. "She may have broken our hearts, but it's our own fucking fault for turning to anger instead of understanding. Violet is a *victim*!"

"Don't fucking look at me like I'm the only one who was hurt and pissed at her!" Ellis bellows, but his eyes look red like he's on the verge of crying, which makes me pause and let him continue. "I wasn't the only one who laughed about fucking around with Jamie to get back at her! I'M NOT THE ONLY BAD GUY!"

I watch my best friend, my eternal love, slam a fist into his chest. That pained move combined with his words makes my breath stutter.

"I'm. Not. A. Bad. Guy." Ellis changes his wording and says it quietly, slowly, like he's trying to force himself to believe his words.

"Damn it," I curse and rush forward to hug him. He doesn't break down in tears, but he does swing his arms around me and holds on to me like I'm his lifeline.

I don't say anything for a few minutes. Gathering my thoughts before I speak this time is really important because I'm now realizing just how fragile Ellis is feeling. Hell, he's been fragile ever since we saw Violet at the coffee shop. I just really fucking wish his fragility didn't make him sharp when he breaks. But that's hard for me to ask of him when it's who he is.

Fuck. I came at him guns blazing and throwing out accusations. Just like he did with Violet. He's right—he isn't the only one who made bad choices and treated others poorly.

The thing about heartbreak is that it can change brain chemistry. My required psychology course in college taught me that dopamine and neurotransmitters are affected, altering pain and attachment. This can lead to intense emotions or withdrawal. Obsessive thinking, grief, anxiety, and depression are all symptoms of a breakup. We experienced them all.

Ellis never knew such pain until Violet shattered our future by running away. He lived a slightly sheltered, loving life with encouraging parents and two younger sisters who adore him.

When Violet ghosted us, Ellis changed. Of course I've loved him the same and even more through the heartache, but sometimes competing with his heavy emotions triggers my own.

I may be the leader in our relationship, but I'm human too. My feelings get the best of me sometimes as well. I'm not just a dominant machine that keeps my man in line and loved. I need something similar in return. Something I think Jamie might be for me if he gives us a chance.

Together when in pain, Ellis and I have a high probability of weaving toxicity. Which we did after we saw Violet and Jamie at the coffee shop. It was clear they were in some kind of relationship. Add a little alcohol to our open wounds? Well, we fucked up. *Bad.*

"I'm sorry, darling," I coo in his ear, letting the emotion slip through a little so he can hear my truth. "You're right. You aren't a bad guy. Neither am I. We made a bad choice fueled by anger. But," I hesitate, not wanting to sound too sensitive or weird.

I have a beard, I cut wood for a living, and I wear big bulky work boots everywhere I go. I'm outwardly masculine, which always makes me hesitate to share thoughts or feelings that might seem more attributable to a female. Societal norms for someone who looks like me do not include knowledge about feelings or vast insight. At least in my experience. I was made fun of in high school and college for expressing myself because no buff kid with a lot of hair should *feel* apparently.

"But?" Ellis encourages, knowing I'm struggling a bit.

I take a deep breath, accepting that I'm in a safe place with my partner. "But there's more than anger. Honestly, I don't even think I'm mad at her anymore. I'm sad, Ellis. I miss her."

Ellis pulls back and studies me. "I miss V too. But I don't think the girl we fell in love with exists anymore."

"She does," I reply resolutely. "Violet's a victim whose trauma forced her to retreat and withdraw. I believe she's still in there. We saw it before we interrupted her date with Jamie, remember?"

He nods slightly, but there's still a heavy dose of

uncertainty in his eyes. Honestly, I really do see the girl we knew in the older version we keep hurting. She has purple streaks in her hair for fuck's sake. If her quirkiness still exists, then other aspects are still there.

Slumping against my chest again, Ellis groans. "I miss her so much, Nate."

I palm the back of his head and allow my sadness to swallow the anger inside me. "I know. Me too. The least we can do is relieve her of the guilt she showed us the other day. We need to tell her we forgive her. Maybe even that we miss her."

"Even if she never wants to see us again?" Ellis mumbles into my dusty shirt.

Nodding, I answer him. "Even if she doesn't want to see us again. We need to set her free, darling."

"Okay," Ellis whispers, sounding worried.

I'm scared too, but one of us needs to stand tall for a bit, and Ellis slumped over before I could so it's up to me. "We'll go see Jamie tomorrow and try to convince him to get us into contact with Violet."

Ellis snorts and shakes his head, obviously feeling as hopeful as I am. We'll be lucky if Jamie even opens the door to see us.

Twenty-Eight

JAMIE

With my eyes closed, I imagine the warm water circling the base of my hardening cock is actually Violet's little tongue. Just thinking about her is enough to make me tremble and act like a fucking teenager in the shower.

She's coming over soon, and my body can't control itself and wait for her before it starts getting greedy.

Groaning, I grip the back of my neck and tilt my face into the spray. I can wait for Violet to give my cock the attention it craves. Or if she doesn't want to tonight, that's fine too. I'll just have to fuck my fist as soon as she leaves.

Shaking my head at myself, I finish rinsing away the suds clinging to my skin. After a day at work touching too many bodies as I tatted them, I *needed* to shower before Violet came over.

I'm not sure what she wants to do tonight. A few weeks ago, if she had texted me at five in the afternoon asking to come over I would have immediately thought she was looking for sex. Now I'm not so sure. We went on a date. She's slept over. *Shit!* I took her on a date and didn't ask her out again.

"Goddamn it," I scold myself and turn the shower off.

I'm such a dumbass. Violet doesn't know I have plans for our birthday in a few days. Does she think I don't want to date her because I haven't asked again?

As I'm contemplating the odd situation I've put myself in, I rub my towel against my scalp. When I bring my arms back down to wrap the towel around my waist, the sound of knocking rings through my apartment.

Confused, I cover my goods and leave the bathroom. I told Violet to just walk in since I needed to hop in the shower. *Maybe I locked the door.*

My frown only deepens as I swing the door open to usher my sweet woman inside. Mainly because the two people on my doorstep are *not* Violet, and I'm not entirely sure I want to talk to Ellis and Nate.

"Okay, wait." Nate puts his hands in the air as if in surrender. Ellis glances over at him and frowns but otherwise keeps his sass to himself when Nate continues. "I see the look on your face. You're not happy to see us, and we get it. But can we please talk?"

My forehead throbs with a building headache just looking at them. I can fucking *feel* Ellis devouring me with his eyes, reminding me I'm naked beneath my towel.

Motherfucking son of a—

"It's about Violet," Ellis adds, sounding far more reserved than I've heard him before. "Please, Jamie."

Teeth clenched, I eye them. I haven't said a goddamn word yet they seem to know exactly what to say to wrap me around their fucking fingers. Ellis eyeing my abs and watching the water drip between my pecs disarms me a little too.

Shit.

"You have five minutes," I grit between my teeth and step aside so they can enter. Surveying the hallway to ensure Violet isn't here yet, I close the door and turn around. Their low muttering comes to a halt when the door snicks shut.

I fucking *hate* how the sexual tension immediately snaps into place. What a cliché right? I should hate them, yet I'm eager to pound Ellis' ass while Nate fingers mine.

Crossing the space quickly, I hide my growing erection behind the island. My placement also serves to put some space between us. Putting clothes on right now is low on my list because I have to get these two the fuck out before Violet gets here.

Ellis smirks, and Nate slaps his ass in warning. My own lips twitch because I desire their relationship. I love their dynamic even if I despise their attitude toward the woman I love.

"Right," Ellis grunts, palming his sore ass cheek. "We want to apologize—"

My frown comes back with a vengeance. "I'm not the one you need to fucking apologize to, Ellis."

"If you'd let me fucking finish, *Jamie*—" *Whack!* "Ow!

Fuck, stop spanking me. Or at least alter cheeks so they're even."

"Don't fret." Nate rolls his eyes. "I'm sure you'll be an ass twice more, *then* I'll make it even. Don't be a prick. We're not here to fight." Nate says to me, "Even if Ellis makes it seem that way."

Crossing my arms, I bite my tongue. I'll let them speak their piece, then they can leave. The more I interrupt, the longer this will take.

Ellis rolls his eyes but nudges his shoulders back in confidence. "We really need to apologize to Violet. Acting out of anger is always easier, but the more we really paid attention to her, the faster we realized she would never intentionally hurt us. We would appreciate your help in getting in contact with her. Again, to apologize, not antagonize. We understand she too was a victim of what happened to Blue, and she lives with her own scars. We just wish she had let us battle alongside her."

My eyebrows rise with each word he says, and now I can't keep my mouth shut. "Did you practice that speech?"

To my complete joy, Ellis blushes. "I—Yes." He sighs.

"I made him." Nate chuckles. "His mouth runs away from him sometimes, so he needed clear boundaries."

While humor makes me want to smile, I think about something that pisses me off. "So you didn't actually mean it? Your boyfriend gave you a script, and you just pushed through it to get what you want?"

"What the fuck?!" Ellis looks surprised and offended. "No, asshole. Those are my words, and I meant them with my whole heart. I feel really fucking horrible for how I've treated Violet. Seeing her cry and freak out because of *me* was a wake-up call. I'm trying to be better."

I don't know Ellis very well, so I'm having a hard time letting him near my woman because of what I *do* know. But he seems genuine in what he's saying right now.

"I'll help you," I relent, looking both of them in the eye. I'm pleased to see the hope and happiness bloom in their eyes. No malice or odd glint to make me question their motives.

"Thank—"

I cut Nate off. "On one condition. I'll be there the whole time."

Ellis butts in, sounding offended once again. "We won't hurt her."

I raise a brow that says *you already have,* and he looks away. "While that might be true, Violet needs me too. I walked away the other day at the restaurant, and you triggered Violet."

"It wasn't intentional," Ellis protests, but it's weak.

"Exactly," I confirm. "You definitely know more about the woman Violet was seven years ago, but I know her now. I was sidelined and only offered a window into who she is, but believe me when I tell you I know more about who she is, what she needs, and what might send her running."

They share a look, then nod at me. Nate adds something important that I wholeheartedly agree with. "If she asks you to leave, you'll respect her choice to be alone with us."

I smile, feeling our dominant energies swirling around each other in an attempt to coexist. It's hot not knowing who might top in different scenarios. *And now my dick is hard. Fuck.*

"I think he liked your demanding tone, babe," Ellis teases, eyeing me. Groaning, I roll my eyes and watch as Ellis prowls toward me so damn slowly. There's plenty of time for me to stop him, yet I don't. Something about his bratty, teasing, ridiculously sassy attention drives me crazy in a good way. Especially after he opened up about his feelings, I'm feeling incredibly attracted to him right now.

My dick twitches, and his eyes immediately drop to the rising tent in my towel as he rounds the island. Stealing a quick glance at Nate, I see he's resting his elbows on the counter and his dark eyes are filled with lust.

Ellis' large hand sliding around my waist brings my focus back to him. His smile slips as he presses his crotch against mine. Eyes heating, his challenge melts into need. But I'm not doing shit for him right now. Not until he fixes things with Violet.

"Not so funny now, huh?" I taunt, voice thick with need and the desire to bend him over and show him who's in charge.

Click.

"Jamie! I'm here! Oh."

Violet.

Journal Entry

Fact or lie? Fact/Ramble version.

I turn twenty-six this weekend. Fact.

Jamie turns thirty on the same day. Fact.

I've turned down his offer to celebrate four years in a row. Fact, and I feel bad about it.

He hasn't mentioned celebrating with me this year. Fact.

I have plans that are a surprise from Cassidy. Fact.

I'm thinking about celebrating with Jamie after Cass. Surprising fact.

He hasn't asked me out again though. Fact.

It worries me a bit. Fact.

It makes me overthink. Fact.

I miss him. Fact.

It's only been a day and a half since I saw him. Fact.

I've kept myself busy with planning my next work trip. Fact.

It hasn't helped keep the anxiety at bay. Fact.

It's almost February, and I'm starting to stress about Valentine's Day plans. Fact.

I actually want to celebrate with Jamie. Fact.

I'm worried he will want to spend it with someone(s) else. Kinda fact.

Overall, I'm feeling pretty anxious. Fact.

I'm heading over to Jamie's to hopefully calm some of my worries. Fact.

Twenty-Nine

VIOLET

"Oh."

Jamie literally chokes and tries to step away from Ellis who won't release him. As if I just walked into a lion's den, I slowly hang my purse on the hook by the door. Jamie's state of undress is the main reason I close the door, but I'm not sure I'll be staying.

"Should I go?" I ask, taking in the three of them. Sheesh, the sexual tension in here is wild, and I have to admit that seeing Ellis with his hands on Jamie makes me a little squirmy but also sends my anxiety skyrocketing.

Jealousy, uncertainty, and horniness make my hands tremble ever so slightly. One thing I miss the most about the bubbly girl I used to be is how confident I was.

If there weren't feelings involved, I'd probably whip my shirt off and seduce them into action. Except, that's not what I'm doing because I'm pretty sure I'm in love with Jamie, and all the love I had for Nate and Ellis never received its closure or found an end.

Thus, I'm freaking out on the inside. I don't know where I stand with any of them, especially when I saw the way Jamie melted into Ellis before he noticed me.

Maybe I should go...

"NO!" Jamie shouts, panic lighting up his eyes as he tries to get to me. Although I know for a fact he could break free from Ellis' hold, he just doesn't want to.

"Alright," I drawl, attempting to pull up my big bitch panties and deal with this. While I remove my jacket, I question what I just walked in on. "What exactly am I looking at here?"

"Ellis pushing boundaries." Nate throws Ellis under the bus so easily.

I nod, understanding as I kick off my shoes. "Jamie likes to do that too."

Bantering with Nate relaxes me just a bit, but I'm still nervous as heck. *Fake it 'til I make it.*

"Shit," Ellis grunts, and I watch in fascination as he thumps his forehead onto Jamie's shoulder. He seems so comfortable when he looks up at the man I'm falling in love with. "They're always going to gang up on us, aren't they?"

What an oddly intimate statement. *Always?*

"Probably," Jamie murmurs, looking down at Ellis with a frown on his face. Their lips are inches apart, and just as I think they're about to kiss, my shuddering breath snaps Jamie out of his trance.

"Fuck," Jamie literally shakes himself, which dislodges Ellis. "V, it's not—"

"What it looks like?" I finish for him, damning the ball in my throat for making my voice sound so tight. *Don't cry, don't cry, don't cry.*

Jamie looks worried as he walks toward me. "Nothing was—"

"Going to happen?" I finish for him while eyeing his boner.

Nate snorts and struts into Jamie's living room. *Why does he look so natural in this space?* "Does she always complete your sentences?"

Jamie ignores the man and stares at me. Thankfully, he's stopped coming toward me, and hasn't touched me. I feel a little nauseous about the idea of him touching me right now since Ellis just had his hands on him.

Yet, I'm also a little annoyed he *won't* touch me.

I raise a brow and cross my arms. Careful not to wrap them around my waist so I don't look as insecure as I feel, I cock my hip to hide behind my sass.

"Violet," Jamie starts, shifting toward me. I'm not surprised when his hard cock slips through the crack of his towel. "Fuck. Be right back."

As Jamie rushes down the hallway to his room, Ellis watches him go. "Did you see how red his face was?" Ellis asks me with a shit-eating grin on his face.

My heart twinges, but I force my arms to relax. Ellis is like a dog with a bone. If he so much as sees any kind of feeling on my face, he will sniff out its origin and demand its context.

"I did," I confirm, avoiding his probing gaze. Instead of taking Nate's offer of sitting on the couch beside him, I take the solo recliner by the window.

Their gazes stay on me as the minutes go by, but neither man says anything. Shocking, especially for Ellis. Hopefully it looks like I feel indifferent as I watch the snow fall through the orange light of the street lamps.

Jamie's steps sound hurried, drawing my attention to the room at last. "Thank fuck you're still here," he breathes, rushing to me.

Tingles race from the kiss he places on my forehead to the tip of my nose. Blinking, I find myself studying his facial expression as he pulls back and seats himself on the armrest beside me.

Walking in, I immediately felt like an intruder. Like a fourth wheel. Jamie's actions just now rewire my brain, offering comfort and the reassurance I need that I still have a place here. With him.

"Alright," Jamie announces, voice hard as he acknowledges the other two. "I'm going to talk first, then you may have the floor."

Ellis and Nate nod, but I'm frowning. "What about me?"

"You just sit there and look pretty," Ellis replies with a wink.

"Damn it," Jamie mutters and takes over before I can spit something rude. "Ellis. Less condescending. Especially when I know you're itching to hear what she has to say to you."

Ellis blinks. "I was just teasing."

Nate sighs and grabs the back of Ellis' neck. "Not the

time for jokes, remember? We have a lot of work to do before you can try to make her laugh."

"Sorry, Violet. Please interrupt us at any time. I really was just trying to lighten the mood. I'm nervous as hell and—fuck, now I'm rambling and ruining everything. Somebody else go."

A short while ago Ellis made fun of Jamie's blush; now he's the one with fiery red cheeks and shifty eyes. My gaze is slow to move to Jamie even as he starts talking about how he didn't invite the other two over. There's a new complexity in Ellis that wasn't there before. He always felt things the most out of the three of us, and his coping mechanism always resorted to rambling or blurting things without thinking.

That hasn't changed, it seems, but Ellis has an edge I'm not used to, and it scares me. I never know when he'll snap at me or accuse me of something. Maybe it's not fair to him considering this is only the third time I'm seeing him, but he's made an impression. Not a good one. His lack of filter makes him seem cruel when he's mad, and I don't like it.

"Alright, you go." Jamie gestures to Nate and Ellis.

Total shock ripples through me when they both stand up and kneel at my feet. Nate starts with his soulful eyes locked on mine. He doesn't dare touch me thankfully. "We're sorry for how we've been treating you, Violet."

I feel my eyebrows pull together, but Ellis picks up where his partner left off. "We've been holding on to a lot of hurt that was easier to morph into anger. We never should have taken it out on you. Honestly," he murmurs, and reaches out to touch my knee. The contact makes my breath hitch. "We should have hugged you and told you we were never letting you go now that we found you. Please forgive us."

I'm stunned absolutely speechless. *Why the fuck are they talking about hugging me and never letting me go? I broke their hearts, and I'm definitely not the same person I used to be.*

"You're confused," Nate observes with a sad nod. "That's our fault. We've made you question our words and feelings. You must have whiplash. But the honest fucking truth is that we miss you so damn much."

There are many paths in front of me, and I've already proved I'm terrible at making decisions. So of course, I stick to the road I know best.

"I forgive you. Really, I understand why you must have hated me. I do too." I shrug, as if I didn't just implode our conversation with my self-hatred.

ELLIS

W*hat the fuck did she just say? Violet hates herself?* That's far more fucking concerning than trying to convince her that Nate and I don't hate her.

My gut is protesting the gentle look she's giving me. In no way should she look so calm while spouting the shit she just did. The longer the silence drags on, the more her face shifts with worry.

I can practically feel the anger rolling off of Nate beside me. Hell, my teeth might turn to dust any second here from how hard I have them clenched.

Unable to form words, I snap my focus to the one person who *might* deserve my anger. Jamie. "Did you know she felt this way?" I grit out.

I swear to god, if he tells me he knew, I might punch him. We all know I'm not the most dominant man in the room, but it's common fucking sense to put an end to negative self-talk and feelings immediately with your partner. You're supposed to build them up, show them they're more than what they think, and help them see how amazing they truly are. How long has he let her fester in this horrible feeling?

Jamie looks absolutely gutted. So much so that he doesn't even spare me a glance since he's so locked in on staring down at Violet. "My love, look at me," he pleads softly.

Violet shimmies in her chair and leans back to look up at him. "Yeah?"

"You don't mean that, do you?" Okay, I no longer feel the need to punch Jamie. He looks like Violet just told him something truly devastating.

"I mean," Violet murmurs, glancing at me and Nate still kneeling in front of her. I squeeze her calf to give her some reassurance. "Yes. I don't really care for who I've become, but I've been working hard to find the parts of me I miss."

Be still my breaking heart.

Jamie reaches for her and tucks a lock of hair behind her ear. Envy scratches at my breastbone—I would like to feel their ease of intimacy. As much as I like fucking with Jamie, I hate how he freezes when I'm near now. And Violet...I saw her flinch when I first grabbed her leg.

Jamie looks ready to go to war with her demons. I can't say I blame him, because Nate and I will be right fucking there with our swords and arrows. *Cool weapons only.* "Violet—"

"Please don't try to force me to shake the thoughts away," Violet interrupts, sounding stern. "They're mine and have been incredibly motivating to open up to you. I used to be a very happy, open book kind of girl, and I'm trying to find that again. So please just leave it. I swear to let you know if my icky thoughts get out of hand."

I know she's only talking to Jamie, and promising him these things, but goddamn it, I plan to do whatever I need to do to make her include me.

It's taken about forty-five minutes for my adrenaline to settle. After Jamie agreed to give Violet the mental space she requested, Nate and I slowly moved away from them.

We sat back on the couch, and I ordered pizza while Jamie offered to get everyone a beer. Well, Violet received a White Claw. Once again I was struck by their closeness because I learned Jamie has a whole shelf of things Violet likes in his fridge.

He's practically moved her into his kitchen, and she doesn't bat an eye at it. I half wonder if she even realizes.

Dinner has been a silent affair, but now that we've polished off the slices, the air shifts. Nate tucks me into his side, and I curl my legs up on the couch beside me. I'm shocked Jamie hasn't kicked us out, actually. But if I'm here, I have no problem getting comfortable.

"So Violet," Nate says and continues even when she jumps and eyes him warily. "What do you do for work?"

Jamie smirks and leans back against the wall. With him sitting on the floor across from us, it gives me the perfect view to read his facial expressions. His reaction to Nate's question makes me excited.

"Um. " Violet sips her drink, seeming to need a moment before sharing. "Do you know what a ghost-writer is?"

"Like people who write books for the authors but don't get credit or share their name?" Nate clarifies.

Violet nods. "Yeah, well, I guess you could say I'm a ghost photographer."

"What?" I gasp, sitting upright. "That's so cool!"

She blushes, but Nate steals the happiness from our interaction with his next question. "So nobody knows it's the amazing Violet Bennett behind the images? Everyone thinks it's someone else?"

"Yeah. I want nothing to do with social media or the spotlight. I've had enough to last a lifetime, and I learned my lesson." Her voice shifts to monotone, making me anxious.

Nate doesn't let it go even though it's obvious she's shutting down."V—"

"So I take monthly trips and do a lot of hiking, which I've always loved. Only now I take my camera with me and take the images that feel good. Then I load them up and send them to my employer."

"Who posts your stuff? What's their handle?" I'm so invested. I'm eager to see the work she's done.

Jamie snorts, and my hope fizzles when he says,

"I've tried to find that out for four years. Good luck getting her to tell you."

Violet rolls her eyes and tucks her legs beneath her. My heart pitter-patters happily at the relaxed way she's presenting herself. "Jamie's right. I also take images for a few businesses' social media."

"Can you tell me which ones those are?" Batting my eyes at her, I try to put her at ease. I don't want her to think she has to tell us everything, but I need her to know I'm curious about her life.

She smiles a little at me, and I swear I die on the spot. Violet actually looked happy to have me near for a moment! How could I ever have convinced myself I hated her?

"I work for three places in Detroit while I'm in town. Club Surreal is a nightclub. Strands and Stories—a hair salon. And most frequently is a coffee shop. Espresso Yourself."

"Oh we've been there!" I blurt out not thinking about the repercussions of sharing that piece of information.

Nate pokes my back, and I fight like hell to keep the blood from draining from my face. Violet can't know we saw her and Jamie there, and that's what set this all in motion. That finding her sitting across from an attractive man sent me into a tailspin of rage and revenge.

My throat closes over as Jamie and Violet wait for me to continue. *Fuck, did my eyes widen in panic?* They must have, because there's no way I could control my worry.

Thankfully, Nate steps in all smooth and ready to cover for me. "When we moved to Ferndale, we were looking for the best places for a date. Espresso Yourself caught our eye. Your photos brought us there, V. They are amazing!"

Violet blushes so prettily, and she takes another sip. "Thank you, Nate. Their coffee and pastries are amazing. I love bringing in more business for them."

I make a mental note to give Nate a lengthy blowjob later. He saved our asses with his explanation and praise.

"When is your next trip again?" Jamie asks this time, and I'm struck by their odd relationship. They're so comfortable with each other and move like they're in love, yet Jamie doesn't know some of the most basic things about her.

Violet frowns and pulls her phone out. She fiddles with it for a few moments, and I imagine she's checking her calendar or something.

Her lips twist in concentration, then she answers Jamie without looking up. "End of February, then another one mid-March."

"How long are you usually gone for?" I ask just as Jamie narrows his eyes at her.

"A week or two," Violet says, still focused on her phone.

Jamie taps her knee. "This will be the longest you've been home in a long time. Then two closely scheduled trips after. Is something going on with your boss?"

Violet glances at him. "They are working on their new vibes, and direction for this year. I won't waste my time taking photos until we have our meeting about what they're looking for."

"Okay." Jamie nods like he gets it. I'm sure he does. He can't create a tattoo design until he knows what his customer is looking for.

"So anyway—"

"What are you doing for your birthday?" I ask at the same time, unintentionally cutting Violet off.

"Well, I was going to ask Jamie if he wanted to go out to eat after I'm done hanging out with my roommate."

"You were?" Jamie looks like a kid who got a load of candy dumped on his lap. "You want to celebrate together this year?"

"Jamie and I share the same birthday," Violet explains before nodding at Jamie. "Please?"

"Of course, Sweets!" Jamie beams and kisses her hand once he steals it from beneath her blanket. "I would *love* to. Thank you."

Jesus. If I wasn't sure before about their love for each other, I would be now. The way they're looking at each other is the same way Nate and I do. The same way Violet used to look at us and us at her.

The night continues with surface-level conversation. Sharing more about our work lives, what brought us to Ferndale, and upcoming vacations. Once the topics fizzle out, leaving us with a strange tension, Nate and I decide it's time to head home.

Maybe in the future we can do something about the tension we felt. Whether it's having a deeper talk, or acting on our attraction, I hope we can make it there.

As much as I want to stay with Jamie and Violet, tonight went way better than expected. So leaving V feeling positive about us is the best choice, especially when she starts to yawn.

I didn't get a kiss or a hug, but Jamie did shake my hand, and Violet offered us a small wave. The small wins are enough for now.

Thirty-One

VIOLET

I feel like I can't breathe.

The unknown is a suffocating void, and the only thing that can give me oxygen is having my mama back.

A flash of a black hoodie rushes past me, making me choke on a terrified scream. I'm not scared for myself, but terrified of what he finds as he crashes to his knees a few yards away from me.

Where's Mama?

I swear I just saw her a few minutes ago. She said she would follow. Mama told me to go inside, so I did. I should have stayed with her. Maybe then she wouldn't be missing and I wouldn't feel like I'm going to die without her.

MAMA! Nothing comes out, only a pained whimper. A plea for someone to fix the mistake I've made. Someone bring Blue back! I need her.

Suddenly my throat begins to burn, and bile rushes past the barrier of anxiety. I turn to hurl into the nearby bush, but

I'm shoved off balance and struck in the hip with something solid.

Vines of horror wrap around my throat, halting the fiery bile where it rose. It feels like my esophagus is burning, which only heightens my fear.

My vision swirls as worried eyes stare down at me. I can't make out who they are, but they aren't helping me anyway.

Just as I lose sight of the murky world around me, the sound of someone talking jolts me awake for a moment longer. "You are the only one who can help yourself, Violet."

My eyes fly open at the sound of the voice ricocheting through my brain. Mama? *I can't fucking speak! I can't shout for her to come get me. Words don't make it further than a terrified croak at the back of my throat.*

Tears blur my vision as I rapidly look around to see her. Maybe Jared was wrong and he didn't find her blood on the ground. Maybe Mama was with me this whole time, and I just got lost. When I'm lost, she's always there.

But she wasn't. She went missing. And it was all my fault.

"Breathe..."

A muffled curse follows Mama's encouragement. "Breathe, my love."

The endearment slams a shocked gasp into my lungs.

"I want Blue!" I scream on my exhale, lunging for the sound of my mama's voice. "I want my mom!"

"Whoa, Sweets..."

Warmth rubs lines up my back, and something encompasses my chin, making me screech and rip to the side. *Where am I? Why am I sitting up?*

"Hey, hey, hey! Careful," the masculine voice warns me right as the touch on my chin snaps to my bicep.

"Is she okay?" a quiet voice asks. "Here." Just as the new voice says that, a lamp is flipped on. *Cassidy.*

As if Cassidy flipped a switch inside of me, I release a big breath and slump forward. With my face in my palms, I finally register the fact that Jamie is sitting on my bed, chatting quietly with my friend.

Once I hear Cass leave and close my bedroom door behind her, I peek between my fingers to glance at the man in my bed. A man who has never once been in here, let alone inside of my apartment.

"I'm too tired to ask," I murmur when he just continues to stare at me.

He winces and moves to petting my thigh. "Sorry, Sweets. Cassidy texted me. You were screaming in your sleep, and she didn't know how to help."

I blink. He should know what I'm going to ask now.

"She has my number because she was helping me plan a birthday surprise for you. Nothing more. I'm glad she had it for tonight," he whispers, plucking my left hand from my face. "What were you dreaming about? Your mom, right?"

Tears immediately fill my eyes as I recall the warped

dream I had. Two different traumatic scenarios wove together to create something truly awful.

"Come here," Jamie coos, tugging me onto his lap so I'm cradled sideways in his arms. "Just please keep breathing. You stopped for a moment there, and it scared the shit out of me."

"I'm so—"

"Don't apologize. Just tell me what your nightmare was about if you feel comfortable to. Or just rest and try to fall back asleep. Here, take a sip." He presses the spout of my water bottle to my mouth, and I greedily suck the cool liquid down.

"Thank you," I sigh once I'm done.

Curling up on him is becoming so natural, and I can't say I'm mad about the trajectory of our relationship. If only there weren't two complicating factors. But Nate and Ellis aren't here right now, so this can be as simple as I want it to be.

I'm just a woman being comforted by the man who owns a part of her heart. *And it's okay*. It's okay because I know I'll never do anything to hurt Jamie, and pushing him away would go against my silent vow to protect him. Once my heart has calmed, I offer him a bit of my trauma.

"I was reliving a mixture of when we found out Mom was missing, and how I felt when I was mugged."

Jamie tenses and hugs me closer. "Fuck, Sweets. We haven't really talked about the mugging, have we? I'm so sorry."

I'm a little confused about why he's apologizing, but

I don't want to get into it right now. Our birthday is tomorrow, and I'd rather not drag us down. "Can we talk about it later? I don't want to rehash everything right now."

"Of course." Jamie is quick to agree and allow me time to process. I appreciate his maturity in knowing when to push me and when to let me be. "Do you think you'll be able to sleep?"

I sigh, knowing it's unlikely. "I'm not sure. You can head home, though. You know, if you want." My tone sounds sad and small, like I don't actually want him to leave. Which is true. Maybe if I weren't so frazzled by the nightmare, I'd be kicking him out and feeling horrified by the fact that he's seeing my depressing bedroom.

"I'm not leaving you," Jamie declares firmly. "Which has multiple meanings again, but for now I'll just say I'm not going anywhere until I know you're okay tonight."

I should tell him that I'm fine and he doesn't need to stay, but damn it feels good to have him here. "Okay," I whisper and wiggle on his lap.

A rumbly sound vibrates through his chest, and I gasp when he slips a finger through the side of my panties. "First, let's take care of your restlessness, hmm?"

I'm pretty sure I was about to say something in response or feel embarrassed about only wearing one of his T-shirts that I stole last week with a pair of bright purple cotton underwear, but everything flees from my mind when his thumb brushes over my clit.

"Jamie," I gasp, arching and spreading my thighs for him so easily.

He shushes me and presses his lips to the top of my head. "Just relax, my love."

My toes curl, and the stretch of the fabric accommodating Jamie's hand heightens my arousal. Just that slight bite of pain along with his finger dipping into my pussy has me thrusting against his expert touch.

"So wet, V. You're doing so well. Breathe in and hold it," he commands so gently I have no issue obeying when he's being so sweet. "Good girl. Now feel your little clit pulse against my thumb. And as I enter your tight cunt, suck me in just a little. *Goood.*"

The breath in my lungs begins to burn, but I'm quickly forgetting the need to breathe as my desire trumps all other bodily functions. His fingers slip and glide inside and outside of me, bringing me to the edge. The encouragement and praise make my lips tingle with the urge to kiss him or express my love for him.

Just as I feel like I'm about to burst, I clench my pussy at the same time Jamie curls a finger against my walls. "Now breathe out, Violet. Now. Breathe for me, my love. Come for me."

My exhale tumbles out of me with a choked cry. Every muscle in my body tightens as if struck by lightning which sends white dancing across my eyesight. Then my whole body slumps with a wave of exhaustion and satisfaction.

"Sweet girl...you sleep now," Jamie murmurs. He moves a little and covers us with my big comforter. "Sleep. I'm not going anywhere."

I really hope he means that because I know when I wake up in the morning, my first instinct will be to reach for him. So as I let sleep claim me, I clutch him just a little tighter. Just in case.

Thirty-Two

JAMIE

I have never been so at peace in my entire life. After so many years, I finally get an inside view of who Violet is.

Except what I'm seeing is *not* her. I think her bland bedroom has been her attempt to block out everything she used to be. There are signs of the bubbly part of her that has slipped through though.

Purple comforter, purple robe, purple panties...Violet definitely had a hard time completely locking herself away. There are small pops of color, but what really stands out are the excessive stacks of notebooks she has on her dresser and on the floor near her bed. She's even using one stack as a makeshift nightstand.

Oh how I fucking itch to crack them open and see if she's used them all. There's one on the actual nightstand beside me with a pen marking a page near the center that really intrigues me.

It's beautiful. White and purple with flowers decorating it. *What does she write about? Are they journals? Windows into her soul?*

The early morning sun highlights my woman sleeping soundly in her bed. I may be beneath the covers with Violet, but I haven't done more than snuggle her and jump awake every so often to check on her.

When Cassidy called me at half past midnight last night, my heart about beat out of my chest. I was already up and tugging my clothes on to get to Violet. There was no doubt in my mind that Cassidy's call had to do with V.

On the speedy drive over here, I kept replaying Cassidy's description of Violet's nightmare. *Thrashing around, crying, screaming, gasping, not being able to wake her up.*

I about busted down their door, tripping through the hallway to get to Violet. Fear and so much determination propelled me forward, but as soon as I kneeled on her bed, a sense of calm washed over me.

It was as if my instincts told me I needed to be gentle and soothing. She was in distress, and no matter how much I wanted to snatch her up to beg her to open her beautiful eyes, I couldn't. She needed my patience, and, fucking hell, I've proven I have enough to last at least five fucking years.

So I did what I felt was best. Then I fingered her because fuck if I knew anything about getting someone back to sleep after such a horrible nightmare.

All I knew while she was in my arms was that I could help her body succumb to the exhaustion her brain was fighting. A new, warm, comforting side of me came rushing to the surface when I touched her. Our intimacy shifted in that moment, and all I wanted to do was praise her for letting me into her bedroom, into her heart, and into her mind.

Sitting here now, counting her dark eyelashes and smirking when she huffs a snore, I think about ways I can get her to let me into her soul.

Breakfast. Worth a shot.

Alone in the women's kitchen, I can't help but worry I'll mess something up. My presence here is meant to be helpful and supportive, not hinder anyone's schedule.

I may be a confident man, but everyone has a weakness and a worry. Mine is Violet and ensuring I give her no reason to push me away.

I thought for half a second this morning that I should leave and not overstay my welcome but decided that was dumb as shit. Violet has been allowed enough space for a few different things. Now that I'm in her home, there's no way in hell I'll leave voluntarily.

Cassidy took one look at me flipping pancakes on her stove and walked right out the door. She wished me luck at least, so I wasn't offended by her disappearance. I'm glad, actually. Violet and I took a new step last night, and today is the day I'll solidify my place in her life.

I hear Violet's bedroom door open before I see her, and I shit you not, I stop breathing for a second. Dressed in my T-shirt, and her purple panties with her hair in half a rat's nest, I completely fall head over heels for Violet.

The times she's slept over at my place, she's always been up before me, and once I see her, she's already looking *proper,* you could say. I love this version the most. Especially the rasp of her voice when she speaks due to snoring all night long.

"Cassidy? Are you making breakfast?" she murmurs, rubbing both of her eyes. When they blink open, they're red and watery. I immediately drop my spatula.

I'm around the counter and lifting her onto it within moments. Ignoring her squeak because of the cold marble on her bare thighs, I grab her cheeks in both of my hands. "Did you have another nightmare? Why have you been crying?"

"I...What? I thought you left," she says, a little stunned.

Worry churns my gut, which is super fucking unfortunate because the bacon burning on the other side of the kitchen smells amazing. "That's why you've been crying? Because you thought I'd left?"

Violet twists her lips, and I notice a drool stain running from the corner of her mouth down to her jaw. *So fucking beautiful.* "Well, you didn't leave, so it doesn't matter."

"Hmm." I cock my head and take a risk to kiss her nose. Every kiss I give her outside of sex feels like a risk, but she's accepted every single one. "It definitely matters, my love. I told you I wasn't leaving."

"I know." Violet blushes but doesn't break eye contact. "You will be if you ruin my bacon."

A bark of laughter escapes me as I rush away from her to be her knight in shining armor. "Anything for you," I say, still laughing. Christ, I love her sass.

"Jamie..." Small arms circle my stomach when Violet hugs me as I flip the bacon. "Happy birthday."

My throat closes over just enough for me to know how much she means to me. With one hand on hers, and the other taking care of her bacon, I repeat her words back. "Happy birthday, my sweet love."

Thirty-Three

VIOLET

There's something refreshing about the silence between me and Jamie. It's peaceful and offers an air of comfortability I never thought would be possible with us.

Jamie is an artist as well, but his focus isn't to stand in awe about the way the sunshine sparkles in the snow; his attention is in the details. So much so that he hasn't been afraid to kneel in a snowbank and study the lines of a dead leaf.

I'm not focused on the sun anymore either. No, I've found myself stealing photos of Jamie. Normally, portraits aren't my forte, but his passion and curiosity about how he can use this experience to enhance tattoos is stunning.

"This is so cool. Violet, come look at this, please."

With his hands on his knees, Jamie's face is inches away from a particularly rough-looking tree. He's studying the bark and tracing his fingers through the grooves. It's impossible to keep my camera from rising to my eye and my finger from clicking the button.

Immediately his head whips around to see what I'm doing. Caught red-handed, I just go with it and continue snapping my shots. His beaming smile jolts me forward and makes me put my camera down.

"Sorry," I apologize and actually walk toward him. "Here I come."

Jamie watches me like a hawk as I sidestep mounds of snow. Once I'm close enough, he reaches out a hand to help me over a prickly bush. I don't need his help, but his actions are sweet. When he tucks me into his front and starts telling me about the depth he could create with some tree tattoos, I feel like crying.

Why have I been keeping myself from experiencing these wonderful things?

"Alright, up you go. We have to keep you moving so you don't freeze." Jamie once again helps me over the small bush as if I'm not a daredevil hiker. I'm a cliff girly, and definitely enjoy the thrill of going off the beaten path.

Humoring him, I let him warm up my hands while my camera rests around my neck. We've started up a hill, and my heart is thumping harder with the slight exertion. Hiking will always be therapeutic for me, and my camera helps me slow down to enjoy the spot I'm at. Internally, I scold myself for not going on a hike sooner this month. With everything being thrown at me, I really freaking needed this.

"Thank you," I murmur, not wanting to disturb the

serenity of nature. "For surprising me on our birthday." We don't need gifts for each other; this is perfect.

Jamie squeezes my hand and looks at me. "Thank *you* for agreeing to spend your day with me, V."

Guilt coils tight in my belly. Glancing up at Jamie, I admit, "I hate you have to thank me for spending time with you. I'm sorry for my distance over the years."

Jamie doesn't let a moment of pause come between us. "Are you here with me now though? Close and ready for more?"

I give him the courtesy of thinking about it for a moment. He's asking me a serious question, and I must handle it with care. "I'm here with you," I whisper in confirmation. "No more distance. But I don't know what *more* means when everything feels so complicated."

"You mean everyone?" he questions, knowing where I'm headed with this.

As he grabs my elbow to help me across a patch of ice, I think about what to say. *The truth is a good start I guess.* "Nate and Ellis really like you. I've seen how you are with them too. They're good for you, and I think you'd be good for them."

"There is no me without you, Violet."

I cringe, my mind taking me to the place I don't really want to go but have to anyway. "Jamie." I sigh, shaking my head. "They hate me. I would just cause more problems if you keep thinking that way."

"And what way do you assume I'm thinking?" He sounds so calm and confident it riles me up just enough to actually have this conversation. At least we're doing my favorite activity during it.

"You think we can all just be one big happy family, the four of us. That's simply not true. Nate and Ellis don't want anything from me. Heck," I huff, throwing my hands in the air. "I think they only forgave me to get in your good graces again."

Now Jamie lets the silence stretch, and this time I hate it. Who knows what exactly I want him to say, but he needs to say something. The longer this goes on, the more my mind will fill in the blanks. *Woohoo for anxiety.*

"Interesting." That's all he fucking says!

I try to tug my hand free, annoyance flaring hot in my chest. When he doesn't release me, words tumble out of my mouth in a case of word vomit. "Really? That's all you have to say? Jamie, I'm willing to share you with them, and as much as I would love to be involved with the three of you, Nate and Ellis wouldn't want that. So I'll just enjoy the time I have with you, okay?"

We've stopped walking, and Jamie turns to step in front of me. His gloved hands pull my winter hat back into place, warming my right ear again. Smiling softly, he presses a gentle kiss to my lips.

"My sweet woman. Violet, there's no *you* sharing *me.* Let me prove to you it's the other way around, please? In no time you'll realize Nate and Ellis still have feelings for you."

I'm already shaking my head, but Jamie continues, still so calmly. "Yes, I like them. I don't like how hotheaded they've been, but I empathize with their hurt. It's true they like me. But their love for you is still very real."

My mouth is wide open. "I feel like we're a couple that's talking about opening our marriage up to them or something."

Jamie barks out a laugh and kisses me again. "Oh how I love the word marriage on your lips. And yes, my love. You can think of it that way because no matter what, it's you and me. Got it?"

I'm a little too dumbstruck by the way this conversation has gone to say much more, so I just nod.

"Good," he hums and kisses me again. "You'll trust me to prove to you this is a very real possibility?"

I nod, entranced by the way he's taking control. My gosh, it feels so nice to just let this go and allow Jamie to handle this twisted situation.

"Beautiful. I'll have rules though."

At that, I roll my eyes. "I may be letting you take the lead, but rules? Come on Jamie, you know I don't follow rules."

Playfully biting at my nose, Jamie laughs and starts our hike again. "I meant for Nate and Ellis. I'll require full respect and kindness when it comes to you. Open communication and total honesty. They've started at a low fucking bar, so they should have no issue rising to the top to be a good partner to you."

"You've thought a lot about this..."

He looks down at me with so much love I choke up a little. "You're my love and my life, Violet. Of course I've thought about keeping you safe, happy, and healthy. If they aren't on board, I won't be throwing any buoys."

I laugh at the cheesy metaphor but am quickly shut

up by a black squirrel cresting the hill in front of us. My gasp is loud enough for Jamie to release me. I feel his eyes on me the entire time I capture my images.

It would take something big to knock me off the happy cloud I've found myself on.

Thirty-Four

NATE

"Better?" Ellis asks, licking his lips and leaning back with his hands on my knees.

"Fuck," I groan, rubbing my face. After such a powerful orgasm down Ellis' throat, I should be feeling relaxed. But I'm not. "No. Shit, I'm sorry, darling."

Ellis rubs my legs a little. "Hey, it's okay. Nothing can compete with the feeling of urgency. Let's go."

When I pull my hands from my face, Ellis steals a kiss and pulls me to stand up. "What?"

He's already dragging me to the front door after pulling my jeans back up. "We're gonna go check on Violet. You really want to see her, make sure she's okay, so that's what we'll do. Plus, it's their birthday, so we *should* go. Maybe this time we'll get her phone number," he grumbles and steps into his boots.

Not one to deny the opportunity to see Violet again, I shove my feet into my shoes, grab my jacket, and rush out the door after Ellis. The usual twenty-minute drive it takes us to get to Jamie's apartment is closer to a half hour as we're getting close to dinnertime and the snow is tripping people up.

I'm itching to get there, and the whole time Ellis drives, he peeks over at me with worry. "Nate, what's going on? You're restless."

I sigh so big it borders on rude. "We don't have birthday gifts and haven't seen them for a few days. We need to be around them more if we're going to solidify our place in their lives."

Ellis glances at me again. "So then why the hell have you locked yourself in your garage? And their gift will deliver next week, so it's fine."

"I have a lot of orders from Christmas, you know that." It's bullshit but also true.

"Bullshit. Why have you been avoiding everything? You've even pulled away from me, which we agreed years ago was never allowed."

Fuck fuck fuck. The guilt that has been eating me alive doubles because not only are we lying to Jamie and Violet, but I've also hurt Ellis.

Steeling myself, I turn in my seat to watch him as he navigates downtown Detroit. "I'm sorry. I just—there's so much I'm worried about. Like what if they find out what we did that set this all in motion? I'm battling that and being angry at both of us for doing something so immature."

Ellis swallows. "I know. Me too. But I *need* you, Nate. We need each other to get through this and move on from it. The more you pull away, the longer it's going to linger."

Nerves have me reaching up and putting my shoulder-length blond hair into a bun. The last thing I need is to feel overstimulated with hair on my neck. "You're right," I acknowledge. "I'm sorry. I'll keep this in mind, darling."

Nodding, Ellis pulls into Jamie's parking garage. Once in a guest parking spot, I grab the front of his jacket and yank him toward me. "Forgive me?" I whisper, needing *someone* to.

"Always," he murmurs.

Ellis melts into my hold, allowing me to give him a possessive kiss that tells him we'll always be a team, even when one of us is being a dumbass.

It's time to figure out how *not* to be an idiot.

Walking into the fancy lobby of the apartment complex, I never thought I'd see Violet backing away from Jamie. In my mind, I figured that man could do no wrong when it came to her, but I guess I was wrong.

Ellis growls low in his throat when we get close enough to see the tears rolling down her cheeks. I have to grab the back of his jacket to keep him from attacking Jamie.

"El, wait. Let them work it out," I murmur in his ear and shuffle us forward so they both know we're here.

When Jamie glances over at us, his eyes show so

much feeling my breath catches in my throat. Worry and desperation widen his gaze and turn his lips down.

"Violet, it's not a big deal, my love," he tries to reason once he turns back to her.

Cringing, Ellis and I both know that was the wrong thing to say.

Violet takes a shuddering breath and raises her chin. "It's a big deal to me!"

"What's going on?" I ask, stepping in because Violet's close to yelling in a public space. And honestly, I don't like that Jamie's hurting her. Someone needs to be there for her to lean on, and I intend to be that person. But to be here for her, I need some information.

Jamie looks at me, slight annoyance now playing in the crinkle of his nose, but he still answers my question. "I told her about my MC friends keeping an eye on her for me to keep her safe."

"Oh, like Bash?" Ellis blurts, and I have half a mind to fucking spank him when Violet looks at us with hurt.

"You knew?" she accuses.

Ellis pales, realizing his mistake. "Bubbles, we thought you knew."

Violet steps away from Ellis now and places a hand on her chest like he struck her. "Don't call me that," she says, pointing at my partner.

"And you," her voice trembles when she turns to Jamie again. "You should have told me a long time ago you were having me followed!"

"It was just for your safety, Violet. You would have told me to stop, but you fucking walked home from my place every weekend in the dark. No, I didn't tell you.

But that was a safety choice I made for *you*." Jamie isn't budging, and while I don't blame him, I think he's coming at this from the wrong angle.

"That's not the point." Violet confirms my suspicion. "I'm mad you kept it a secret. Secrets get people hurt, Jamie."

Fuck. My heart clenches and my brain tumbles through all the hurt Ellis and I could cause if *our* secret ever came to light.

"You *did* get hurt. It's a good thing Bash was trailing you." Jamie reiterates the wrong statement.

"Hey," I interject, stepping forward only to be ignored as Violet snaps.

"That's not the fucking point, Jamie!"

"Then what is the point?!" Jamie does well keeping his voice low, but the exasperation in his tone makes it *feel* like he's yelling.

I'm about to suggest we go upstairs to talk this out when Violet deflates with tears running down her face. "The point is this is just another thing thrown at me that I don't know how to cope with immediately."

Jamie frowns, but it soon morphs from confusion to realization. I feel for the man, I really do, but this was his fault. He sounds pained as he reaches for her.

"Violet—"

Unfortunately for him, his movement triggers Violet to turn to me with big pleading eyes. "Can you take me home, please?"

"Violet," Jamie gasps, like he can't believe what he's hearing.

My heart is in my throat. She's asking me to be her

safe space right now, and, fucking hell, it feels so good. I clear my throat and hold my hand out to Ellis for the keys. "Of course, baby. I'll drive you home."

"Come get me when you're ready," Ellis murmurs to me with a nod of acceptance. He can hang out with Jamie for a while, maybe help him figure out how to fix this.

"Thank you," she whispers, fidgeting with her hands. "I just need time to think," she says to Jamie and gives him a little smile.

Poor fucker looks ready to cry or tie her to his bed, whichever it is, I feel bad for him. This time his loss is my gain.

Jamie seems to gather all of his courage, because he nods. "I understand. I'm very sorry for throwing this at you right now."

"Thank you," Violet offers like the sweetheart she has always been. "Good night. Happy birthday."

"Good night, my love," Jamie responds, sounding so pained I don't want to take her from him at all. Violet shuffles toward me and tugs on the arm of my jacket to get my attention, but Jamie tells me, "Text me when she's safe."

I nod. "Of course." To Violet, I smile and grab her hand to lead the way. "Come on, baby. Let's get you on Ellis' heated seats. They can fix anything."

She nods sadly, seemingly lost in her head already now that I've walked her away from the reason for her pain. That's okay, I'm just happy she feels safe with me for a while.

"You can be as quiet as you'd like, but I'll need your

address somehow," I tease and tickle her cheek to get her attention.

My God, the way she looks up at me as if I'm her hero steals the breath from my lungs. I'll drive her *anywhere* in complete silence as long as she wants to be with me.

Stay with me forever, baby.

Thirty-Five

VIOLET

"You must think I'm overreacting." It's possible I'm projecting how *I'm* feeling. My current worry beyond how overwhelmed I am is how much I hurt Jamie by leaving in the middle of an argument.

Did I run away? Or did I take the space I needed? I feel like I left respectfully and gave him the reassurance I could in the moment. But jeez, a girl can only handle so many curveballs in one month.

"I don't think you're overreacting," Nate replies firmly. I can feel the glances he's giving me as he drives, but I'm too embarrassed about my behavior to look at him.

Swallowing, I try to imagine what he's thinking. "This must bring up all your anger with me, huh? Watching me run away all over again."

"Baby," Nate scolds gently, all the while my heart flips happily at the endearment. "Don't put words in my mouth. No, I wasn't thinking that at all because the clear difference with what just happened with Jamie is you communicated your needs."

"You think so?" This time I do peek over at him because it turns out I'm starving for some reassurance that I'm not ruining everything good in my life.

Nate nods. "I know so. You know what, this was because of Jamie's lack of communication and what I'm guessing was poor delivery before we got there."

"Very poor." With a sigh, I recall Jamie's nonchalant response when I asked him how he knew the guy who saved me when I was mugged.

"Hearing that Jamie kept a secret from you, even if it was one with good intent, must not have felt nice."

Nodding in response to Nate's guess, I find myself wanting to open up to this man like I did in the past. There has always been a comfortable connection of understanding and support about Nate.

Jamie and Nate have strong energies, but while Jamie is wilder and more commanding, Nate exudes calm confidence and a grounding presence. They complement each other very well.

"Violet, are you okay?"

"What?" I snap my head up, realizing I had placed my face in my palms. "I'm so sorry. My mind is messy, and I can't get it to stop."

"It's a good thing you'll be home in a few seconds," Nate assures me, though he sounds a bit disappointed. Once parked, he turns to me with the most open expression on his face. "Can I walk you up?"

Probably against better judgment, I say yes, but I've been struggling with feeling safe walking around at night. Nate provides safety and an easy space to feel my feelings as he escorts me to Cassidy's and my apartment.

"This is me," I murmur, already feeling disappointed about him leaving me here.

"Can I hug you?" Nate murmurs, looking unsure, but at the same time he seems prepared for any answer I could give him.

Tears immediately fill my eyes, and before I can even nod, I'm diving into his wide embrace. A sob explodes from my chest as if I've reached my breaking point. Nothing more can fit inside my head.

"Oh baby..."

"It's too much!" I cry, feeling like my chest is going to explode. The pressure in my forehead and my heart makes me ache, so I cling to him harder.

Nate's large hands rub my back and cradle the back of my head. He surrounds me and holds me up all the while my sanity collapses to its knees.

A creak sounds somewhere, and suddenly I hear Cassidy. "What's going—Oh! Oh shit. Bring her inside."

Nate thanks my friend and doesn't hesitate to lift my feet from the ground. Wrapping them around his waist feels easy, and honestly I don't have any mental capacity to second guess my actions anymore.

I'm too checked out and lost in my suffocating thoughts to listen to their soft voices, but I love the way Nate's chest vibrates against mine. When we were together and excited to meet for the first time, I was so excited about our size difference and to feel his arms wrapped around me.

Now, finally having him, I don't want to let him go. *How could I have ever let him go?!*

"Baby, shhh. You need to calm down before you make yourself sick," Nate coos.

I realize we've stopped moving and my knees are helping to support my weight on the couch. The scent of brownies perks me up a little. *Did Cass make our special brownies?*

Nate chuckles and nudges my chin up so he can see my face. "I'd love to hear about these special brownies, but first you need to take a deep breath."

I'll blame my heated cheeks on all the crying. I don't love when I accidentally mumble my thoughts because they're usually embarrassing.

Embarrassing, like crying all over the man whose heart I broke. Tears well in my eyes as the feeling of being a burden rises.

"I'm sorry." Though I try to wiggle off of his lap, he holds me firm. "I can't believe I did that. Of course you don't want me crying on you. You hate me. But jeez, you are *so* nice for comforting me."

Word vomit. That will get me in trouble every darn time.

Nate's eyes narrow, and though he might be blurry, I can still see the dominance rising to the surface in his features. "Violet. How many times do I have to tell you Ellis and I do *not* hate you? We miss you so fucking much I literally couldn't relax tonight without coming to find you."

I open my mouth, but he's not done. "And I've already told you, you're forgiven. Apologies are not necessary. Especially not for hugging me like I've always dreamed of you doing."

"But I soaked your shirt," I whisper, sniffling.

Nate smiles and raises his hands to wipe my tears away with his thumbs. "Is it weird that I don't want to wash it? So I can keep it as a token of your trust."

Those are big words with deep meanings, so I'm not sure how well I'll be able to comprehend them tonight. I file them away to think about after I snack on Cassidy's brownies.

Instead, I huff a small laugh and slump against him once again. "I miss you too."

Nate sucks in a breath and hugs me so hard I feel my bones creak. "Fuck baby. Thank you. I'm so sorry for how we treated you at first. There was so much heartbreak clouding our judgment."

"I know. It's okay." I mean my words. I'd probably react the same way if our roles were reversed.

Nate stiffens slightly. If I weren't as close to him as I could get, I might not have noticed it. But soon he relaxes and begins to rock us slightly.

"Violet?" he murmurs after a while of me snoozing on his lap. My brain feels calm in his embrace, and that's way more than I can hope for.

"Hmm?" I snuggle deeper, knowing this is about to come to an end.

"You need to get some sleep. But may I take you out for breakfast in the morning? Please. There will be coffee, bacon, and hash browns."

"Cheesy hash browns?" I tease.

"Anything you want."

I smile into his chest. "Then yes. Is it a date?"

"How 'bout we decide that in the morning once you've gotten some rest?"

So thoughtful. As I see Nate out with a whispered goodbye and a lingering glance over his shoulder as he walks down the hall, I decide I really need to call my mom.

Thirty-Six

BLUE

I could scream. Not only because I'm pissed at three men, but because I feel fucking useless. Literally, the scream is building in my throat.

All I want is to hold my kid and tell her everything will be okay. Saying it over the phone isn't the same. Hearing her cry and tell me how confused she is, broke my heart. I know how she feels even though my situation was very different from hers.

She broke two people's hearts. I had mine broken by four men because they disappeared. Ghosted me. Whatever.

Now they're back, and my sweet Violet is trying to keep her feelings buried to give everyone what she thinks they need. I haven't even met this Jamie guy, but I know for a fact he is irrevocably attached to her.

She seems to have accepted that she's in love with Jamie, and maybe it could have been easy, but now there are more factors. Two more, and a whole fuckload of history.

"Do I need to get my shovel?"

I snort into my glass of wine and glance over at one of my best friends, Janine. She's a hardass, and completely amazing. Janine helped Violet a lot before V went on her never-ending road trip, so she would understand my feelings fairly well.

I shake my head and take one more sip. "No shovel this time. Sorry. Violet just told me she's terrified that she has feelings for three men."

"No shit?" Janine's eyes widen a fraction, but I doubt she's all that surprised considering we're watching my *four* men take down my Christmas lights outside.

Sighing, I try not to get too lost in staring at Declan and Felix making out by my glowing snowman. "Yeah. It's complicated too."

"Shocking," Janine scoffs with a grin. "Three dicks and one hole to stick it in? Tough cookies, yo."

Swinging my foot out, I kick her in the thigh and quickly cover back up with my blanket. She laughs, and I can't help but join. "Well, it sounds like the three guys are all together too."

Janine's eyebrows actually fly up this time. "Damn. Go Violet."

Cringing a little at the image, I try to move past the sexual preferences part. I tell Janine about Violet's history with Nate and Ellis, and how things have progressed with Jamie. Janine listens throughout the entire story, and we work some of the tangles out together.

"She has a lot going on. Especially when she just started trying to figure herself out and work on the lingering effects of what happened to you," Janine reflects, sounding concerned and sad.

"I want her to come home," I admit. "If she were here, Roman would make her food, Declan and Jared would make her laugh, and Felix would make sure she never felt the need to cry again."

"Yeah," Janine snorts, "because Felix would need my shovel. No men, no tears, amiright?"

I shush her and roll my eyes. "I want to fix it, Janine. It's tearing me up inside. My bubbly girl, the one who used to dance around my kitchen and take silly videos, disappeared. I love Violet like she's my soulmate, but I want her to grow and find herself again."

Janine nods. "She's been hiding for a long time."

"Exactly! It's my fa—"

"Stop right there," Janine snaps, pointing at me. "We don't say the word *fault* in this family. That word, that *feeling,* is what popped all of Violet's bubbliness. Enough. It's not your fault."

Growling a little, I know she's right, but I still feel so guilty. As a mother, it fucking sucks that I can't whisk away all my daughter's pain. I want her to live happily and love fully.

"That doesn't stop this raging need to fix Violet's problems though." If I were standing, I might stomp my foot. "It *is* really nice that Jamie and her roommate seem to be really supportive and challenge her to grow. I'll need to meet Jamie soon. Maybe invite them for dinner. But they have a lot to figure out, so I'll wait."

Janine pats my foot, smiling at me like she thinks

my rambling is cute. "You just keep answering your phone, Mama. Violet will figure it out."

Yes, she will. I just hope her *figuring it out* doesn't result in a broken heart, three holes in the ground, and Janine's shovel. Those boys better not hurt my girl. If they knew the legion she has behind her, they wouldn't even think about it.

Broken heart or not, Violet will find her way.

Thirty-Seven

ELLIS

Something about the way Jamie's looking at me makes my dick hard. The combination of his clenched jaw, crossed arms, and messy long hair fanning around his cheeks, makes me a little weak in the knees.

"You have my goddamn number. Why the hell can't you fucking call before showing up?"

"Goddamn, hell, fucking." I tick off my fingers to count the number of times he swore. "You must be having a bad morning."

"Ellis," he grits out in warning. "What do you want?"

I sober a little, realizing a bit too late that now is not the time to fuck with him. Well, not with teasing words at least. Probably should have realized as soon as I saw his disheveled appearance.

"Can I come in?" I ask politely, knowing damn well he's alone because Nate is currently on a date with the only person Jamie would want to see right now.

"No."

"Can you bring me home then?" There are really only two options.

Jamie scowls, face turning thunderous. "What the fuck are you talking about?"

Sighing, I squeeze past his tense body and kick off my shoes. "Nate dropped me off on his way to pick Violet up. He's taking her out to breakfast."

The slam of the door and the following silence behind me make the hairs on the back of my neck stand up. I've poked the bear; I'm just not sure which statement triggered this deadly quiet response.

"Jamie?" I'm hesitant to go near him, but I feel bad for the poor bastard, so the least I can do is try to calm him down. "You okay?"

Stance wide and hands fisted, Jamie looks ready to do some damage. "He took my woman on a date?"

"I mean, can't she be our woman? 'Cause you know, we did have her first and all."

Wrong thing to say. Jamie lunges for me, but my agility helps me dive over the back of the couch. "Woah, okay. I'm sorry," I plead, hands in the air as if in surrender.

Jamie doesn't say a damn word, just jumps over the couch like I did. "Shit!" I curse and bolt toward the back hallway. Not a good plan, but I never said I don't love being hunted down.

"When you catch me, will you fuck my ass really good?!" I shout over my shoulder, hoping he will do as I ask.

He still doesn't say shit, but my dick is raging hard in response to the sound of his stomping footsteps.

Adrenaline pumping, I bolt through his bedroom door and twist to lock it behind me. Only the feral fucker shoves it back open, sending me crashing to my ass.

"Ow! Fuck," I hiss, already turning to stand and run away, but Jamie's faster and stronger.

He snatches my ankle in a firm grip and drags me back toward him. "You are such a fucking shithead," Jamie growls, actually looking like the feral beast he's acting like. Wavy long dark hair hangs around his cheekbones while he looks down at me, eyes wild.

"Listen—" I start, trying to talk my way out of whatever plan he has cooking in his brain.

"No."

"Okay, so we're back to one-word answers," I murmur, only kind of trying to kick my foot loose.

Him standing over me, my boner standing proud between us, and Jamie's heaving chest makes me ache. The scene is hot and kinky, giving me ideas that involve us being naked in an empty forest. I'm open to trying new things, and maybe I'd like some primal play in my life, who knows. What I do know is I'm severely hot and bothered by his anger and power.

A rumbly sound from Jamie makes me almost moan in response. Fuck, I'll push his buttons every day if this is the result. Although I know most of his take no shit attitude is due to how he upset Violet last night.

"So…" I start, feeling a little antsy and nervous. I'm not sure I like that he's not moving, but he shuts that worry down when he drops my foot, leans down, and grabs me by my sweatshirt.

Mindlessly, I help him pull me to my feet. I even stumble toward the bed as he pushes me there.

"Shirt off. Pants down," Jamie demands, and when I start to do as he says slowly, he raises an eyebrow. *So now is not the time to challenge him.*

Quickly, I undress. I keep an eye on him as he stomps to his nightstand and grabs a bottle of lube.

My dick stands high in the air once I release it, and the promise of Jamie's lube makes me tremble with excitement. *Holy shit, is he going to fuck me?*

Jamie looks his fill of my toned thin body, and just his attention on me has my balls tingling. Chills race down my spine, and my lips suddenly feel so chapped, like the only thing that can help them is his cum.

Still dressed, he stands in front of me. His clothes don't do anything to hide his boner, though. The sight makes my mouth water. "Turn around. I want your tight ass in the air and your face pressed into my bed. Got it?"

"Yes, Sir," I obey, giddy as hell. The comforter smells clean and faintly of Violet which only makes me harder.

Faintly, I hear him tug his zipper down, but the rustle of clothes never comes. Then he speaks, and goosebumps spread to the top of my head. "You're about to learn what happens when you tease an angry man, Ellis. I'm going to fuck your tight hole with my fingers, and while I plan to come all over your back, you won't get to so much as touch your cock. Understand me?"

Alarm shoots through me, and I try to sit up to demand he doesn't edge me. I'm terrible at edging. I turn into a horny pile of mush for the rest of the fucking day. But he just shoves me back down and swats my ass. "But—"

"You have two options, Ellis. You say 'yes, Sir' and get finger fucked in the ass or you say 'red' and I pull my pants up, then make you a coffee."

Well, that's sweet and makes my answer much easier. "Y-yes, Sir."

"Good choice," he praises, and I shit you not, I feel like my insides glow in response to his words.

My knees tremble when the lube cap pops open, and the wet noises behind me make me guess he's fisting himself. I'd like to look, holy shit do I want to see the way his massive hands squeeze the base of his cock and work the cum out. What I wouldn't give to lick the precum from his tip and feel the way his cock gags my throat again.

He doesn't let me. "No peeking. You just fucking lay there and let me use your hot body."

Muttered curses tumble into the blankets beneath me. I should keep my cool, but Jamie makes it almost impossible with his filthy mouth, then he *touches* me. A cool finger slides between my cheeks, and I naturally tense.

Judging by the slick sounds behind me, Jamie hasn't slowed down fucking his fist even while he offers encouraging words. "Push out. I know for a fact Nate fucks your ass frequently, so you should have no problem taking a few fingers, right?"

I—Holy shit. The dirty talk mixed with praise is energizing as fuck.

Shock and sheer pleasure rip all thought from my mind as Jamie slips one finger then two inside of me. He pumps into me like he's on a mission to drive me crazy all the while he moans and pumps his cock just outside of my eyesight.

No matter how much I desire to see his glorious body, I'm trapped. He demanded that I not look, and for once I obey. Listen and feel, that's all I can do.

"Take it," Jamie grunts, and my confusion at his words goes up in flames when he fits a third finger. "That's it. So greedy."

"Fuck! Jamie!" Fisting the sheets, I try to contain the ache in my balls and the pleasure of having my prostate massaged. Craving more and not getting it makes my insides burn and my body twitch incessantly.

Flexing my hips, I aim to hump the sheets like the greedy fucker Jamie said I was, but all noise suddenly stops, and a sharp slap rings down on my right cheek. *Yesssss.*

"Don't you fucking dare," he growls, knowing where my throbbing dick was headed. "I'm close, then your pleasure will end."

Pleasure?! I'm pretty damn sure this is just torture now.

"Jamie. Fuck. Please let me come. I'm sorry for pushing your buttons. I won't do it ag—AH!"

Just as I'm about to finish my promise of something I'll never be able to follow through on, his fingers disappear, leaving me empty. But that sad feeling is soon swallowed by a firm grip on my balls, and the speed of the sexy sounds he makes increases. The threatening pressure makes me pause, and it's just what Jamie needed to come all over my back.

"Ellis!" he roars, warm liquid dripping down my ass. I swear I feel some of it swirl into my butt dimples as I slump onto the bed in frustration and exhaustion.

I must black out to protect my poor horny body from more torture because I don't realize Jamie grabbed a wet rag until he's wiping me clean and telling me I took my punishment well.

As he dresses and helps me stand, I'm stuck wondering what the fuck just happened and begging Nate to get here ASAP to help me.

Thirty-Eight

VIOLET

Apparently my guilt knows no bounds. I'm shaking like a freaking leaf in Nate's passenger seat. The poor man just continues to hold my thigh and reassure me that leaving our date early is totally okay.

He's not mad or disappointed. When he tells me he's proud of me for being open about my worries, I want to hit him. Not because what he said was bad, but because I feel like I don't deserve his leniency.

"Nate, I bailed on our first date. Right in the middle of it because I couldn't stop thinking about another man. Stop trying to make me feel better."

"Just the fact that you're calling it a first date makes me the happiest man in the world," he retorts, winking at me. Damn him for knowing how to respond to me so well. "Also, I was completely aware of your emotional dilemmas when I asked you out. I'm not dense enough to think you don't need to make amends with Jamie."

"But I should have been thinking about you.

Responding to you, Nate. Instead, I pushed the food around that you bought me and zoned out for half the time."

His response isn't what I expect it to be. "What would Jamie have done if you were on a date with him but you really needed to talk to me? So much so that you were in distress and shaking."

"He—" *Shoot*. My shoulders slump, accepting defeat. "Jamie would do the same thing you're doing. But I would feel just as bad."

Nate nods and rubs his thumb along the outside of my thigh. "Then it's up to us to show you what a secure relationship between the four of us could be like."

Stunned silent, I move on autopilot as Nate parks the car and holds my hand the entire way up to Jamie's apartment. Outside the door, Nate stops and crowds me.

"One moment," he murmurs, tucking a lock of purple hair behind my ear. "I won't ask for a kiss this time, baby. But I will ask for a second date. If you need Jamie there, I'm happy to have him too. We may need to bring Ellis along as well if it will be a group deal, but I'll do anything to see you again in a date setting."

The complete respect he has for my connection with Jamie baffles me and makes my heart feel close to bursting at the same time. How can this man be so selfless?

"I'd like that," I whisper, raising up onto my toes to kiss his jaw. It's padded by a beard, and the hair tickles enough to make me smile. His hair is in a bun at the base of his skull, and he's wearing his clunky work boots. His jeans and tight black shirt beneath his jacket were appreciated for as long as I could focus on him.

Nate deserves a kick ass date, and I will deliver once my brain sorts through the mess life has created for me. As I follow Nate through Jamie's apartment door, I can't help but think about how Nate doesn't feel so scrambled in my mind anymore.

I definitely still have feelings for him, and somehow I feel like they could grow to be even stronger than before. Staring at him as he helps me take my shoes and coat off, I'm ready to give him an actual kiss when Ellis interrupts my thoughts.

"Thank fuck." Ellis sighs, face red and body fidgety as he rushes toward us. "Can you take me home now?"

Frowning at him, I wait for Nate to say something, but Nate just looks his partner up and down and smirks. So I say the first thing that comes to my mind. "Did you terrorize your babysitter or something?"

"Yes," Ellis groans and tugs on his hair.

Nate bites his bottom lip and glances down at Ellis' waist. I follow his line of sight and suck in a gasp when I realize Ellis is sporting a boner. I'm still staring at it when Nate must see Jamie because they start a conversation as if this is all normal.

"Did he deserve it?" Nate asks.

Jamie chuckles darkly. "Oh yeah. Fucker earned it as soon as he opened his damn mouth."

Earned what? Nausea swims at the base of my throat, and I suddenly feel like Nate is the only safe place right now.

Nate has questions, but I'm confused as to why he

sounds amused and a little turned on. "How long has he been like this?"

"An hour and a half," Jamie replies as Ellis mutters something about a million years.

Nate nods but doesn't seem to notice me inching behind him. Something clearly went on here. Something sexual and intimate. Between Jamie and Ellis. Nate's acting like it's okay, and I feel like I might be sick. Tears are already burning the backs of my eyes.

I'm so fucking sick of crying.

"Alright. I usually max his edging at three hours."

I feel faint at Nate's words, so I quickly grab the back of his shirt. *Edging.*

While I was thinking about Jamie so much that I ruined my date with Nate, Jamie was edging Ellis.

Wait, every part of that statement is so fucked up.

What am I doing? What is going on here?

My brain conjures up every icky message it can spare to tell me I'm not wanted. I need my journal. I should organize these feelings, these thoughts.

"Baby, look at me."

It's those words that force me to blink. Realizing Nate is crouched in front of me while I'm sitting in the entryway, I suck in a shaky breath.

"Hi," Nate says, smiling. "You zoned out for a minute there, so I had you sit. Are you okay?"

Baffled, I answer him. "Me? Am I okay? Are *you*? Ellis and Jamie screwed around while you were gone."

Am I in some kind of alien world where this was just a normal day? Because let me tell you, this has been the most screwed up month of my life. I miss the void I lived in for so long. The one that kept my anxiety at bay and my life a stagnant pile of nothing.

"Violet," Nate coos, ready to school me on the ways of polyamory, I bet. News flash, my mom has four dicks, and two of them dick each other down too. "I took you on a date this morning."

Scoffing because I knew he would resort to mansplaining, I stand and walk to the kitchen. I don't look at the three of them as I grab a glass and fill it with water.

Jamie tries to get my attention. "V, my love." His approach annoys me a little too.

"Am I?" I snap. "Your love I mean."

Jamie has few triggers when it comes to me and how I can treat him. But the main one is questioning his feelings for me.

And I just yanked on that fucking thing.

Toxic V is in the house, and I'm ready to ruffle some feathers to get some answers. Because I won't have *any* kind of relationship without communication.

I've broken enough hearts and ruined my soul because I was too chickenshit to talk to the people I loved the most.

That ends now.

I'll throw down the gauntlet myself since nobody else will. "Because I seem pretty replaceable where I'm standing."

Thirty-Nine

JAMIE

Did she just say that?

I have an emotionally intellectual mind, so I can see where Violet's coming from with her question. But fuck does it piss me off to no end.

The deep breath I force myself to take does nothing. I try to convince myself it gives me time to say something good back. *No such luck.*

"Of fucking course you're my love!"

Shit. Ellis stiffens and shifts to face me a little as if he needs to keep an eye on me. I don't blame him.

"Don't say *of course* like it's obvious, Jamie," Violet responds with a roll of her eyes. I'm not sure I prefer the look in her eyes over her crying. The one right now is far too similar to the one she used to wear when she was keeping me at arm's length.

"Of course it's obvious!" I have no filter, and the words I'm using are those of a child throwing a tantrum. I'm a complete and utter asshole. My dumbass didn't even think fingerfucking Ellis would be a problem at the time.

Even an hour and a half later, I didn't think it would be an issue. Hell, Violet was on a date with Nate this morning!

"It's not! Not when they're here!"

Her furious eyes pin me in place, and I force myself to swallow the words that accuse her of going on a date with Nate without consulting me either. Defensiveness roars inside of me. Years of being rejected by Violet's heart force my vocal cords to spout my ugly truths.

"I love you! Can't you fucking see that, you stubborn, beautiful woman?!"

I'm lost in the relief of admitting my feelings to her. So much so that everything else comes pouring out.

Violet's face is flushed, and Nate and Ellis have closed ranks around me because I might as well be spitting fire with the pent-up emotion in my voice.

"I may not have as much going on or tears to cry, but fucking hell, Violet! Don't you think I'm confused too? That maybe I'm just going with what feels right?!"

She takes a step back, and the way her chin wobbles makes my heart clench. But all that does is release more things I should keep to myself.

"I'm a man. A fucking tattoo artist. I have powerful, dangerous friends. My tattoos, long hair, and dominant disposition are the surface. Below, I'm confused as fucking hell about why I can't keep away from Nate and Ellis. They're under my skin just like they're under yours."

Whipping around, I break eye contact with the woman I love and yank on my hair. It's a plea to make myself stop, but I can't. I've cut myself loose from the chains of what I'm expected to be. My love, my *life,* will know how I feel even if I have to shred my tatted skin and growly voice.

"*Yes,* I should have talked to you about all of this before I fingerfucked Ellis in the ass—"

"Could have left that part out..." Ellis mutters.

"*Yes,* I should have hijacked your date and demanded we figure our shit out before bringing them into it—"

"Glad you didn't..." Nate murmurs.

"*Yes,* I love you with all my heart and soul!" I stress, turning around and rushing toward Violet. Bypassing Nate and Ellis' worried grabs for me, I grab V's wrists and pin them above her head against the kitchen cupboards.

"Jamie," she breathes, eyes wide, chest heaving.

"*Yes,* I thought about you the whole time I was with him." Before Ellis can comment this time, I continue fast. "I thought about how much I would love to see him eating your pussy as he was bent over my bed. Imagining his tight ass hugging my cock while Nate fucked your wet pussy, and I held your hand was the fantasy that had me shooting my load onto Ellis' back."

"Holy fuck," one of the guys groans, and I can't help but smirk a little.

With Violet pressed between me and the counter I make her breakfast on every opportunity I get, I release my final words. "This situation is fucked. *I'm* fucked for how I've gone about my attraction to them. For that I am *so* damn sorry. I swear, from the bottom of hell to the top of heaven, that I *love* you."

She opens her mouth, but I'm not finished. "And I *love* the way they've challenged you and pulled more emotion from you. You are far more than a woman who I enjoy spending time with and warms my bed. Violet, you are *mine*. Your heart, soul, mind, and future are mine. But," I hesitate ever so slightly because my next statement will set our trajectory, "you can't have a future without a past. And your past is one you *love*. Especially the people who were a part of it."

Truthfully, I'm glad Violet isn't crying because I would start retracting shit I have no business retracting. She just blinks up at me, looking between my eyes like she needs to see the emotion behind my words to make this feel real.

I feel like I'm not breathing as I await her response. Shit even the other two don't make a peep. We're waiting on the edge of something profound and life changing.

You know what my sweet Violet says?

"Can we go get some waffles?" Her eyes widen as if she can't believe she just said that. "I mean, I love you too. *So much*. Of course I still have feelings for Nate and Ellis. But I'm starving, and I fear I'm too hangry to have this deep conversation."

For the love of everything good and holy... "Don't ever change, Violet Bennett." Kissing her after giving her my everything feels like something new.

One of the new parts of our lives chooses that moment to speak up and explain why he didn't feed my girl when he took her out. "She was worried about you so much that she couldn't stomach much food. That's why we're back early."

Nodding in thanks to Nate, I nudge my face into the space between Violet's jaw and shoulder. Keeping my voice low, I ask her, "Would you like them to join, my love?"

She hesitates for half a second, and I shit you not, I about come in my jeans when she grins. "Ellis still has an hour and a half, so why not."

"I fucking love you," I declare and squeeze her until she relents and tells me she loves me too.

Forty

NATE

I had every intention of leaving Jamie and Violet alone. Professing their love in front of me and Ellis was intense and I'm sure unintentional. But their invitation to go get something to eat with them was not.

Violet clung to Jamie a bit tighter on the drive to lunch. She only allowed him his hand back when the ice on the road required more attention.

I'm not one to talk because Ellis and I held hands the entire way to the restaurant. Ellis could very well be thinking about when he can orgasm, but I'm almost positive he's stressing over how serious everything is becoming.

Not because we don't want our relationship with them to grow, but because there's a big fucking secret making us sick to our stomachs constantly. Who knows how long I can hold on to this deceit.

My stomach growls in agitation; instead of thinking about lunch, I'm stuck remembering why I couldn't eat breakfast. The entire time I watched Violet fidget and worry on our date just reminded me I have the power to hurt her worse than a slight miscommunication she and Jamie had.

I don't want this power. I never should have stolen it. Selfishness and childishness have tainted our meeting. My sweet, bubbly woman doesn't even know we are building this relationship on lies and betrayal.

Fuck, I have no clue if I can even eat lunch at this point.

Seated at our table after the short drive, Ellis shifts in his chair beside me, and Violet giggles quietly. Jamie smirks and nudges his knee against mine. His touch brings me back from the depths of my guilt. I don't deserve to, but still I soak in her laughter and heated gaze she's giving my partner.

"Shush, Bubbl—Violet." Ellis pales, realizing his mistake with his words immediately. "Shit, I'm sorry. I need a new nickname for you."

Violet doesn't seem too bothered by his slip. Instead she just cocks her head and waits for Ellis to continue running his mouth. It's a good tactic if you want to hear some wack ass shit.

"How about Streaks?" he offers.

Violet scowls so hard I can't help but snort into my beer. I wasn't planning on having a beer with lunch, but the awkward silence and my thoughts drove me to drink.

"Absolutely not." Violet protests the nickname. "I've never streaked."

Ellis smiles and tugs on a lock of purple hair. Her

breath catches with his closeness as he explains, "I was referencing the purple streaks in your hair."

"Oh," she exhales as he leans back. "Still no, though."

"I'll think of one you won't be able to say no to," Ellis declares with a wink just as the food arrives at our table.

Silence descends around us once again. The sound of other people talking and the football game on the TVs in the restaurant saves us from talking while we eat.

It's not that we have nothing to say; it's that there is *so* much to say.

Eating feels like the last thing I should be doing, but damn does it taste good. The burger and fries are fucking amazing; before I know it I'm completely engrossed in my meal.

Around the last few bites of my food, Ellis murmurs something to Violet. The concerned lilt in his tone draws my attention to them. He's leaning toward her again and talking softly.

Violet's lips are twisted as she shakes her head. Jamie's tense beside me, but I bet he can't hear the conversation either.

Ellis nods and leans back, looking serious. "V is too anxious about the talk we need to have. So let's get it out of the way while I feed her," he explains to me and Jamie.

Then, to my surprise, he shuffles his chair closer to her and picks up a slice of her quesadilla. "Alright, someone go," Ellis demands, looking ready to go to battle for Violet.

V stares at him, seeming a bit exasperated, but her lips are curved up in a smile of appreciation. I too am shocked by his intuitive desire to guide us in the right direction and take care of her.

Ellis can be a selfish man, thus needing a more dominant hand frequently. Seeing him step up and take on a more mature role with Violet gives me hope that we *can* make this work.

"Well," Jamie drawls, wiping his hands on his napkin. "Violet found a good description of what this feels like yesterday on our hike."

"Was that just yesterday?" Violet gasps. "Jeez. So much is happening all the damn time. No wonder I'm tired."

"Well, you also haven't eaten anything yet today," I deadpan and look at Ellis. He follows my silent command and gives Violet a bite of her quesadilla.

She munches on her small bite and seems to relax at the burst of flavor. Ellis watches her and doesn't break his stare as Jamie continues to speak.

"She said it feels like we're two separate couples coming together. I'd say that feels pretty accurate to me. Thoughts?" Jamie gives me the floor with a glance.

I take a moment to think about it. "Yeah, I'd say so. You and Violet have been with each other for years, maybe not in the official sense, but you're comfortable with each other. The trust is there, as is the love. It's the same with me and Ellis."

Ellis and Violet continue listening while he nudges more bites into her mouth. It works that she's distracted by our conversation so she can ignore the food going into her mouth.

"Then there are other connections that need to be built," Jamie continues. "But I really appreciate the respect we all have for the established couples' dynamic."

"This sounds like a business deal," Violet grumbles, pushing Ellis' hand away. "Why can't we talk about it normally? Like establish rules or something?"

"By all means." Jamie waves a hand at her and leans back in his chair.

Glaring at him, Violet rolls her eyes. "I mean like Jamie and I aren't official—"

Jamie sits up straight at those words. "Watch your mouth, Sweets. As soon as you told me you loved me, we became official. I've been yours for a long time, and now that you're on board, it's official."

Their staring contest goes on for a few seconds before Violet relents. "Fine. We're official. So are they. How do we make this fair?"

"Maybe we should call your mama," I suggest, only kind of joking.

Violet waves her hand through the air and admits, "Already did. She said we have to treat every relationship as its own. But the group has its own space that needs to be paid attention to and nourished too."

"Eat," Ellis commands, pushing a chip into her mouth. When she leans away, he says, "Eat, Violet. It's my turn to talk anyway."

The intense vibe coming off of him is kind of sexy. He won't get away with talking to me like that, but I love seeing it directed at Violet. She needs some guidance too.

"Thank you," Ellis mutters when she takes a bite. "Can I just say, I'm fucking flattered that you've already talked to Blue about us? She's definitely right about each dynamic being its own. Every relationship is different. So how about we just date and let it come naturally?"

Jamie shakes his head. "It can't be that simple, though. We need to communicate and build trust."

"Alright," I butt in. "We can do that. But first we need Violet's phone number."

Violet rattles it off, and Ellis orders another round of drinks as I input it into my phone. "There. Expect us to text and call you both a lot. We're in this for real, and we don't want to step back. Is that okay with you two?"

Jamie and Violet make eye contact before nodding. "Yes," Violet says, but I can see the questions in her gaze. I know she has a lot going on in her mind lately, so I don't pressure her to talk quite yet.

At some point she will trust herself and us to express her worries. It's up to us to show her that we can be trusted.

Even if we can't be.

Forty-One

VIOLET

It's been a few days since what I believe was an unproductive conversation about our relationship changes. What I hoped would be a talk about boundaries and rules, like deciding how much time to spend together in a week, when to have sex, when to kiss, etcetera, ended up being an agreement to date each other.

I've been trying to calm my questions and keep them to myself to try this whole "let's let it all happen naturally" thing, but it's hard. The flashes of insecurity and jealousy that jolt me out of our group chat bother me.

I'd love for this to feel completely equal between the four of us, but it doesn't. Maybe that's because I'm subconsciously holding back, while Jamie seems to just take the flirting in stride and give as good as he gets.

Now don't get me wrong, I'm a very sexual person, but this is completely new territory for me. I think I've done decently well in keeping my concerns to myself even though we agree communication is key.

Sometimes I just need time to figure things out on my own, so I'm not that worried. Part of figuring things out is following their lead.

Which is why I'm clicking through photos on my camera at the nightclub I take images for while waiting for Ellis. He texted me separately yesterday asking if I was free. I wasn't. At the time, I was at the hair salon accepting apologies from the manager for her teasing remarks a few weeks ago.

I had some edits to do and emails to catch up on, so Ellis had to wait for our date. Which is why he's meeting me at the club for a drink and a chat after work.

Date. I can't believe after all these years I'm finally going on a date with Ellis Perry.

Work has helped keep my mind off of some stuff, like wondering if Jamie has people watching me. I should feel weird about that, and I do, but I have to admit it makes me feel safer when I walk from my car to my destination. I wonder if I'll get to thank Bash someday.

Too many things...

I'm so darn nervous my knee hasn't stopped bouncing. The bartender gave me a water and a lemon drop to calm my nerves, which I appreciate. He's handsome, and I may have given him the time of day if Jamie hadn't made it clear last year that I was his and no bartender was allowed to bother me for my cell number.

I was pissed for a while after that because who the hell was Jamie to decide who I spent my time with? Of course, I got over it because the thought of undoing the claim he forced on me here made me feel sad.

So I left it, and the sexy bartenders have left me be. My artistic focus tonight has been on the wall of liquor and neon lights, so I've carved out my small corner. Now I'm waiting.

It's an awesome club, but it's nowhere near as kick ass as the club my mama works at. She mainly manages security for the young bartenders now because that place has only skyrocketed in popularity.

"I'm surprised you aren't surrounded." Ellis' voice warms me before his heat does. Behind me, his chest presses against my back, and his arms bracket me as his hands land on the counter outside of mine.

Turning toward him so he can hear me over the thumping music, I explain. "Jamie's fault. I'm not to be approached when I'm working."

Ellis' laughter in my ear makes me shiver delightfully. He presses a light kiss to the side of my neck and shifts to sit on the stool next to me. "I'll thank him for that later," he teases with a wink.

The reminder of his own relationship with Jamie sends an uncomfortable feeling through me for a second before it's gone. "Jamie and I actually met right here." I tap my finger on the bar.

"No way, really? So he was one in a long line of men who tried to get your attention?" Ellis looks genuinely interested in this story, so I tell him about how Jamie spilt his drink close to my camera and apologized profusely, then proved himself to me with the highest orgasm count in one night.

"Three doesn't sound like a lot, but it is for me." Blushing, I scold myself for sharing that piece of information.

Ellis leans closer to me and kisses the side of my neck again. His rumbly whisper in my ear makes me melt. "Challenge accepted, angel."

Rapidly shaking my head, I deny his claim. "I'm not an angel. Don't call me that."

Ignoring my protest, Ellis looks down at my camera. "Tell me about this beauty."

His question lights me up from the inside out. "Oh! I love her so much. She does all my work. Very dynamic and flexible with my needs. I don't need other lenses on my hikes since I prefer to use my feet to get closer to the view and vision I want to capture."

Ellis watches me gush over my camera like he's mesmerized. "What do you like most about it?"

"This style fits my minimalistic needs. I don't want a flashy camera that takes extra time to set up. Enjoying my job is my main goal, and this one helps me do that."

Ellis nods, seeming to really soak in my words. I appreciate his curiosity about my camera. I've always been passionate about creating content, and he knows that. The fact that he wants to know more about how I adapted to my hangups means the world to me.

"What kind of pictures do you take on your hikes?" He hasn't even motioned for a drink. Ellis is completely locked in on me, making me feel special and important.

Excited to tell him without showing him, I dive into

my love of thrill. "Cliffs are my favorite, but from the top. I lie on my stomach and capture the image from the top. Sometimes I can get a really trippy depth that makes the viewer feel like they're falling."

"Have you?!" Ellis sounds a bit mad. "Have you ever fucking fallen? V, that's dangerous."

I shrug, acknowledging his worry. It's the same fear Jamie has, so I'm used to this kind of response. That's the actual reason I've never shown Jamie the pictures from my hikes. Some of those were really risky.

"No, I've never fallen, Ellis. It's okay. That's why my camera is small and easy to travel with. There was a close call with a waterfall once, but I caught myself on a vine."

"A close call with a waterfall," he repeats slowly. "Violet, you can't—"

"Careful." I smirk and kiss his cheek. "Jamie tried to tell me I couldn't do those anymore, and that didn't work out well for him."

"Fuck," he curses and finally motions for a bartender. "Just promise me you'll text and call as much as possible when you're on your trips so I know you're safe."

Beaming at his perfect response, I nod. "Promise."

"Or better yet, I'll come with and tether you to me so I know you're safe the entire time." He's grumbling, but his warm hand on my upper thigh is gentle.

"Maybe some day but I really enjoy going on my own. It's therapeutic being out there by myself and finding my own way. I'm good at it, but I promise I'll keep you updated on my safety," I offer, trying to diminish the sting of my rejection.

It's not that I don't want to go on a trip with the guys. It's just that it's *my* thing. The road and endless hiking opportunities were my constant for a long, *long* time.

"Alright, Sugarbloom," Ellis relents and kisses my cheek.

Laughter bursts from me as my head furiously whips back and forth. "NO. Not Sugarbloom!"

"Hmm. Someday I'll find the perfect one for my perfect woman."

He spends the rest of our date making me feel special and wanted. I'm not perfect, but maybe I can accept that he believes I'm perfect for *him*.

Forty-Two

ELLIS

Holding myself back has caused one of the biggest, most painful boners I've ever had the displeasure of dealing with. For two fucking hours.

"Were you a gentleman?" Nate asks as I slam our front door closed behind me.

He's the one who dropped me off at the club and picked both me and Violet up. My knee hasn't stopped bouncing with pent-up energy since we got in the fucking car.

After walking Violet up to her apartment and coming back down to see Nate's smirk, I've been on the verge of explosion.

"Yes," I grit out my answer, kicking my shoes off. "The perfect fucking gentleman."

Nate's chuckle is quiet as he rummages around in our kitchen. I'm practically vibrating with need for his attention, but he takes his time. When he brushes past me with a glass of ice, his grin is still there.

He knows exactly what my fucking dilemma is. *Fucker.*

I don't hesitate to follow him to our bedroom, but the stairs up make my dick chafe on my jeans. "Nate," I moan, closing our bedroom door behind us. He still hasn't said anything as he puts his cup down.

My heart skips a beat when he kneels beside the bed and pulls out his box of toys. "Fuck yes," I breathe, already stripping my clothes off.

I'm literally panting like a bitch in heat as he lays out a few sets of black rope on our bed. A bottle of lube joins them. I can almost feel his slippery fingers teasing me just by watching him with a damn bottle of lube. That's how horny I am.

"I'm proud of you for being a gentleman, darling." His deep eyes flash to mine as he puts the rest of the toys back under the bed. "But why are you still standing there?"

My breath whooshes out of me as urgency drives my motions. Climbing onto the bed, I assume the position I know he likes. With my back to the headboard, I rest on my knees and keep my arms loose at my sides.

Over and over again my muscles clench and release. It's a test for me to stay still and allow Nate to guide our pleasure.

Sometimes Nate and I delve into BDSM when we both need stress relief. While it's pretty tame in comparison to what else is out there, it's so amazingly intense for us.

Almost reverently, Nate unravels his ropes and methodically ties them to the first bedpost. The only time he lays eyes on me is when he moves around the foot of the bed to get to the other side to tie another rope.

My cock throbs between my thighs, and when Nate bites his lip, it jerks. He smirks, knowing exactly what he does to me. I want his cock in my mouth, in my ass, or spurting on my face. Honestly, I don't fucking care. I just need him.

I can't tell if I'm freezing or burning up. The chills and sweat make me fidgety, but I know from experience that if I move, he'll delay touching me.

"Ellis, how much would you like?" Consent and communication are key when we do this. There have been a few times when tying me to the bed was too much.

Sometimes I struggle with feeling like I'm too big for my body. That's where the rambling and crappy filter come from. When I'm like this, sometimes I really, truly need to move. In those moments, being tied me up sent me into a panic because it felt like I was about to burst out of my skin.

As much as Nate knows me inside and out, I'm still the only one who can feel my limits.

I'm worried I'm too riled up to handle it right now. Violet's arms are branded around my neck, and I can still feel the way her ass swirled against my cock on the dance floor. "I'll hold on to the ropes, Sir. But I need all of you."

Nate nods, and that's my cue to grab both ropes. Shifting onto my ass, I wiggle down so I'm lying there like a meal waiting for Nate to devour me.

"You're very warm," he comments, dragging a hand across my stomach. He moves back toward the glass of ice, making my abs and thighs bunch with anticipation. Silently I curse the freezing cubes because I know what he's going to do next. "Cool off while I get ready."

A hiss escapes between my teeth as he places one between my pecs and another in the grove of my abs beneath my belly button. My dick grows, betraying my dislike for this new form of kinkiness.

As much as I want to watch Nate reveal his large, muscular body, I can't. The cold has me squeezing my eyes shut and breathing through my teeth. *This is fucking freez—*

"AH!"

My eyes fly open and connect with Nate's between my legs. The heat of his mouth is a total contrast to the ice cube he swirls around the head of my cock with his tongue.

"Nate. Shit, that's good." I feel the moisture of the melting cube drip down my balls. It's thicker than water thanks to his spit and my precum that is most definitely coating his tongue. "I'm gonna come!" I wheeze, yanking on the ropes.

My warning makes Nate sit up. "No," he growls, slapping his hands down on the insides of my thighs. The sting makes me gasp and lurch toward him. "I want to feel you clenching around me when you come."

I knew that. I knew he wouldn't let me come so soon, but the pout that I feel rising as the pressure lingers in my balls is hard to contend with. The need to come is insistent and consuming.

"Now, please. Sir," I add, hoping to appeal to his dominant side. *Fuck, I'm going to come as soon as he enters me.* "Just fuck me!"

I don't think I can handle his fingers right now, and thankfully he seems to understand. Watching him lube up his cock, I recall the curve of Violet's neck as she flung her head back with laughter tonight. I can still feel the way her thighs flexed when I ran a finger closer to her pussy.

"Keep thinking about her while I fill you up," Nate encourages. I lift my thighs to give him access to me, and when he nudges my entrance, I suck in a breath of pleasure. "What did she do to get you so hot and bothered?"

The reminder of why he put ice on my heated flesh makes me shiver as I focus on the water dripping down my chest and waist. It's an added sensation that helps me adjust to Nate's thick cock as he enters me.

"There you go," he groans, seating himself. With his weight pressing against me and his long blond hair hanging between us, I completely give in to whatever he wants to do now.

All I know is his dick is finally inside of me and I'm being given what I've craved all night long. "Nate," I moan, trying my damndest to keep hold of the rope. I want to grab him and force him to fuck me hard, but the rope is there to contain me.

"Did she rub her thighs together at the sound of your voice?" he asks thickly as he drives in and out of me. It's a tight fit, but he always keeps me well prepared to allow him to take me whenever he wants.

"Yes," I sigh, my head falling back onto our pillows. "Her little gasps of pleasure when I kissed her neck drove me wild."

"Mmmm, like this?" Nate rumbles, and the next thing I know, he's putting his weight on top of me and nibbling on the column of my throat. Noises escape me unbidden, but I'm unable to control them. With his stomach rubbing my aching cock and the friction of his hair adding more sensation, I'm about a moment away from losing all control.

"Come for me. I need to feel you strangle my cock, Ellis. But don't you fucking let go of those ropes."

His demand is what tips me right over the fucking edge. One final drag of his abs and spattering of hair against the tip of my dick rubs the orgasm right out of me.

Faintly I hear the headboard creak and groan with the force of my pull on the ropes. "FUCK! FUCK!" Roaring out my release, I relish in the way Nate's body pins me to the bed as he bucks and paints my insides.

Slowly, and reluctantly, I float back down to earth and find myself in Nate's arms as he pets my back. He knows me well enough to know when I need aftercare and a cuddle.

"I love you," I murmur into his heaving chest.

"And I love you," he whispers, hugging me tight and giving me exactly what I need. Like he always does.

Forty-Three

JAMIE

"I have an idea," Violet announces, turning to me on the couch. She crosses her legs and waits for me to respond.

Smiling indulgently at her, I grab her fidgeting hands and set them on my thigh. "What's your idea?"

After a long day of work, I could listen to her talk about literally anything and be completely content. My schedule is jam-packed lately, like it always is after the holidays. What better way than to spend your gifted cash?

Violet takes a deep breath like she's gearing up to say something important. Her body language puts me on high alert, then she blurts out, "I want to have sexy time as a group before I leave for my trip in a few weeks."

I open my mouth to say something along the lines of fuck yes, but she keeps talking like she needs to explain herself. "It's just that I think we need to figure out if we can actually do stuff without bad feelings before taking the emotional next step, you know what I mean?"

"Bad feelings?" I ask, still holding her hands. If I let go, I worry she will stand and start pacing.

She nods her head. "Like jealousy and insecurities."

Now I do sit up straight and abandon my peaceful idea of just listening to her talk. "V, have you been feeling jealous and insecure?"

Her shrug annoys me because I don't want her to lie to me, but she warms my heart by telling the truth. "Sometimes. It's odd reading your flirty text messages to them in the group chat. But I also worry about what you send separately. Because what if you decide you don't want or need me anymore? Nate and Ellis are very forward and available in this dynamic. I'm over here hesitating."

Son of a bitch. I should have been paying more attention. "Why haven't you said anything?"

"It's only been a week. I figure I'll get used to it at some point. But back to my idea—"

"No," I growl and lift her onto my lap. "We aren't done talking about your feelings. Why didn't you tell me, V? We're partners. I'm here for you, yet I've been hurting you without knowing."

"Jamie." She sighs, sounding tired of me always trying to help and love her. "You're not hurting me. I'm just adjusting, and sometimes I need to think things through on my own. If I start saying everything I feel, you'd have no time or space to flirt with my exes."

"Jesus, don't say it like that." Cringing, I spank her

ass a little which makes her laugh. "I always want to know how you feel, my love."

Violet raises an eyebrow. "And sometimes I don't want to tell you how I feel because I don't know how to articulate it. I'm still an individual, Jamie. I love you, and that's why I'm talking to you about it now."

Damn it all to hell. I want to wrap her up so tight she will never think of being independent again. But that's fucked up, and I keep the thought to myself, which now makes me feel like a hypocrite.

"Alright, so your idea," I steer us back on track.

Violet smiles and wiggles on my lap. "I want us to try to see how we all feel. If there's a problem or bad feelings, I think it's best we find out now before we all go falling in love."

Falling in love...Am I capable of falling in *love* with Nate and Ellis? I like them and I'm attracted to them, so maybe she's right. I may not be in love with them yet, but I could be.

"No more broken hearts." Violet sounds pained, and I understand given their history.

I pull her down for a soft kiss, but it quickly shifts to something hotter when I get my first taste of her. She tastes like mint, and my tongue seeks out more of it. Hers battles mine like we're dueling for the upper hand, but when her hot cunt presses against my cock, I grab her by the throat and push her back.

A puff of air explodes from her like it always does when I grab her in such a vulnerable place. "More?" she pleads, eyes lidded.

Out of the corner of my eye, I watch her hands raise, but before she can enchant me with her fingers in my hair, I ask her my final question. "What do you need to feel ready to try the next step, Sweets?"

"A date," she replies quickly, like she's already thought about it. "With Nate and Ellis. Then meet you after for a drink. I need to know if our feelings are really still there as a throuple too."

Her words trail off, and I allow her attention to shift to my body. Her blunt little nails massage my scalp and tug my hair tie free. Moaning, I use my hold on her throat to pull her back to me so we're sharing the same air.

"I have an idea too." And fuck is it a good one.

"I'm not wearing that!"

Laughter shoots from my mouth since I automatically think Violet's joking. Yet, her face never changes from horrified at my idea.

Interesting. Have I found a limit in what Violet Bennett will let me do to her? Let's see...

"My love, you have exactly three minutes to fit the cute little vibrator into your thong before I put it there myself."

My tone is one that's not to be fucked with, but I'm happy to announce that Violet is definitely getting her sass back. "*My love,*" she mocks. "*You* have exactly three *seconds* to shove it up your ass before I do it myself."

I cock a brow and bite the inside of my cheek to keep from snorting. "Do you really think you can win this battle, V? Be honest with yourself."

Fuck, arguing with her and battling for the upper hand is always such a turn on with her. We both know I'll win, but Violet has me by the balls in every aspect of our life. I'll bend over backwards while burning the fucking world down for her.

She scowls, and I'd bet she's about a moment away from stomping her foot. I don't know if she sees the hard set of my jaw or the determination in my eyes, but she sighs. Eyeing the small device in my hand, she asks, "Why do you want me to wear that on my date with Nate and Ellis?"

Easy question. "So you'll have the sexiest reminder I could come up with on short notice for you to remember who you're coming home with at the end of the night."

Pulling my phone out of my jeans, I show her the app that controls the vibrator. It's long distance, but not super long, which works fine because I'll be meeting them at the bar next to the arcade.

"Jamie, that's so fucked up."

"Really? This is the line then? A vibrator to make your clit tingle every once in a while during your date with two other men?" I'll be shocked if she says yes.

"Well, no..." she mutters, much to my delight. "But we'll be at an arcade! It's super inappropriate."

Okay, I hear what she's saying, but... "What's the difference between this and you stroking my cock in the line at the coffee shop this morning?"

Now she stomps her foot. "Nobody was looking, and I was covering myself the whole time."

"Great so we're in agreement. Nobody can see the vibrator through your jeans, and I'll keep in on low. Just enough to tease and tingle like you did to me before nine in the fucking morning."

"Damn it Jamie!"

I'm getting hard even as my impatience rises. "What's your color, Violet?"

Seething, she sucks in a breath through her nose and has a staring match with the vibrator. "What is it called?" she grits out.

"Ferri."

"Of course it has a cute name. Green, damn you. Give me it."

With a cheesy fucking grin, I slide my new best friend into her outstretched palm. Before she can slip away from me to get dressed, I snatch her around the waist and press my lips to hers.

She moans and opens her mouth, allowing me to taste the mint of her toothpaste. Soft caresses of my tongue soon turn to a devouring of her sassy fucking mouth.

With one grind of my cock against her, she turns to putty in my hands. *Perfect*. "Good girl," I whisper, pulling away a fraction. "Don't forget about me, 'kay?"

Wanton and panting, Violet simply nods and tries to kiss me again. Except a knock at the door forces her to suck in a breath and rush to the bathroom.

Not before she peppers two final kisses on my lips.

"Don't worry," I tease as she slams the bathroom door. "I'll let our boyfriends in!"

"Not our boyfriends yet!" she shouts, making me laugh as I leave the room.

Not yet.

Forty-Four

VIOLET

I have never in my entire life been so fucking happy as I am right now. Like truly happy.

Of course I know what happiness is and have had plenty of it in my life, but tonight encompasses all of those moments. The arcade has brought me so much childish joy I haven't stopped smiling.

Thankfully, it's more of an adult arcade at the back of the bar, so I'm not as disgusted to be wearing my Ferri. Yes, it's mine now. I love it. I claim it because I love the reminder of Jamie's claim.

Nate and Ellis love guessing when Jamie's teasing me too. So not only am I having a blast kicking their asses in Skee-Ball and Piano Keys, but I'm horny and excited for some more kinky shit.

Also, I have never sworn or threatened someone so much in an evening. Nate and Ellis think my competitiveness is funny, so that's good. Green flags all around.

The only red flag I've felt is all on me. Nate and Ellis have been together since high school. I know their background, how they met, and the complete love they have for each other.

Witnessing their public displays of affection and feeling their connection literally inches away from me is...I have no idea how to explain it. I'm not jealous, per se. Left out maybe.

I made it a point to tell Jamie that they are not our boyfriends yet. Which is totally true because it's way too soon to tell if this will work, but I'm worried.

The complications keep adding up, and without taking action to figure my shit out, I'm just going to keep questioning things. I'm starting to wish we had canceled tonight's plans and just stayed home to fuck to see where the jealousy comes from.

Am I being toxic? Or just horny?

It sounds like a good plan to me, and Jamie didn't say no, so who knows.

Ellis for sure wants to have sex with Jamie, and I know for a fact Nate wouldn't mind watching.

Is it just me? Am I the only one with stupid insecurities and hesitation?

Except, Nate and Ellis have made no move to kiss me or initiate anything beyond simple touches. So maybe, much to my anxiety's pleasure, they aren't actually attracted to me as much as they are to Jamie.

Once again, my anxiety steals a wonderful evening from me. I'm hiding in the back corner, playing a lonely game of Skee-Ball with only my thoughts to keep me company. And that's never good.

I could have gone to find Jamie in the bar section of this place, but he's not meant to be *here*. I'm on a date with the other two to see if this can work. So that means not running to Jamie every time I feel sad.

"Do that again," a raspy voice says behind me, and my skin breaks out in goosebumps.

I had left Nate and Ellis behind during one of their sweet kisses to play a game alone so I could chill out. Turns out being alone was the last thing I needed to make myself feel better. Because as soon as Nate's pelvis lines up with my ass, I whimper and all thoughts flee from my mind.

"Do what again?" I rasp, eyes still locked on the Skee-Ball lane.

His beard tickles my neck, and I kind of hope I'll have a rash there in the morning. Now to just keep him there. "Stick your ass out like you're begging for my cock."

"Oh." I couldn't sound more needy if I tried, but my hips sure think that's a challenge because I immediately bend at the waist to grab another ball.

Nate curses as he moves his hands to grip *very* low on my hips just above my pussy. Just as I'm about to toss my ball, Jamie does something new to my vibrator, and, the next thing I know, Nate's hand is covering my mouth as I lose all composure.

Each pulse of my Ferri starts to slip and glide as I soak my panties. My thighs clench and my eyes roll. The neon lights of the arcade blur, making me feel like I'm flying through space. When Nate's other hand grabs my pussy outside of my jeans, I spasm and thrust against his palm.

"Someday, you needy girl, I'm going to fill this ass so full I'll be dripping out of you for hours."

His words really do make me see stars as I go crashing through time and space. I want his fingers in my pussy as I clench around nothing over and over again. His tongue would feel so good slipping through my folds and around my clit. I wouldn't even care if it felt like too much because I'd have more of him.

More. More. More.

I just need more. More of Nate. More of them. Jamie brought me to the edge, and Nate sent me crashing into an orgasm so hot it stole my scream from my lungs. Ellis carries me back to earth with his grin and relaxed composure against the wall. He blocks us from the rest of the arcade all the while holding his phone up to his ear.

"Yeah, man. We got her. Damn is she beautiful when she lets go." Ellis nods while I try my best to comprehend what he's saying. "Yeah. Turn it off. We need her to get points so we can get some candy at the ticket shop. Yep. See you soon."

His phone comes down just as I'm beginning to relax my muscles. I miss the heaviness of Nate's hand on my pussy and the reminder of Jamie there too, but Ellis makes it easy to shift back into date mode.

"Alright, pretty lady." Ellis gently pulls me from Nate's raging hard on and tucks me in front of him instead. "Think you can get a few more in the fifty slot so I can get you a bag of candy with our tickets?"

I don't promise anything, but I do grind on him with each ball I throw. These positions give me some really good ideas on how to test myself and this new budding relationship.

It's much different from what we used to be, but I didn't give us a chance back then. This time, I plan to give Nate and Ellis my all, and that includes sharing Jamie. This dynamic is like offering the ultimate trust. It's us acknowledging the love we can have for one another while believing we're loved equally.

Am I too damaged, too deflated and detached from the girl I used to be to actually believe I could be loved the way they love Jamie and each other? Or am I too messed up to see myself the way I hope they see me?

Jamie, Nate, and Ellis keep saying it's up to them to show me this can work. That they all have feelings for me.

I haven't said anything, but they're wrong.

They can't convince me if I'm not ready to be convinced. I love Jamie, and I *know* he loves me too. But I'm just not sure I'm in the right headspace for this level of commitment and trust. I don't remember the last time I trusted myself in any way.

I'm a mess. A mess I'm trying to sort out and love.

But how does someone who doesn't love themselves, allow three others to and actually believe their words? Time might help, but I know for a fact that if I go on this trip with questions, I'll fuck everything up like I always do.

So while Nate gave me the reassurance that he wants me, I need to know if I'll feel like I'll always be competing with the others.

Maybe I should call my mom again. How the hell

does someone love *one* person and feel confident in their relationship, let alone one from a why choose novel?

This sucks.

I suck.

Anxiety sucks.

Sex is good, though. Sex is the answer. If I run away puking, angry, or crying, I'll have my answer.

Let's hope the only things burning my throat on Valentine's Day are thick cocks and shrill screams of pleasure.

Forty-Five

NATE

Valentine's Day always has a sexy feel, but the charged energy in our living room is off the charts. I wasn't surprised when Violet requested we all just stay in tonight instead of going out for the holiday. What *did* shock me was when she asked if she and Jamie could come see our home and hang out.

Jamie's been keeping an eye on her way more than usual, and Violet hasn't stopped stealing glances at us. I swear I've been holding my breath since they stepped through our front door an hour ago with pizza and wine.

Ellis feels it too. Whatever Jamie and V have planned, they aren't being discreet in their nerves. All I can do is sit back and let them do their thing. Am I hoping this turns into a sleepover? You bet your fucking ass. I'd even settle for a family cuddle and a few kisses.

But, and this is just a guess, I'm almost a million percent positive Violet's panties are *drenched*. She hasn't stopped fidgeting since we sat down to watch a movie, and nobody's even touching her.

This is the easiest edging I've ever done, but I'm not one hundred percent sure if this could be considered edging. Nobody's actually paying attention to the movie, that's for sure. Especially me, because all I want is to feel her tiny hand wrap around my rigid cock and ask me if she's doing it right.

Or I'm a fucking asshole for reading into our tense Valentine's night.

Horny or not, I don't like the nervousness radiating off of Violet. It goes against all my instincts as a protector and lover *not* to give her some guidance to make her feel better.

"Violet baby," I say gently, trying not to startle her. "Come sit with me and Ellis please. We missed you."

It's true. We haven't seen her for exactly two days since our arcade date. Ellis has been teasing me about already planning our big family bed frame. I haven't denied it though. There are multiple ideas already forming in my head for the furniture I could make to accommodate all four of us easily.

I haven't told him I have an inspector coming in a week to check if we can knock out the wall between our room and the guest room. It would be the perfect space for all of us to fit.

The blush Violet tries to hide behind her long hair is adorable, and when she peeks at Jamie, I smile. I love how naturally submissive she is, but there's also a beautiful level of independence and pushback she gives that makes her utterly perfect for me.

Relationships are not one size fits all, but I'm fucking ready to see how I fit into Jamie and Violet.

Violet stands and drags her blanket with her. Her feet shuffle a little as she approaches, and a battle goes on behind her eyes. I hope one day she will share those warring thoughts with me.

Today's not that day. I'm just fucking thrilled when she plops her pert ass in the space between me and Ellis.

"Good," I mumble and help her situate her blanket.

Once I'm satisfied she's warm enough, I rearrange her so her knees are crisscrossed and pressing into both me and my partner. I must have been too distracted by ensuring Violet's comfort because when Jamie speaks low and growly in my ear, I jump a little.

"This okay?" he rumbles, lining his body up against mine and placing his big hand on my thigh.

Swallowing the groan that threatens to burst out of me when his heat seeps through my sweatpants, I nod and clear my throat. Except the sound quickly turns into a gargled choke.

Violet huffs a small laugh as if she's not dragging her pinky finger along the head of my throbbing cock. Ellis makes a similar sound, and I reach for him behind Violet's back. She's small enough between us that I can wrap my fingers around the back of Ellis' neck.

That's all they fucking do. Jamie doesn't even move his damn hand; just the weight of it makes me a little feral. Still the movie continues to play, and Jamie laughs at the right places.

Violet peeks around me for the third time in what

feels like an eternity. She catches Jamie's eye, then he gives her another nod and smile. My brain is screaming at me to ask them what's going on. Yet my body is forcing me to keep my mouth shut and see where this goes.

Two very different hands are on me, teasing me, and Ellis is fighting the same battle I am. This is torturous heaven, and I'm kind of fucking here for it. Violet hums when the couple on the screen begin to kiss. Teeth grinding, I grip Ellis a bit harder like he's my personal stress ball.

At the halfway point, Violet moves. She rotates her legs and wiggles her feet beneath my left thigh. Jamie also adjusts his position, but I think his goal is to watch Violet.

My theory is proven correct when Ellis sucks in a gasp of pleasure, and Jamie stiffens. It's my turn to hold his thigh and keep him grounded. My attention is half on the way Violet's arm flexes and moves beneath the blanket on Ellis' lap and half on trying to figure out what's going on in Jamie's head.

His eyes are fixed on our partners, but they hood ever so slightly when I caress the inside of his thigh. The muscles ripple beneath my touch, lighting me up inside with confidence. I have the same effect on him that he does on me, I know it.

"Violet, I need—"

Ellis' pleading moan snaps me out of my moment with Jamie and I squeeze Ellis' neck hard. "No, darling," I admonish, voice thick with my arousal. "They're leading tonight."

Ellis clenches his jaw and glances around at all of us. I don't see what look Jamie gives him, but Ellis nods and relaxes into the couch. Violet slows her movements and sits up.

The way she nibbles on her plump bottom lip is so sexy I can barely control myself. Then she narrows her eyes at Jamie. "Did you tell them?"

"No," Jamie responds patiently. "I think Nate's a pretty smart man, though."

Violet turns her narrowed eyes on me. "What do you know?"

I lock eyes with Ellis for a second, and I'm pretty sure he's thinking *what the fuck* do *you know?* Unable to help myself, I reach for her mouth and caress her abused lip with my thumb. "I know that you want to experiment. Considering you keep checking in with Jamie, I'm guessing it's to make sure he's okay with all of this?"

Again, Violet glances at Jamie. Neither say anything, and I wish I could have been a fly on the wall for their conversation about this.

"Baby, would you like to talk now?" I tug on her shirt to get her to lean back, but my pretty woman shakes her head.

"No," she whispers, "I want someone to take me to bed."

Ellis. Motherfucking Ellis screams, "DIBS!"

Forty-Six

VIOLET

My nerves feel like they're short circuiting. One moment I'm buzzing with excitement and need, the next I'm zapped with uncertainty. It's jarring and incredibly frustrating when all I want is to make this work.

I want to fuck all three of them, watch them fuck each other, and be totally cool with it. Because if I'm not, I should think even *more*.

I don't want to lose them. I don't want to end this and hurt them again because I can't get control of my anxiety. *Hurting myself isn't an option either.* And my gosh, I think losing them might ruin me for life.

I can't do it again.

"Ellis!" I screech, blood rushing to my brain. Hoisted over his shoulder with my ass in the air, Ellis rushes up the stairs.

"CAREFUL!"

"NO RUNNING!"

I don't have a chance to laugh before I'm flipped

onto my back. Bouncing on the mattress, I look up at the handsome man who looks ready to eat me.

Then, Ellis opens his mouth and all my worries fly away with the giggles that burst out of me. "Do you get daddy vibes from them too?"

My chest aches with the force of my delight, because *yes. Yes I do.* "Did they sound the same to you just then?" I ask, loving that we can bond over our overbearing men.

*Our...*Maybe this won't end in tragedy after all.

Ellis smiles down at me and tugs his shirt over his head. Saliva pools in my mouth at the sight of his ripped, lean frame. His dark hair is mussed to perfection, and his cheekbones are shadowed in the soft glow of the lamp beside the bed.

"Ellis," I breathe, reaching for him.

The tight feeling in my belly isn't nervousness. No, I'm aching to be filled by this beautiful man who can make me laugh like nobody else. He makes me feel like I have a best friend who would do anything for me. He feels so deeply, so I know if he loves me, he *loves* me.

Loud footsteps startle us both. Jamie and Nate are coming up the stairs. Ellis lunges onto the bed and rushes up to sit against the headboard.

I'm jostled around by his quick movements and end up scampering off the bed to give him space. "Quick," he hisses. "Get naked and come sit on me. I don't want my ass spanked again."

Lips twitching again, I pull my shirt off like he did and quickly tug my leggings down. One thing I'm not very self-conscious of is my body, so that's a relief.

"Violet," Ellis whines as the murmuring deep voices get closer. "Get your wet pussy on my dick before Nate yanks me off the bed."

"Pretty sure this is a terrible way to encourage me to fuck you, Ellis," I scold, but still I climb back onto the bed and crawl toward him.

His eyes heat, and the humor in them burns to lust. "Fucking hell," he moans.

"Stay right there, baby," Nate demands as he and Jamie enter the bedroom. The latter closes the door and unbuttons his jeans, but doesn't remove any clothing as he goes to sit beside Ellis.

I'm frozen on my hands and knees. My tits sway as the bed dips with Jamie's weight, forcing me to acknowledge how heavy they feel. *Why did I leave my bra on?*

The room is silent while three sets of eyes burn into my naked flesh. Nate has the perfect view of my ass and lacy black thong. The longer I stay like this with my thighs spread, the more I feel.

The cool air kisses my pussy lips. My thong no longer holds all of me in its tiny fabric. My clit tingles, and my hole aches to feel the scratchy material move. Even just some slight friction would be phenomenal.

Throb after throb, I become a needier mess, and nobody's even touched me. They haven't moved or said anything.

With each inhale of my chest, my nipples graze the small lacy bra. Goosebumps and chills roll through my body, but the sweet torment doesn't end there.

What really makes me whimper is my other

entrance. The empty, aching pulse of my pussy pulls on my ass each time, forcing my thong to massage me back there. I love some kinky ass play, and just the fact that Nate has a front-row seat to it makes me moan.

"You are so fucking desperate right now," Nate growls.

The broken silence makes me gasp out my desperate pleas. "Nate, please. Please do something."

"Baby girl, we haven't even fucking touched you, and I can see your pussy and tiny asshole quivering." Nate's filthy mouth will surprise me later. Right now it's so fucking hot I arch my back to show him how needy I really am. Maybe he will finally help me.

"Someone please touch me," I whine, throwing my head back only to find myself staring directly at a thick cock. The space separating me from my treat is gone within an instant, because if nobody will touch me, then I'll touch them.

"OH fuck!" Ellis cries, and the cock in my mouth plunges to the back of my throat as he fucks my face.

"Whoa, careful," Jamie coos, calming Ellis. But his voice has the opposite effect on me.

Stiffening, my eyes shoot open as I'm reminded I should be anxious. I should feel horrible for doing this. So why don't I? Why did I present myself like that to Nate and jump on Ellis' cock without thought while Jamie was sitting right there?

"Hold on, Ellis," Jamie murmurs, and the hips beneath me settle onto the sheets, but the cock never leaves my mouth. Before I can pop off of it and start apologizing profusely, a hand pushes my head back down.

Jamie's voice is so soft and honest as he addresses me next. "You are doing so well, my love. *I'm* good. Seeing you get all worked up with nothing but our attention was the most beautiful thing I have ever seen in my life. Your desire to please me warms my heart, but I want you to focus on Ellis right now. I want to play with your wet cunt with Nate, okay?"

Humming my agreement, desire zips through me when Ellis groans at the vibration. Grinning around his thick cock, I peek up at him and do it again.

"God fucking damn it. Stop that," Ellis snaps, but the bite in his tone is gone. In its place is a breathlessness that makes me preen. "I can't be the first one to come, V. Please."

"That's right," Nate says, and a snap rings out through the room as he rips my panties off. Hot on its heels comes a burning sensation around my hips and along my slit from the fabric. Screeching, I try to wiggle away from the sting, but heavy hands grab my hips and force me to stay still.

Whipping my head around to shout my indignation, I'm stunned into a choking fit when I see them.

Nate and Jamie are completely naked, kneeling side by side behind me. Thick thighs hold them tall and proud as their cocks point menacingly at my bare pussy.

Jamie's abs are more pronounced than Nate's, but Nate is wider. Neither man is sexier than the other. I love the tattoos and dark long hair on Jamie. He's my biker-looking baddie. Nate is my hunky, complex, mountain-looking protector.

With their hair down and their hands on each other's dicks, I feel like I'm about to combust. My pussy clenches, but I'm not sure if it's in fear or anticipation.

"Want to play a game?" Ellis asks with a grin on his lips. I don't know where to look or what to do, but Ellis has a plan. Any plan has to be better than the rising uncertainty I'm feeling so I look at him.

"As long as I get to come," I declare and wiggle my ass. Two sets of groans behind me help to calm me again.

All three of them want me.

Forty-Seven

JAMIE

I'm shaking. In a good way, I think.

Other than the subtle hints of *she's mine,* I'm enjoying the fuck out of this. My woman's dripping pussy is in the air, and her lips are swollen from sucking Ellis' cock.

She's stunning. A goddess.

When Nate and I undressed before kneeling behind her to share, I hesitated only a moment because this is the biggest step we can take. Nate giving me a condom while keeping one for himself was a mindfuck. Another man's dick will be in the love of my life's pussy. The lube beside him gave me some other ideas too.

How can I be okay with this?

Then, the sexy bastard reached over and grabbed my dick in an all-encompassing hold. My lungs constricted, and I grappled for him immediately. He stroked me, and I followed his lead.

He was right. When we walked up here, I explained what Violet had been worried about because I felt like he could help her, but he said helping *me* would help her.

My slow nod and thick swallow was as close as I would be getting to agreeing to bottom for him tonight. I trust Nate. He always has everyone's best intentions laid out on his sleeve.

He saw right through my desire to help Violet and knew I was also struggling with the thought of this relationship.

I'm most definitely not going to complain about his firm, hot hand jacking me off while we stare at my woman's wet thighs. *Jesus, I don't think I've ever seen her so turned on before.*

"Want to play a game?"

My eyes immediately narrow on Ellis because what the fuck? I was about to fuck my girlfriend, and now he wants to mess around?

But my bad mood deflates when Violet's body does. *How did I not notice her tensing up again?*

Nate's hand releases me, allowing the bad thoughts to seep in. I should have noticed when Violet was feeling off. I thought when she saw me and Nate tugging each other's cocks that I saw lust in her eyes. Have I been reading her wrong all night?

I watch aimlessly as Nate swipes his fingers through Violet's wet pussy lips. She gasps and grinds on his palm, but he comes back to me.

"Enough," he whispers in my ear and coats my throbbing dick in Violet's wetness. "She needs all of us, and Ellis picked up on something I didn't see either.

Another reason we're good together. Let me show you a few other reasons why we fit."

My hand clenches on his cock as he glides up and down my length. The roughness of his calluses mixed with Violet's creamy arousal makes me hiss between my teeth.

"Harder," I demand and thrust forward. All the while Ellis is explaining to Violet that she needs to guess who's fucking her.

"No. You aren't in charge here," Nate snarls and bites my neck. It's primal and different from what I'm used to, but I don't fucking care because the next thing I know he's wrapping my dick in a condom. Violet moans around Ellis' erection and Nate guides me into her hot cunt.

Nate groans right along with me even though I drop my hold on him to hold V steady. She's so wet I slip right in. I'll never get over the way her walls stretch and flutter around me to make room. She grips and pulls on me as if her body instinctively knows how to wring every fraction of pleasure from me.

"Jamie. It's Jamie!" Violet gasps, making me realize that it's not just my time with her.

"Fuck!" I snarl and pull out of her. I don't move until I've peppered her back with kisses and called her a good girl at least twice. "So sweet for knowing it's me."

She pops off Ellis' cock once more to give me a big smile over her shoulder. "I'll always know it's you."

"I love you," I blurt out, needing to say it because this is a vulnerable as fuck position we're putting our relationship in, and I need her to know nothing has changed. Hell, it feels like shit just got better.

"You too," she murmurs and mewls when Ellis tugs on her hair.

Unable to help myself, I reach forward and return the favor to him. I yank his face to mine and relish his choked gasp. I don't give him a chance to figure his shit out before my tongue slips through his lips and I devour him like a starving man. Just like my starving girl between his legs.

"Alright," Nate snaps, and the three of us pull apart. We're panting and ready for more. "Get your fat cock back inside our girl, Jamie."

Our girl...alright...that didn't piss me off, so that's good.

Not one to ever skip out on being inside of Violet, I sink right back in and snap my hips forward. She convulses around me, and the slight tickle of sweat dripping down my back makes me shiver.

"We're close," I force through my teeth, needing Nate to hurry the fuck up with his plan. I hear the rip of the condom wrapper behind me and I check to make sure Nate wraps himself up. *It's on, so why isn't it inside of me?*

"Same," Ellis breathes. When I look up at him, I see he's watching me fuck myself into Violet. The same woman sucking his cock. *Holy shit this is hot.*

"You like this?" I ask him, wanting to tease him for just a second. It's sexy and will help keep me from coming too soon.

"Fuck yes," Ellis says, not skipping a beat. "Rub yourself, Violet." He has no reservations as he makes V gag on his cock. The wet sounds of her saliva mixed with the slippery sounds her pussy makes is divine.

"And you?" Nate growls low in my ear as his chest presses against mine. "Do you like this?" Just as he asks, a lubed-up finger swirls my asshole and pushes past my outer ring with ease. "Oh yeah, you do. You pulled me right in, didn't you? Just as greedy as your girlfriend huh?"

"Motherfucking son of a—" I grunt.

The burn in my ass increases as he adds a finger, then another, making me slow down before I lose my load in Violet. She sputters at the same time a strangled shout leaves me because I was *not* ready for Nate's thick cock, but he was, I fucking guess.

"You know what to do, you horny fucker. Let me in." I'd like to tell him to fuck off and shove my dick in his ass with no warning to see how he likes it, but I have Violet under me bouncing back on my cock like *she's* in control. Thank fuck for the lube because, holy shit, it's a tight fit.

All I can do is hold on. There's literally no way I can do anything but allow them to use me for their pleasure right now. As Nate drags along my prostate and snaps his hips forward, I thrust so far into Violet she screams around Ellis' cock, then absolutely shatters around me.

My head rips backward as pleasure shoots through my balls and up my chest. With Violet strangling my cock and my ass clutching Nate's like I could keep him there forever, I come so fucking hard I swear I destroy my vocal cords.

I'm a loss of heavy limbs as I bounce between Nate

and Violet, but Nate's warm cum inside of me is soothing as fuck.

Soothing. Sexy. Damn near life-changing.

Yeah, this dynamic won't be a problem for me at all. Next time I'm going to ask Violet to hold Ellis' cum in her mouth so I can sweep my tongue in there and steal a taste.

Not a problem at *all*.

Forty-Eight

ELLIS

We were—*are*—on the verge of something amazing. I'm just having a really hard time believing that when the two people we have developed feelings for are brushing us off.

For two days in a row, Violet has declined our request to hang out. I even offered to go to her apartment with food, and she flat out said no.

She did say thank you, so she must not be mad at us. But who knows what else could be wrong. Valentine's Day was the most incredible night of our lives. She even said so herself, and now it feels like she's pulling back.

Jamie too. Neither of them have sent me and Nate much more than short, unreliable messages.

Violet leaves tomorrow. Her only lengthy message to the group chat was to let us know that her deadline moved up and she has to leave a week earlier than planned.

Jamie didn't say anything in response, and judging

by their synced response time, I'm guessing they're together.

Are they talking shit about us? Have they decided they don't want us? Is Jamie leaving tomorrow with her and disappearing like Violet did the last time? Did they find out about what we did?

I'm spiraling.

"You're in love."

Glancing at Nate, I frown when I see him watching me. I've been pacing for a while and checking my phone repeatedly. "Obviously," I retort. He knows I love him.

He chuckles, but I see the worry lines around his eyes and mouth that haven't disappeared all day. "I mean, you wouldn't be this worked up if you weren't in love with them, Ellis. Jamie and Violet."

Scoffing, I go back to pacing. It feels good to do something because I'm pretty fucking useless otherwise. I still don't have a job, and we've been here for months. We may not be hurting for money, and I know I'm helpful to Nate with his business, but I'm literally doing nothing with my life besides pining over two people who clearly don't fucking want me.

"Ellis, you need to stop. Your brain is going to destroy you if you let it." Nate's voice is soft, and it grates on my nerves.

"I don't need to stop. I need them to break it off with us if that's what they want to do!"

Nate stands up from the couch and approaches me like I might bite him. His posture and tone are strong, though. "Enough. I know this is bringing up some horrible shit, and I don't blame you. I'm worried and a bit self-conscious too, but there are many things that could be happening."

Fear twists my gut, forcing me to blurt out, "Oh my god, do you think one of them is hurt? Should we go over there? I can't believe I thought the worst again. Fuck!"

Just as I'm whirling around to grab the keys, Nate grabs my bicep and pulls me back. "El, breathe. You're losing it a little. Not everyone is used to being in constant contact with each other."

I cough with the force of my inhale, and release it shakily. "Fuck. Okay. I can’t pinpoint why I'm so anxious. We are so close to being *more,* you know?"

He nods and swallows. Our phones ping at the exact same time, and I swear to hell my heart tries to fling itself from my body.

I reread the message over and over again, trying to use logic and not be swallowed by insecurities all over again. It's not working, so I repeat the message out loud even though Nate has already read it over my shoulder.

"So she's on her period and that's why they've been distant?" It even sounds stupid coming out of my mouth. My anger flares at the excuse, and when I turn to tell Nate it's bullshit, I see a similar frown on his face. Only his looks a little more thoughtful.

Another message comes through, and I read it out loud again, ready to tear into Jamie for dodging us while using feminine shit as an excuse. But his message takes the wind out of my sails.

"He said she has severe cramping, nausea,

headaches, and is exhausted. He did some research and thinks it could be dysmenorrhea, but Violet rolled her eyes and kicked him out of her room. Now he's making her dinner." I reread. "She's like really not feeling well, then..."

I'm such a fucking dick. I need to do something about the anxiety I have. Nate thinks it's a response to losing Violet when we were younger, but Jesus, I'm thirty years old, I shouldn't be reacting so immaturely.

Before either Nate or I can say a word, my phone blares with an incoming video call from Violet. I'm so quick to answer I almost hit decline. My heart is pounding, and Nate is plastered against me to fit on the screen.

Violet finally loads onto the screen, looking sleepy and pale in the low lighting of her bedroom. "Hey guys, I'm so sorry."

She sniffles, and I try to work out a way to kick my own ass in my head. Cursing myself out silently, I ache at the tear that slips down her cheek.

"It's okay, baby. Jamie told us what was going on." Nate is quick to soothe her.

She groans and moves her face away from the screen. I have half a mind to elbow Nate in the gut for making her go away, but she's back quickly. "That dick. He's been smothering me with heating pads and chocolate."

"Why didn't you ask us to help?" There go my insecurities again. Did she not want us to help her?

Violet wipes her cheeks. "Well, I didn't ask Jamie either. He just showed up yesterday when I wasn't answering my phone. I was taking a hot bath and left it in my room because the screen was hurting my head."

"Are your periods always this bad?" I ask because I have two younger sisters, and they never spoke a peep about their cramps or anything like that. It's also possible I tuned it out.

Violet shuffles around in her bed and lies on her side, taking us with her. "Yeah. Some are worse than others. Stress can affect them too. I'm used to it, but driving tomorrow and the next day will be a pain."

"Can't you stay?" Nate worries, probably ready to lock her in a room and feed her all her cravings with Jamie.

"No," Violet sighs, sounding exhausted. "This is my high profile client, and I at least need to have three good images to her by Friday. Three days isn't a lot of time, so I have to be on the road early."

I can hear Nate grinding his teeth behind me, so I speak up since I'd rather he not go all caveman on her. "Maybe one of us should come with you?"

Please say yes, please say yes.

"No," she declines. "Really, I'll be okay. Jamie's packing for me, so I know I'll have everything I need to get through the drive. And I'll be driving all day tomorrow with my heated seat on my lower back, which sounds heavenly."

I don't like it.

"I don't like this," Nate grumbles my exact thought.

Violet laughs a little, and it lights me up inside. *I love her*. "Too bad, big guy. Boss Ellis around instead for a while. You can borrow my Ferri."

Narrowing my eyes at the little minx, I say, "That's rude as hell, Bubbles."

All three of us suck in a breath at the same time, and I immediately want the ground to swallow me whole. How could I be so careless again? "Violet. Shit. I'm so sorry. I didn't—"

"No," she rushes out. "No, it-it's okay. I think—You can call me that."

"Really?" I'm fucking stunned. She has been so against us calling her that she's even had physical negative reactions to it. Why is it okay now?

Her eyes sparkle with emotion through the phone. "I feel like I'm getting some of those bubbles back, and you helped me manifest them. It feels right."

I could cry. I really, really fucking could. Instead of saying something epic or beautiful, I joke, "SO does that make me the bubble maker?"

Violet snorts an unladylike sound that has me smiling so big I decide I don't regret my stupid mouth. I have no filter, but I'll opt never to have one again if it makes her laugh.

Nate squeezes my hip, and Violet's laugh turns into a yawn. My partner leans in and says her name. "You should get some sleep, baby. We will be there in the morning to say goodbye and give you kisses, okay?"

"Yeah," she replies around a yawn so big I think I hear her jaw crack. "Okay. Good night you two."

"Good night, baby."

My heart knits itself back together. "Good night, Bubbles."

Forty-Nine

VIOLET

I thought driving away from them would be the hardest part of this trip. My cramps were nothing compared to the pain I felt in my chest as I waved goodbye one last time.

Jamie, Nate and Ellis kissed me like I'd been theirs for an eternity. There was no hesitation or side eyes as I embraced each of them separately and together. It was everything I had hoped for. Leaving what we've built for six days felt like I was ripping my heart out and throwing it through the sunroof.

What good is the beating organ if it doesn't work properly without them, you know?

Alas, my heart stays in my chest because I am still an independent woman who is working on loving herself. That's what I had to tell myself an hour into my drive. Since then, I've been determined to get my work done, enjoy nature, and maybe head back a day early to surprise them.

I've promised to check in with them at every stop,

and every other time I can. Having a big family and a lot of family friends back in Chicago means I'm used to the demand.

I considered just putting Jamie, Nate, and Ellis in my family group chat so I don't have to send multiple messages, but I don't think any of us are ready for that can of worms. Yet.

Feeling incredibly positive and hopeful about life and relationships for the first time in seven years has made this work trip feel different. I've caught myself wishing I had them with me to make memories with.

Of course the fresh air and alone time are great for self-care, but damn it, I miss them.

I thought leaving would be the hardest part, but I'm living through the worst right now. Standing in front of the most stunning view I have ever seen, I realize *this* is the hardest part. The picture I took on my phone and tried to send to our group chat failed. No service. It's a bummer that I can't connect with them at all right now, but maybe this time I'll share my good images with them.

I want them here with me so much my eyes begin to well with tears. Honestly, I'm not entirely sure where I am, but it has become a monumental marker.

This is the spot where I realize I'm madly, truly, deeply in love with three men. Two from my past who let me get away, and a new one who chipped away at the walls around my heart for far too long to be normal. Jamie's patience and care opened me up to the relationship I lost years ago.

"I love them," I whisper into the early morning glow

of sunshine. My breath puffs into the chilly air around me, and I curl into my jacket a little more while wishing it was their arms.

A slight breeze teases my neck, and if I close my eyes, I can imagine it's Nate's beard when he comes up behind me for a cuddle. Or to whisper dirty things in my ear.

Inhaling the scent of pine and waterfall with my eyes closed, I sink into the idea that Jamie and Ellis are standing close by. Maybe making out because why not.

I'm kinky like that I guess.

My eyes snap open at the sound of rocks crashing onto the water's surface near the waterfall. Rushing forward to snap the perfect photo of the splash, I become my own avalanche.

Feet twisting together, I stumble with a terrified screech. My momentum makes it easy for me to lunge for my camera after I've caught myself on my hands and knees. Except, I didn't realize I would be risking myself until I'm tumbling right over the dirt-covered edge of the steep incline.

"AHH!" I scream, grappling for trees and prickly bushes, not caring for a second how much it hurts when they rip my skin off. Over and over again I'm slapped across the face by branches while getting the wind knocked out of me by logs and rocks.

"STOP!" Screeching, I wrap my arms around my head as I feel something crack in my side. The only sense I have is to protect my head, the thing I should have used once I saw my camera go flying over the edge.

Stupid stupid stupid.

Somersaulting and rolling through dirt and dead trees has stolen the breath from my lungs. It's jarred me so deeply I don't even realize I've stopped in a puddle of freezing mud until the chill nips at me through my jacket.

"Fuck," I groan, voice hoarse from my screams. I really don't want to try to sit up, but I've taken enough survival courses to know I need to get out of the cold puddle and figure out where to go from here. I'm afraid to take stock of my injuries, though I know I should.

Time is of the essence in situations like this.

Just like proper gear. Hissing and wincing, I roll over and slowly push myself into a sitting position.

"Yes," I breathe in relief once I notice my hiking-approved fanny pack is still intact. For shits and giggles, I pull my phone out and cringe at the crack in the screen. Thankfully, it still turns on. Unfortunately, I wasn't lucky enough to land in a spot with service.

"Okay. Alright." My eyes burn, and my cheeks are itchy and wet with my tears. Hell, my voice barely even works. It's wobblier than I've ever heard it, but I'm doing my best to psych myself up for the trek ahead of me. "I can do this."

NOPE.

My ankle protests so vehemently that I collapse back to the ground when I finally work myself up to stand. "Oh god. This isn't good. It's not good."

Step one, make sure I'm not bleeding and no bones are protruding.

Done. No bones. A lot of trickles of blood from cuts

on my hand and my face is definitely not good, but I'm not bleeding out.

Step two, figure out where I am.

Glancing around, I have no fucking idea where I landed. There are no trails I can take a guess at in my line of sight. Turning my glare on the hill that put me through the wringer, I groan. It's not horribly steep, but it's *tall*. Any steeper and I would have seriously injured myself. I can move my foot enough, but it hurts so much I'm trembling.

I can do this if I get mad. There isn't an option for me to call my family or the guys. Nobody's here, and I'm all alone. Mama always told me anger is easy because it's fuel. Fuel to conquer and continue. Well, I need to do both, so this Bubbles is pissed. Let's fucking go.

"Bitch," I hiss at the pile of dirt and trees. That's all it is, and it thwarted me today. Of course, the hill doesn't respond. Just taunts me and waves its trees around.

The tears continue to fall as I drag myself on my hands and knees as I take my first portion of the climb. It's all I can do not to crumble and cry for someone to help me. It hurts to breathe, everything burns, I'm freezing, and I can't walk.

I'm all I've got. And I know what to do. So now it's time I put my trust in myself to the test.

"The guys are going to be so mad," I grumble. Fucking hill is going to get me in trouble.

Fifty

NATE

I am incapable of tearing my eyes away from the paper in front of me.

When we told Cassidy we hadn't heard from Violet in almost six hours, she flipped out.

When Ellis expressed his concern that she might have run again, Cass told me to go through V's journals to see if there could be any clues of that being the truth. I refused, saying that was a horrible breach of privacy, but as six hours became eight, I couldn't refrain. I had to know whether Ellis was right.

Was she saying goodbye to us when she left?

She's been gone for three days, and her texts have become fewer. Cassidy said it's probably bad service, but Jamie has looked sick to his stomach ever since Ellis mentioned her running.

Not even Jamie knew if this was normal behavior for her because she's been distant as hell with him until last month. He knows nothing. We know nothing.

All we have is the trauma of the last time she left us

in her rearview mirror. Is this time the same? She just couldn't commit? Jamie's barely said anything to us since we got here, but now I'm the one incapable of speech.

Seeing her room for the first time was like a fucking punch to the gut. It's scarce and depressing, like she packed up and is planning to leave. All except her notebooks.

Over and over again she jotted down her worries, thoughts, and fears. When she told us she hated herself, I didn't believe it. Not until this moment. Violet has to convince herself that her bad thoughts aren't true.

Does Jamie know about this? About how deep her pain runs? It's practically in her veins. No part of her life is untouched by this sheer anxiety. She even wrote about taking a nap one day not making her a lazy person. Who has to tell themselves it's okay to rest without feeling bad about it?

Violet second guesses every single choice she makes. It would make sense she's second guessing our relationship change. It's not the norm in society. Even though her mom lives in a polyamorous relationship, Violet is a different person than Blue.

Tossing another notebook to the side, I grab the most recent one on her nightstand and take a deep breath. My eyebrows furrow as the script changes. She's no longer questioning who she is as a person, but it looks more like a list of things she needs to think about and process.

Her birthday and Jamie's is on here. Then her need

to ensure she can handle a relationship like ours. The last entry makes my shoulders slump in relief.

My worries and insecurities were soothed by Jamie, Nate, and Ellis. Fact.

I can confidently say I am comfortable moving forward with this relationship. Fact! :)

I'm happy. Fact.

I'm bubbly. Never thought I'd say this but fact!

Leaping from her bed with the notebook in my hand, I rush into the living room. Excited to share my news, I give the book to Cassidy first and turn to my partners.

Jamie's phone is against his ear like it has been all morning, and Ellis is pacing, trying to rip his hair from his skull. I clear my throat, and Jamie turns around, not dropping the phone. *It must be ringing.*

"I—"

I'm cut off as I realize Ellis is talking. No. More like he's rambling, getting louder and louder. He's closer to Jamie, and when Cassidy speaks up behind me, I startle.

But what she has to say doesn't matter because then I hear the fucking words that Ellis swore never to speak. Nothing matters because I'm getting a front-row seat to Jamie's heart shattering.

"She found out what we did. She ran again. I knew I shouldn't have felt bad for sleeping with Jamie to get back at her. How could she do this? She couldn't have. She cares about us. I *know* she does. We do too. We love her!"

Every atom in my body pauses as I watch the life we planned go crashing to the ground again in the form of a cellphone with Violet's name on the screen.

Voicemail sent.

Epilogue

VIOLET

I've learned four things in the past eight hours.

One, I love three men so much I was too distracted to follow safety procedures on a risky hike.

Two, never *ever* judge a hill by what you *think* the incline *looks* like.

Three, next time I hurt myself, I need to make sure it's not a mile and a half into a hike.

And four, not every stick can be a walking stick—I learned this one by face planting six times due to shitty sticks.

Oh and five, pain and frustration really brings out my potty mouth.

Which is probably why when my car comes into view, glowing like a knight in shining armor through the trees, I rasp, "Halle-fucking-lejuh!"

It's not my cutest moment, dragging myself out of the hiking trail with a walking stick that truly looks like something out of a horror movie. Hell, I'm sure I look like something that crawls out of a horror movie too. I sure feel like it.

I've contemplated framing my fanny pack for keeping my keys and phone safe, but I imagine I won't trust another besides this one. Miss Fanny is worse for wear, but she's not out of commission.

She's at the peak of her career, thank you very much.

Outside of my car at last, I see my water bottle winking at me in the sunlight, and I cry for it.

Another thing I've learned, when I think I've cried too much, there's always more to cry about.

My eyes feel like I've cried the whole time I've been out here.

Hands shaking, I battle my fanny pack to let my keys free. I appreciate the determination to keep them locked up tight, but I *need* them. Wrestling and cursing a bag also isn't my finest moment, but I'm desperate for safety.

"Just fucking open!" I screech, and my car clicks in response.

Gasping out a breath of relief, I yank the door open and fling myself inside. Obviously, I hurt my ribs and ankle, but I don't give two shits because I'm *alive.* I'm *safe.* Probably will get my ass spanked, but I am totally and a million percent proud of myself for getting myself out of that scary situation alone.

That was life and death, and I conquered that shit.

Blowing a raspberry to calm myself and tone the rage down now that I'm okay, I start my car. "AH!" I bellow, half in pain and half in fear, as my radio blasts to life like I was at a fucking concert.

Clearly, I went into that hike with a different vibe.

"Jesus fuck," I mumble, hitting mute. *Cussing feels good*. I pull my phone out.

SERVICE! I have service!

Then I see all the messages and notifications waiting for me. My chapped lips don't love the way I eat the skin in nervousness, but they're lucky because a new voicemail pings and I smile.

It's from Jamie. I'll listen to the new one quickly, then call him back. Are they worried? It will be nice to know whether they care that much. I could really use the love right now.

I hit play.

"She found out what we did. She ran again. I knew I shouldn't have felt bad for sleeping with Jamie to get back at her. How could she do this? She couldn't have. She cares about us. I know she does. We do too. We love her!"

Is my face numb? My hands are moving. Three numbers are now blocked on my phone, and I don't remember doing it. The car is in drive, and I still can't feel my face.

My ankle tingles, as do my ribs. Is that what's anchoring me to the world? Because I'm starting to wonder why I even climbed up that godforsaken hill.

The GPS is on. It wasn't an active choice. Consciously, I would maybe throw myself down that hill again. Subconsciously, I just want my mom. Subconscious won.

I just want my mom.

Bubbly Duet

COMPLETE ON MARCH 21ST, 2026

Pops of Violet

Part 2

~MMMF

~Groveling

~Emotional glow-ups

Pre-Order Here!

Also Coming Soon...

MAY 23, 2026

Subliminal Bonds Duet

Book 1

~MMMF+

~Omegaverse

~Neurodivergent, selectively mute FMC

Pre-Order here!

Wilted Character Reminder

Wilted character cheat sheet:

Blue (FMC)

Her men:

Jared

Declan

Felix

Roman

Blue's friends who may make an appearance:

Levi & his husband Kevin

Janine

Bethany

Dakota

Also by Y.V. Larson

Always With You duet

(Completed)

A dark, emotional MMFMM romance

Never Moving On

Never Losing Hope

Wherever We Go series

A series of interconnected single mom MMMMF standalones

Just You & Me

Simply You & Me

Utterly You & Me (TBD)

Collapse of the Premuim Designation series:

The Invisible Omega duet

A dark, emotional academy MMFMM Omegaverse

Met Your Match

Met Your Mate

The Torn Omega duet
A dark, post academy MMMFM Omegaverse
Who We Were
Who We Are

Perfidious Passion
A dark, emotional Valentine's Day Novella

Damaged duet
A dark, emotional MMFMM romance
Beyond Repair part 1
Beyond Repair part 2

Wilted duet
A dark, drama filled, emotional MMFMM romance
Petals of Blue part 1
Petals of Blue part 2

Bubbly duet
A dark, angsty, emotional MMMF romance
Pops of Violet part 1
Pops of Violet part 2 (March 21, 2026)

Subliminal Bonds duet
A dark, emotional, MMMF+ Omegaverse
Bound by Trust (May 23, 2026)
Bound by Love (June 20, 2026)

Stalk Me!

Website

Facebook

Instagram

TikTok

Amazon

About the Author

There are so many things I could say but none of the words would live up to the absolute wonderful chaos that is my life. I'm a mother. A wife and daughter. I'm a reader and a writer. I JUST completed my masters degree in marriage and family therapy too. One degree hotter!

I'm a woman who has never forgotten how often her twelve-year-old self dreamed of being an author. I've always said writing is my dream and mental health is my passion. I am motivated and blessed enough to peruse both while loving my family with my whole heart and soul.

The hard days are tough. The lows are pretty deep. And the highs… they are what I live for. Being everything that I am has come with challenges but wow are they beautiful ones.

The pages you'll read show emotion and despair because I am not only the roles I fill for others. I was a kid who felt loss and internal pain. That part of me is still in there begging to be seen and heard… so this is me… my trauma dump in dramatic form. My FMC's live horrible lives, and while their experiences are far beyond mine, their feelings are often my own.

I struggle and I cry. I feel worthless and sometimes

like I'm fighting every day just to be enough. Their stories are mine in a way. Please read with empathy as trauma responses are different for everyone.

My stories and yours are valid and worth being heard. Don't ever lose sight of the battles you've overcome.

And take care of yourself, please.

With appreciation and empathy,

Y.V. Larson